THREE *guilty* PLEASURES

NIKKI SLOANE

Arabesque Edition

ISBN 978-1-9494090-0-0

for my husband

chapter ONE

GRANT

This club looked like nothing.

So much so, I stood on the cracked sidewalk and double-checked the address on the screen of my phone, confirming I was in the right place.

The elusive blindfold club catered to wealthy clients who had deep pockets and a taste for kink. And the operating front for the illegal brothel was supposedly a high-class, members-only wine club. But the nondescript building before me looked like it contained neither of those.

It didn't look like it was in use at all.

I'd been expecting an elegant storefront. For months I'd searched for this place, and once I tracked it down, my speculation went wild. How deep did the wine club charade go? Was it like the movies with an elaborate set-up? Where I'd come in, pluck a certain bottle from a case, and trigger a secret passageway which led to the real club?

The black building had a single door with a diamond-shaped window and no awning overhead. There weren't signs, just the brass street numbers tacked to the side. I stared up at it with a weird sense of disappointment and understanding. It was unremarkable. Exactly what you'd want in this part of Chicago, especially if you were running an illegal operation. It was a place that wouldn't get a second look.

It was a Friday night and the spring weather was decent, but the street was empty. There weren't any bars or restaurants within blocks of this establishment. Just warehouses and stores that were closed. I gripped the doorknob and half expected it not to turn.

It did.

I stepped into the room, which wasn't much bigger than a closet. Or perhaps it felt that way because I was big and took up a lot of space, and the security guy sitting on the stool was even bigger than I was.

He stood and gave me a polite smile, one that seemed rehearsed, as he sized me up. His shoulders pulled back as his posture straightened, making him look bigger still. He wanted me to know he thought he could take me if the situation called for it.

He was underestimating me, though. I was a forward for the Lions, Chicago's semi-professional rugby team, and I was the best prop they'd had in years. I was the perfect combination of big, fast, and reckless.

His gaze noted my suit, and there was a subtle nod. I'd gotten a call from the club owner earlier this week and was told the club rules were "dress to impress."

The security guy was dressed in all black, and his fitted t-shirt was stretched so tight over his muscle-bound chest, it looked like the seams would rip apart if he sneezed. He wore a low-profile communication earpiece that I only noticed because he looked down at the leather-bound portfolio in his hand.

"Name?" he said.

"Webber," I lied.

He scanned the list, shut the portfolio with a snap, and pressed a finger to his ear. "Mr. Green has arrived."

My expression must have been confusion because he shrugged.

"You're a new client." He said it like that should have been obvious.

I was green with newness, but I also felt that way with unease. I'd bent the truth before to get what I needed for a story, but I'd never truly gone undercover. No amount of research could be done to know how the people here would react if they found out I wasn't who I said I was. How likely was it this place was involved with the mob?

I was reckless but usually not stupid. That was how badly I wanted to break this story—I was willing to put everything on the line.

The next door was similar to the first, except the window was replaced with a diamond-shaped logo. The security guard motioned to it. "Julius will meet you at the bar."

A soft buzz rang out as the lock deactivated, beckoning me inside. I pushed the door open and stepped into the next room.

It kept with the theme of not being what I expected. The room was set up like a fancy lounge. Plush couches to the left and a bar to the right, complete with a bartender. Two-thirds of the rails behind him held bottles of wine. Maybe the tall, slender guy behind the bar was actually a sommelier.

"Good evening, sir," the man said. He placed his hands on the bar and leaned subtly forward. "Would you care for something to drink?"

My mouth was parched, but alcohol seemed like a bad

idea. I needed to stay sharp and remember every detail I could. "No, thanks."

"You sure? It's complimentary."

What the hell, I was thirsty. "Water?"

If it was a strange request, the bartender didn't show it. "Of course."

As he grabbed a glass and filled it with ice, the door at the back of the room swung open. The man who came in was built just like me. Tall, wide with broad shoulders. His suit, which was probably custom, fit much better than mine and subtly announced he was a wall of muscle. His head was shaved smooth, and his dark skin gleamed.

He strode toward me, a hand outstretched. "It's nice to meet you, Mr. Webber. I'm Julius King."

Even without his introduction I would have recognized his deep voice from our phone call earlier in the week. "Thanks for inviting me."

His handshake was strong but not overbearing. "I came down from my office, because I like to have a conversation with new members. Get to know them before they go on back."

The bartender set the glass of water down in front of me, and although Julius didn't say anything, I could feel him mentally taking notes about my choice. Men came here to have a good time and spent a lot of money while doing it. Was the bar here to help clients relax, or lower their inhibitions to get them to part with more cash?

"What kind of girls do you like?" Julius's straightforward question made my chest tighten, and my hesitation must have spurred him to continue. "There something in particular you're interested in?"

I forced myself to act natural, even when I felt anything but. "No, just the ordinary stuff."

My answer set off alarm bells, and Julius's expression shifted to a guarded one. "You'll have to explain why you're here, then."

I froze. "What?"

"A good-looking guy like you? You don't come to my club for ordinary. You probably get ordinary all the time." He softened. "If you're nervous, don't be. Trust me, whatever you want—you aren't the first guy to ask for it. But I can't get it for you if you don't tell me."

My pulse spiked. Was I going to blow this before I made it inside the actual club? I was going to have to give him something, but it was hard talking about this with a stranger, and I could hear my feminist friend Ruby's angry voice in my head calling me a pig.

"Blonde," I said. "Big tits."

There wasn't a speck of judgement from him. His tone stayed casual. "Do they need to be real?"

Bloody hell. I felt dirty admitting it. "Yeah."

He nodded. "What else? Any wish list things?"

My head went blank. "Um . . ."

"Anal? Deep throat?" He scanned me from top to bottom. "Pegging?"

What? "No, I'm not interested in that." My words came out tight, and with it, the accent I'd been trying so hard to disguise slipped out.

He lifted an eyebrow like he meant no offense. "It's a power thing. Some of the big guys like being topped by a female half their size."

Julius was a bigger guy.

He must have read my mind, because a slow smile drifted across his lips. "My girl's five-two, and she'd look hot as fuck with a strap-on, but it ain't my thing." The light expression drained from his face. "Where're you from?"

The way he shifted the conversation was impressive. I'd come to the club to research, but he was the one currently leading the interview. I picked up my glass of water and took a sip before answering. "Here."

His eyes sharpened. "No, where'd you grow up? I thought I heard an accent. Australia?"

People sometimes confused my South African accent with an Aussie one. Some even thought I was British. But I'd been living in the Chicagoland area for fourteen years—and as a full-fledged US citizen for the last five—and could mask my accent when I tried hard enough.

I'd had to fill out a mountain of paperwork to get an appointment here, and I wasn't sure how far down they'd dig into the fake profile I'd given them. I had to avoid any hints at my real identity.

I shrugged. "I grew up here."

He gave me the same look my friends did when I told them I was fine following my brutal breakup with Morgan. Julius's dark eyes went heavy with skepticism. I gulped down another drink of water, then redoubled my efforts on sounding as Midwestern American as possible. "So, how does this work? Do I get to pick the girl from, like, a lineup?"

For a moment I wasn't sure he was going to drop it, but he seemed to blink the distrust away. "No. When we're done here, you'll be taken to a room. There'll be a girl on the table and a menu on the wall of what she's into. If you like her? Great. The sales assistant will help you with your purchase. If you don't like that one, keep in mind we have five more rooms."

"What happens if I go through all them and don't see anything I like?"

It was as if I'd just spit on the floor of his establishment, Julius looked that offended. "Then I'd say you're probably too picky." He softened and laughed. "The girls here are fucking gorgeous, and they got wide tastes." He grabbed the sides of his suit jacket and tugged so it would sit straight on his shoulders. "No one's ever gone all six rooms and not found someone they like. Most don't need to see another room."

This was my plan, though. I'd collect all the information I could, then claim I wasn't interested and leave without making a deal.

"You didn't answer my question." Julius kept his voice light and conversational, but the undercurrent was there.

"Which one?"

"Why you're here."

I forced myself not to break his gaze. I didn't need to raise his suspicion any further. My pride would take a hit, but I could give him an extremely edited version of the truth. "My girlfriend cheated on me."

He could probably look intimidating when he wanted, but right now he peered back at me with sincere understanding. It was comforting, like he got it. And the stupid story spilled out of me. "She sent nudes to a bunch of other guys, including ones I worked with. She didn't cheat on me, like, physically, but—it still fucking sucked." I wondered if it would have hurt less if her betrayal hadn't been emotional. "When we were together, she always needed to know she was the prettiest girl in the room."

Like the wicked queen in Snow White, Morgan had to be the fairest of them all. I'd spent the first year not realizing her jealousy of other women was real. I'd thought she was joking, not knowing she was high-maintenance to the extreme. I'd thought I'd been able to keep up with her constant demand for validation, but apparently, I hadn't.

Her cheating started small. A pic to the sound guy, she'd said, just to make sure she was still fuckable. Then a cameraman, because she'd liked the way he'd shot her segment. But her appetite for praise grew until she was sending them to every guy on the crew.

Everyone, except me.

Morgan's insatiable need for attention had humiliated me, and I wasn't going to just take it. If I could break the story on this blindfold club, the spotlight at Channel Five would veer my direction.

Julius put his hand on my shoulder the same way a teammate would. A brotherly gesture, accompanied by a wide, knowing smile. "You wanna fuck a girl hotter than your ex? Yeah. You're definitely in the right place."

chapter
TWO

GRANT

Julius led me into a narrow hallway where we were greeted by another hulking man in all black, wearing a fitted t-shirt and earpiece. He blended in, as the walls and ceiling were dark, and the lighting was low.

"Room two," Julius said to the security guy then turned his head to glance at me over his shoulder. "Enjoy."

He moved down the long hallway and turned right, disappearing up a staircase.

"Sir," the man said, gesturing to the door at his side.

There were doors on both sides of the hall, but the ones I faced were decorated with a large brass number. My heart hummed along at the same quick pace it usually did right before a match. Anticipation and adrenaline coursed through me, bringing everything into clear focus.

I strode toward him, grabbed the doorknob, and pushed it open, ready for anything.

One step was as far as I made it before my brain turned to static.

There was a pedestal in the center of the room, and like everything else, it was black. Wait, no. Pedestal was the wrong word. It was more like a table with drawers underneath. The top of it was cushioned in leather. And on top of that was easily the most beautiful thing I'd ever seen.

A woman with soft pink lips, her blonde hair splashed out in a puddle around her as she lay on the cushioned tabletop, her arms extended and wrists bound by thick satin ribbon. The only thing she wore was a black blindfold, and I swallowed hard as my gaze roamed over all her naked, flawless skin.

Everywhere I looked, there was beauty. Above the table hung a chandelier draped in strings of crystals. There was a tall, white wingback chair in the back of the room, accentuating the lack of color. Even the forearm tattoo trailing up to the girl's wrist was a deep black and paisley patterned.

But there was a bright punch of fiery red seated in the chair, and when my gaze landed on her, the redheaded woman stood. She looked to be the same age as I was, or perhaps older. Maybe even thirty. It was impossible to tell with some women. She was slender and elegant, and just as stunning as the rest of the room, but there was a magnetic force drawing my attention back to the table.

Was it because the redhead was clothed, or seemed to be aloof and cold? It didn't matter. I couldn't stop myself from focusing on the girl. Her tattoo was intricate art, and the shading around the scrolls gave them dimension. I wanted to run my fingers over the ink and see if it was raised.

"Welcome," the redhead said. "Please, come in."

Because I was still standing beside the door, awestruck. I shuffled forward like a big lug, and the door swung closed behind me with a thump.

Like the hallway, the walls and ceiling were black, but in here there was a pattern to it. A closer look revealed it wasn't wallpaper, but textured tiles. Soundproofing?

"Don't be shy," the woman said. Her smile was warm, but her piercing stare evaluated me, and I glanced down for a moment to make sure I wasn't as naked as the girl bound to the table.

There'd been so much competing for my focus when I first walked in, I hadn't noticed the menu hanging on the wall. There it was—all the items the girl on the table was willing to perform if I was willing to buy a night with her. Heat poured down my spine and rushed uncomfortably south of my belt as I read the list.

It took a while because the list was long.

I wanted to do every filthy thing on it. Mark them off like I was completing a dirty, erotic scavenger hunt.

The sales assistant floated toward the center of the room, her heels clicking quietly across the floor. "I hear it's your first visit." She set her hands on the edge of the table and subtly leaned forward. Everything from her body language, her proximity to the gorgeous naked girl, and her tone was pure seduction. "What do you think of our place so far?"

I was thinking I was woefully underprepared for the evening but did my best to sound unaffected. "It's nice."

She smirked. "Hmm. Nice? I think we can do better than that." Her head tipped down, and as she looked at the girl in front of her, her expression filled with desire. If it was an act, then bloody hell, she was amazing. It looked very real. It even *felt* real. Sex hung in the air, so thick it was all I could breathe in.

"Would you like a taste?" she said.

I dry swallowed. "What does that mean?"

She set her hand on the girl's thigh, and as she smoothed

her palm up toward the girl's bare pussy, it squeezed air from lungs. Was she going to—

Yeah, she was. *Fuck.*

My eyes went wide, and I probably looked ridiculous. The redhead watched me the entire time she strummed her fingers between the blonde's legs and pulled a soft moan from her. My knees softened, but my dick had a very different reaction.

"Just so you're aware," she drew her fingers away and sauntered toward me, "you're not allowed to touch me. But I," she lifted her two damp fingers and pressed them to my lips, "can touch you."

The visual of her teasing the girl had been hot, but when her fingers slid into my mouth, I knew I was in serious trouble. The taste and smell invaded my senses, drugging me, and I closed my lips around her fingers like a starved man, so I'd get every last trace.

The sales assistant was diabolical, and her wicked smile said she knew it. Her fingers withdrew slowly, leaving a wet trail across my lips. She stepped back, her gaze flitting down to check the situation in my pants, then rising victoriously to meet mine.

"Looks like we're getting upgraded from 'nice.'" She strolled back to the table and leaned against it, casually folding her arms over her chest. It was a power move, one hundred percent. "You're a big guy. I don't know a lot about football, but you've got the build for it. What position did you play?"

Lust buzzed in my brain and fogged my thoughts, putting me on auto-response. "Prop."

Shit. As soon as it was out, I wanted it back.

Confusion darted through her eyes, then vanished. Even if what she'd said was true, it was clear she knew that wasn't a football position.

I needed to change my plan. The goal had been to get as much info as possible, but now I needed to focus on surviving this room and the smart sales assistant.

I motioned toward the silent blonde. "Is she not allowed to talk?"

"She'll do whatever you want, sir, after we've reached an agreement." The redhead straightened, and her demeanor changed to all-business. "Eight thousand."

I flinched. *Fuck,* that was a lot of money. It came from me with an edge of horror. "No."

Even if I had that kind of disposable cash, I wasn't going to use it. When I had sex, the girl needed to be just as into me as I was her. Fun for everyone involved.

I'd swear the sales assistant could see right through me. Her head tilted a fraction of a degree, and her tone was flat. "Four."

"No." I put my hands up and took a step back. I'd seen the paperwork, talked to the owner, been inside the club, even started the negotiations to purchase. I had more than enough to start writing my exposé. . . right? "I made a mistake. I should go."

Alarm visibly coasted through her as she stiffened. "Just wait a minute. Talk to me. What's the issue?" She ran her hands down the sides of her skirt as if readjusting. She was probably searching for a new angle. "I know it's not the girl. You like her. You've barely looked anywhere else."

Was that true? "No, she's beautiful, but I—"

"It's okay. There's no need to be nervous." A sweet, surprised smile curled on the redhead's lips. "I'm sorry, I didn't know you were shy."

I pulled my chin back. "I'm not."

"Okay." She nodded. "But if you were, that's absolutely fine. If you're worried about her not wanting to—"

"I'm not shy." No one had ever accused me of that.

"All right." The redhead blinked her evaluating stare. "Then, touch her."

Years of competition, and I'd never turned down a challenge. This woman had played it perfectly and gotten me to walk right into her trap.

I drew in a deep breath. "Where?"

She shrugged. "Wherever you'd like."

If I turned the offer down, it would look incredibly suspicious. What guy in his right mind would pass it up? Confusion coiled in my brain as my desire to be smart and walk away fought against the instinct to never back down.

One touch. I could do this and prove I wasn't bluffing, and then decline to negotiate.

I pulled my shoulders back and puffed up my chest as I strode to the side of the table. The redhead's blue eyes sharpened as she watched me lift a hand and gently set it on the blonde's ankle.

It wasn't warm in the room, but I began to sweat anyway. The second I made contact, the girl gulped a breath, and the sexy, startled sound shot straight to my dick. The redhead's relentless stare egged me on. She'd told me I could touch the girl anywhere, and she silently challenged me to do more.

I smoothed my palm along the length of the girl's calf, sliding up to her knee. Her skin was silk, and I faltered when her leg shifted ever so slightly, moving to encourage. The logic in me knew it was an act, like how a stripper plays up she's interested in whatever guy she's dancing for. I knew the only thing this girl was into was the money in my bank account, and yet . . . I wanted to believe she liked the way my hand felt on her skin.

The desire for her was strong enough, it convinced me she wanted more.

I inched my hand along, dragging it up her perfectly toned thigh, while the redhead looked pleased. My breathing picked up, matching the girl's on the table. Her breasts rose and fell with each deep breath she took.

Tension pulled taut between us until it was razor sharp. My palm rested on the top of her warm thigh, my fingertips only an inch from her pussy. The sales assistant arched an eyebrow, one that said, "Go on, then."

I already knew what the girl tasted like. I wanted to know how she'd feel. Would she shift away from my touch? Would she spread wider and welcome it? I'd always been curious to a fault, and this time was no different. I trailed my fingers down, skimming them between her thighs.

She let out a breathy sigh and her back arched, shoving her breasts toward the ceiling. Her reaction was like I'd shocked her, but with a jolt of pleasure. *It's an act,* I repeated endlessly, but no matter how many times I said it, I couldn't convince myself of the truth.

She was hot and damp. One tiny circle of my fingertips on her clit, and she reached her hands back further, gripping the ribbon restraining her. It was as if she needed something to hold onto.

I did it again.

"Fifteen hundred," the redhead whispered.

I froze, and my attention flew back to the sales assistant. Since the moment I'd come into this room, she'd been controlled and confident, but a strange expression was fixed on her face now. Unease?

"You should be aware," she continued, "I've never made an offer that low. And I doubt she's ever accepted one, either. She's worth a hell of a lot more." There it was again, the admiration in her tone. She frowned for a split second before her expression firmed up. "What I'm saying is, this is a limited time deal. I recommend you take it before I change my mind."

Was this a sales tactic, or was she genuine? Her posture was straight and uncomfortable, and I got the sense she was off-balance and overcompensating.

Fifteen hundred, she'd said.

I had more than that set aside for plane tickets to visit my family in Johannesburg. It was a trip I'd been putting off for almost two years. Once Morgan had moved in with me, I'd thought I'd take her and introduce her to my parents, but—no. In hindsight, it was good we hadn't gone. I saw now how Morgan embodied the vain, rude American culture my South African family despised.

At the rate I was going, it could easily be another two years before I got serious about the trip, and in the meantime, that money was just sitting there . . .

Was I insane? Why the fuck was I even considering this?

I yanked my hand off the girl. I wasn't a real customer,

so I had no right to touch her. I should turn and walk away, and yet, I couldn't get my feet to move.

"You look like you could use a drink," the redhead piped up.

"Yeah." I stared at the floor, confused. I considered buying an evening with this beautiful girl, and guilt swam in my head. It was wrong. Illegal. Which only made me more curious to try it.

"What's your drink?" the sales assistant asked. "Scotch? Whiskey?"

"Whiskey."

She touched a hand to her ear, activating the low-profile earpiece I hadn't noticed until now. "Can I get a glass of whiskey to room two?" Her gaze focused on me. "Straight, or on the rocks?"

"Rocks," I croaked out, and the redhead relayed it into her earpiece.

It was harder for me to leave now that I'd ordered a drink, but my mouth was a desert. Each second I stayed in the room, the longer my subconscious had to plead its case it'd be okay to go through with this. The sales assistant had said the girl on the table would do whatever I wanted, including talking, after we'd reached a deal. So, I could look at this as an expensive paid interview.

I didn't have to do anything more with her than what I'd already done.

Although a part of me wanted that very much.

My thoughts were so distracting, it didn't register my drink had arrived until it was cold in my hand. I swallowed a huge gulp while the redhead's expectant gaze seared into me.

She wanted an answer to her offer.

"Fifteen hundred," I announced between sips. "All right."

chapter THREE

GRANT

A startled, pleased smile warmed the redhead's face. She glanced down and threaded her fingers through a lock of the blonde girl's hair, playing with the glossy strands fanned out on the table.

"What do you think?" she said softly. "Do you accept?"

The girl's lush lips parted, and the single word was uttered on a breath. "Yes."

A jolt of electricity washed through me. Was it from finally hearing her voice? Or the power she'd just given to me by agreeing to my offer? In the end, it didn't really matter. As soon as the deal was done, my anxiety and guilt vanished. She could have said no, but she hadn't.

The saleswoman stalked toward the exit on her heels. "Enjoy your evening."

When the door clicked closed behind her, the only sound in the room was the ice tinkling in my glass and the rush of blood pounding in my head. I stared at the girl, lingering over every curve. She was so gorgeous. Absolutely perfect.

But what happened now? I took another long sip of my drink. Maybe the subtle burn of the alcohol would clear my thoughts and give me a better plan. Or any plan.

She squirmed for a half-second, and her face contorted. It put me on alert. "What's wrong?"

She snagged her bottom lip in her teeth and looked embarrassed. "Nothing. It's, uh . . . nothing."

All her answer did was make my stomach turn. Maybe she didn't want me after all—

I took two steps toward the door before she blurted it in a rush, "So, this is really stupid, and not at all sexy, but I have a mosquito bite on my ankle."

I blinked, unsure what to do with the information.

"It itches like crazy," she admitted. To help explain her situation, she moved her arms, pulling against the black straps restraining her. Instantly, the basic voice in my head responded. *Help her scratch her itch, and she can help you with yours.*

"Which ankle?" I asked, moving back to the side of the table. "You want me to untie you?"

"Only if you want to, sir." She wiggled her toes on her right foot, and the glossy red nail polish glinted in the light.

Technically, I didn't need one, but it gave me an excuse to touch her, so I set my glass down beside her knee and peered at her long legs. A faint, pink bump lifted from her skin just above her anklebone.

"I'm told," I said, "they always go for the ankles. Some people are more appealing to mosquitos than others. I'm a lucky one who doesn't get bit much."

Which was great because rugby was played and practiced outdoors. The mosquitos weren't as bad here as they had been in Johannesburg, but I wasn't immune and had gotten my fair share.

I brushed my fingertips over her raised skin, giving her a startle, but she shifted against my touch as if needing more.

When I ran the edge of my fingernails over the bite, her lips parted on a soft sigh.

She'd said it wasn't sexy, but she'd been wrong. Giving her relief was nearly the same as pleasure. Would her reaction be similar if I did?

"I guess I'm a delicious one," she said.

Fuck me. I already knew it was true, but I wished I could confirm it. Press my lips to hers and taste her kiss. Was I allowed to? There wasn't anything on the board about it.

Wait. I needed to focus. It'd be impossible for her to answer questions if I was kissing her, and worse—I was certain once I started, I wouldn't be able to stop. I drew my hand away.

"Thank you." Her voice had an edge of strain, like I'd stopped without giving her full satisfaction.

"Do you like this?" I said abruptly. "Working here?"

"It's whatever you want. If you don't want me to like it, sir, I won't."

I tensed. "No, sorry. I meant it as a question. I'm curious."

Even with the blindfold covering half her face, I could tell she was unsure how to answer. And why shouldn't she be? What was the upside to saying the truth if the answer was no?

I couldn't tell if it was genuine from her flat tone. "Yes, sir."

"Forget I asked." I snatched up my drink and finished it.

In the awkward silence, she moved. She brought her ankles together and ran the side of her foot against the bug bite.

"It's going to keep itching unless you leave it alone," I said lightly. I wrapped my palm around her ankle and held her still.

"Oh," she gasped as I pressed the cold side of my glass

against the bug bite. It wasn't going to be enough to numb the nerves, though, so I put the glass down, dug out an ice cube with my fingers, and set the flat edge against her irritated skin.

She gave a quiet hiss, but there was a faint moan tacked onto the end of it. If someone were to come in right now, it'd look like I was teasing her with ice. I flashed on the idea of dragging the ice cube slowly along her inseam, and lust swamped me. I rolled the melting ice in tiny circles over the spot.

My voice was tight. "Does it still itch?"

"No, sir."

Cold water pooled against her skin before dripping down, and like the slider of a Ouija board, the ice cube moved beneath my touch, guided by an invisible force. It left a glistening path as it trailed up her leg.

Her chest rose and fell with her hurried breaths as I skimmed along, up the side of her thigh, following the same route I'd taken earlier.

"I haven't done sensory play in a while." She sounded excited, even as she squirmed under the cold edge knifing across her bare skin. Like she both did and didn't enjoy it.

I'd never done it before. Was I supposed to say that? Even though I was paying for it, I didn't want her to think I was clueless. I took a detour around her thigh, skirting the edge of her pussy, and dragged the ice cube up over her belly.

Her nipples were already tight and pointed, and I slid the ice over one, then the other, drawing glistening lines across her skin. Her swallow was audible. Her chest heaved. Everything about her response said she was into it. If she liked the cold, would she like heat too? I went in for the kill. I leaned down and swiped the tip of my tongue over one distended nipple.

Her moan was just louder than her hard swallow had been, but her hips shifted, creaking against the leather cushion. She'd brought her knees together, clamping down on her pleasure.

I'd given her just a hint, but now I latched my mouth on her and sucked. Hard.

"*Oh.*" Her soft word was heavy with satisfaction.

My blood heated, boiling through my body. "You like that?"

"Mmm. I do."

Down the ice cube went, faster this time as it slalomed over her curves, racing toward the center of her legs. Her quick breath cut off as I closed in, and it looked like every muscle in her tensed in anticipation of the cold sliding over the hottest part of her.

She flinched and jolted, knocking the ice from my grasp, but I was fine with abandoning the melting cube, because I replaced it with my tongue.

She bowed up, arching her tits into the air, crying out in surprise. Or perhaps enjoyment. I braced my hands on the inside of her thighs and spread her wider, settling in. Whatever plans I'd tried to make, they were pointless. Going down on this beautiful stranger was all I wanted to do.

Morgan's betrayal made me feel inadequate, but I wasn't, and I was desperate to reaffirm it. My curious nature meant I was good at learning new things, and that included in the bedroom.

I flicked my tongue over her, rolling and massaging, and smiled to myself as she quivered. The question was rhetorical, but I asked it anyway. "You like that?"

"Fuck, I do." She moved against my lips, an active participant.

I spun a cartwheel with the tip of my tongue against her clit, and her thighs shook. Above me, she drew in deep gasps of air, strangling back louder moans. It would have been sexy no matter what, but here in this club and with our illicit deal, it made the act incendiary.

"Yes," she whispered. "*Yes.*"

Her shuddering was more pronounced as I picked up my intensity—

A sound rang out from behind us, jarring me. Had someone just opened the door? I turned to glance over my shoulder.

The redhead was there, one hand on the doorknob and a somber expression fixed on her face. "I'm sorry to interrupt, sir, but can you join me in the hall? This will only take a minute."

I wasn't just embarrassed to be caught, my bones turned to lead. I straightened and ran my palm over my face as I cast a final look at the girl panting before me. I'd taken her right to the edge and now was going to leave her there.

Unless what the redhead said was true and I'd be back in a moment. Was there any chance the issue wasn't with me? Doubtful. As I shuffled toward the doorway, the redhead's expression was plain, but her eyes were sharp and angry.

There were two men waiting for me in the hall, Julius and the enormous bouncer who'd buzzed me in. Their faces were full of contempt.

Your cover is totally blown.

Despite the frosty atmosphere, I was able to sound easy-going. "Is there a problem?"

"Yeah, Mr. Kruger," Julius said. "We've got a problem."

A cold sweat broke out down my spine. He'd used my real name. "I can explain," I started.

But he put his hand on my shoulder. The gesture might have seemed strangely friendly, but it wasn't. First, his hand weighed a hundred pounds. Second, it was right beside my neck, and I was very aware of the proximity. His hand clamped on me was a power move, letting me know he was in control.

His tone was firm. "I don't care why you lied. You need to understand what's going to happen now."

My heart banged in my chest, and I tightened my teeth together so hard, my jaw ached.

The redhead slid up beside him, her guarded gaze on me. "We know you work for Channel Five, and you came here to get a story." Her smile didn't reach her eyes. "But you got distracted by what was on the table, didn't you?"

"You knew who I was?"

Julius's hand tensed, his fingers digging into my muscle, and I fought the urge to wince. I couldn't blame him. My thoughtless question reinforced how I'd tried to deceive.

"We're a private club," he said, "with clients who like their privacy."

"Do you think you're the first reporter to come along?" she asked.

"What's that phrase?" Julius's deep voice brimmed with threat. "Catch and kill."

Fucking fuck. I stopped breathing, and when I tried to take a step back, his grip on my shoulder reminded me I wasn't going anywhere.

"This club, and the people here, are important to me. I'm going to protect them with all I got. You feel me?" He slid his free hand into the interior pocket of his suit coat, pulled out my phone, and shoved it painfully into my chest. "You don't come here again. You don't even think about this club again. You so much as say its name, and a copy of the video we took tonight is gonna wind up with someone you don't want it to."

"Like your boss," the redhead added. "Or the Chicago police department."

His expression went dark, and if I were a smaller guy, I might have shit myself. "Or maybe one of the clients here who isn't as nice as I am. We understand each other?"

I eagerly took my phone and jammed it in my pocket. "Yes."

Julius looked barely satisfied. "Good. Then, get the fuck outta my club."

chapter FOUR

TARA

The numbness from the ice on my mosquito bite had worn off, as had the distraction of the guy going down on me, so my ankle itched again. I twisted against the straps, frustrated I couldn't get to do what I wanted, which was ironic. It was precisely why I came to the club, week after week.

To surrender. Being under someone else's control was where I thrived.

What was going on out in the hall? It was always hard to tell when I was on the table, because time seemed to suspend beneath the blindfold, but Regan and the guy had been gone awhile. Definitely longer than a minute.

In my three years at the club, I'd only had a guy pulled from the room once. He didn't have the funds in his account to match his bid, and after some renegotiation, he'd been let back in. Was that what was going to happen? I hoped so. The man tonight knew how to eat pussy, and I wanted him to finish what he'd started.

I couldn't hear anything from the hall once Regan had ushered the guy out and shut the door behind them. The rooms were soundproofed. I never heard moans or screams from the other rooms while the club was operating. While the idea sounded sexy to me, I could understand it didn't appeal to everyone.

Most of the men who came here wanted to feel like they were the center of the universe. It was all about him and how amazing he was at fucking the nearly faceless girl on the table.

Too bad it was hardly ever true.

The door opened with a *whoosh* and high heels tapped across the floor toward me. "Tara, you okay?"

We used fake names around the clients, so the fact Regan had said my real name was a bad sign.

"I'm fine." Except for the stupid mosquito bite. Christ, I was never going outside again. "What's going on?"

Fingers latched onto the end of my wrist strap and tugged the Velcro open with a loud ripping sound. "The guy wasn't who he said he was. Julius threw him out."

I lay motionless in surprise as Regan undid my other restraint. *No,* my body screamed. The anticipation for the orgasm still buzzed in my system, leaving me edgy. "The deal's off?"

"Yeah." She slipped the blindfold up onto my forehead, and I blinked rapidly against the light to bring her gorgeous face into view. Her smile was coy as she leaned in and whispered in my ear. "But there's good news. You'll come over later tonight, and Silas and I can finish what he started."

She didn't touch me, other than her soft breath rolling over my skin, because she never did when we were at the club, but energy ran along my nerves like static electricity. All from the authoritative tone of her command, and the promise of pleasure.

"Yes, Mistress," I whispered back.

No one knew about us at the club. Not that they'd judge us, but because it wasn't their business. Also, as soon as she and her boyfriend Silas had become my doms, their first order was that we kept what we did secret. Regan was the best sales assistant here, and I assumed she didn't want people thinking she played favorites.

I sat up on the table and tucked my legs beneath me as she went to the hook on the back of the door and pulled down the silk robe hanging there. My disappointment vanished that the customer with the great tongue was gone and was immediately replaced with excitement.

It had been weeks since Regan, Silas, and I had gotten to play together. We didn't scene on the nights I took clients, and business had been steady. The plus side was all the work made it easier now to go a night without making a sale.

She handed me the robe as her gaze lingered over me, and I felt flushed. With men, it was different. I was a beautiful woman, and they were hardwired to respond to that. Their appreciative stares gave me power and confidence. But with Regan? It caught me off guard. Like a thrilling, unexpected drop on a rollercoaster.

She left me breathless.

"I've got another appointment at midnight," she said, meaning another deal she'd try to negotiate for one of the other girls. "I'll text you when I'm done."

I slipped on the robe and climbed down off the table, grinning. "I can't wait."

My upstairs neighbors were loud, but it wasn't their fault. I heard them when they were screwing, or fighting, or just putting away groceries in the kitchen, thanks to the thin walls and creaky old floor overhead. We'd seen each other several times in the hallway or by the mailbox, but never officially met. It didn't really matter since I knew everything about Brad and Hector.

As I came in my front door, the chandelier over my dining room table rattled. Heavy, deliberate footsteps stomped out, moving from the kitchen, to the bedroom, and back out into the living room.

Uh oh. Hector's pissed about something.

I set down my purse, fished out my phone, and put on some music to mask the argument brewing upstairs. They were a handsome couple, but theirs was a volatile love. I stepped out of my heels and carried my phone into my bedroom, heading straight for the journal in my nightstand drawer.

The habit had developed way back when I started at the blindfold club. I'd needed to keep track of how many clients I was seeing and how much money they'd bid, because once I got a few regulars, I needed to make sure the offers stayed consistent. If I took one too low, I'd doom myself to that new price point.

I jotted down extra details too, although I wasn't sure why. It felt good to put it all down on paper. Some nights I'd end up with pages and pages of notes. I wrote down everything, even who I thought they might be, since a lot of politicians and celebrities had memberships.

I grabbed the black journal and a pen and flopped down

on my unmade bed. I scribbled the date at the top of the page and put down the original price of fifteen hundred, then scrawled beneath it how the deal had been called off.

In the apartment above, Hector's stomp-fest continued, matching the tempo of the music I was listening to while I wrote. My pen scratched across the blue-lined paper, filling the page with all the details I could remember from the night. How the man had hesitated at first. How he'd used the ice. And of course, how his mouth brought me to the brink of an orgasm.

Damn, couldn't Julius have waited ten more seconds before pulling the deal? Or had Regan pushed for it? The woman did love to delay my pleasure.

Thoughts of her and Silas had me hurrying along. Her text could come any minute, and I needed to get ready. I finished my notes, tucked the journal back into its spot, and hustled over to my dresser.

My lingerie drawer was comical. On the left side, it was sports bras and shapewear and the ugly-ass underwear I wore when I knew no one was going to see it. On the right it was all lace and straps and mesh.

I stared at my options as I shimmied out of the red, low-cut dress I'd worn to the club. Even though the clients never saw our clothes, we girls dressed to impress. What better way to feel sexy before a night of dirty, raunchy sex?

The raspberry colored bra and panty set was my favorite, but . . . hadn't I worn it last time I'd gone over to Regan's place? It'd been so long, I wasn't sure. Instead, I grabbed the bra that was sapphire blue satin beneath black lace.

As I dressed, my gaze drifted over to the full-length

mirror on my wall, and up to the envelope taped to the glass, the words 'FILL ME OUT' scrawled in black marker on the front. Inside was the application to audition for *Dance Dreams*, which was at least ten pages long.

I could pick up complicated choreography in minutes, not to mention wrangle an eight-inch dick, but this application? It was daunting.

Crap, I needed to stop ignoring the paperwork and just do it. I'd already picked my audition music, 'The Scientist' by Coldplay, assuming I'd make it that far in the process. Most people didn't get a solo performance—they were cut in the group round. I told myself I wasn't allowed to start choreographing the routine, the part I was most looking forward to, until I'd finished my least favorite part.

Tomorrow. I'd reward myself when it was done and would book some practice space at my best friend Elena's dance studio.

My gaze dropped from the envelope to the mirror and, as I'd been trained to do for years, I scrutinized my posture and lines. I worked very hard and had a killer figure, but . . . would my twenty-eight-year-old body be able to compete with the dancers in high school and college? I pushed the question out of my mind. Negative thinking wasn't going to help.

My phone chimed with an incoming text message.

Regan: I'm leaving the club now.

I stared at my reflection, all wrapped in satin and lace, and wondered how long I'd have this lingerie on. My cheeks warmed in excitement. Hopefully, not long at all.

Tara: On my way.

chapter FIVE

TARA

Unlike the rest of the girls at the club, Regan didn't sell her body. Typically, we rotated between the jobs, since two gorgeous women put us at an advantage over the men when negotiating. She was exclusively a sales assistant, which meant she didn't pull in the kind of money I did. But she also had a day job as an accountant for some stuffy firm in the heart of downtown, so her apartment was nice.

She was waiting for me at the front door after buzzing me up, a glass of white wine in each hand. She still had on the silk blouse and the short, high-waisted skirt she wore at the club. Her legs looked long and smooth, ending in a pair of strappy heels.

I took the glass she offered and glanced around the large, open living area. "Where's Silas?"

"Still at his gallery, but he should be here soon. He's been working on that piece for forever."

Regan's boyfriend had gotten his start with tattoos, but he used anything and everything to make his art. Paint. Photographs. Sculpture. He was successful enough to own his own gallery, and nearly every wall of this apartment was decorated by something he'd created. Even Regan and I—we both had his ink embedded in our skin.

"Have you seen it?" I asked. "How's it coming?"

Her blue eyes were the same color as steel. "I don't want to talk about his work right now. I want you to finish your wine and get on your knees."

She'd already started her shift into domme, and as I followed her order, I fell into my role. A calm flooded along my body when I set the glass to my lips and drank. There was freedom in being in someone else's control. I didn't have to worry about my safety, my actions, or my enjoyment. That responsibility became hers.

It was almost identical to when I danced someone else's choreography. I was moving under their direction, performing how they wanted, and the better I did, the more pleasure it brought both of us.

The skirt of my red dress rode up on my thighs when I set my empty glass down on the coffee table and knelt beside it, my knees spread and head tipped down. Regan drew in a deep, audible breath, as if the sight of me in my submissive pose gave her power.

For a long moment, there was no sound. She was either drinking her wine, or simply watching me. I grew damp and achy between my legs.

Her shadow fell on me as she finally sauntered my direction, and I stared at the nail polish on my hands splayed out on the tops of my thighs, waiting with tight lungs for her to either touch me or issue a new command.

"The man tonight. How was he?" Her voice was casual.

"He was fine."

She stopped moving, and although I could only see her feet, I knew I'd given the wrong answer. "Hands on the ground," she barked. "Ass up."

I did as told, and once I was on all fours, she walked behind me and yanked up the back of my dress. Cool air seeped through the thin lace of my panties, but only for a second. It was instantly followed by the sharp slap of her palm.

"Don't lie to me, Tara. You fucking liked it."

"Yes," I breathed.

She spanked me again, but this one didn't have the same bite as the first one. "He almost made you come, didn't he?"

"Yes."

She swatted at me a third time and left her hand flat against my backside. "But you didn't. He left you there, hanging."

"Yes, Mistress." My voice was thick with desire.

"You poor thing. Let me help you." Her fingers slid down, caressing the crotch of my panties, rubbing me gently through the damp lace. "There. Isn't that better?"

Heat pooled low in my belly, and I rocked my hips, grinding against her featherlight touch that felt good, but only made me want more. I stretched my back and hung my head, my blonde hair spilling onto the carpet below me.

Maybe she had an advantage because she was a woman, but Regan knew her way around my body. She jerked my underwear down and out of her way as she knelt beside me, strumming her fingers over my clit. She used her other hand to push my hair off the back of my neck and leaned over, setting her lips on the newly exposed skin.

Her kisses and soft bites trailed down my spine and up again as she worked two of her fingers inside my greedy body. *Yes,* I sighed, although I wasn't sure if it was out loud. I swallowed thickly to regain some composure, because the sensation of her moving in me felt so good. "Thank you, Mistress."

"Hmm," she murmured at the side of my neck. "You're very welcome."

She pushed and pulled her fingers, moving faster and more deliberately until I was a gasping, quivering mess, balancing right on the edge of orgasm. We hadn't played together that often, but she must have known, or perhaps I had a very loud signal that I was close. She slapped her fingertips against my throbbing, neglected clit, then abruptly drew away and climbed to her feet.

"The bedroom." Her voice was taut with need. "Everything you're wearing stays here. You'll be ready for him when he gets home."

I wanted to smile as I pushed up to stand and seized the bottom hem of my dress. I knew the lingerie wouldn't stay on long.

She didn't take any of her clothes off. Regan grabbed her unfinished glass of wine from the kitchen table and followed me as I practically galloped down the hall and dove into her big bed.

Her wine was deposited on the nightstand, and steady feet carried her back to the front of the bed where she could loom over me. I was kind of glad she hadn't changed out of her clothes. She looked so good like this, all prim and proper, just a bit too sexy to fulfill a school teacher fantasy. Although, if I asked her to punish me with a ruler, I was sure she'd be happy to.

Maybe next time.

I lay on my back and bent my legs, drawing my knees up,

and bared everything to her. There wasn't shame here in her apartment, or at the club, and I'd grown so comfortable in who I was these days, I doubted I'd feel it anyway. She gave me an eager smile as she placed her hands on my knees.

Had she wanted this as badly as I did? Did she *need* it?

I hoped doing a scene tonight would satisfy our cravings, but was it like a mosquito bite? Where once you scratched, it only itched more?

Down her hands went as she smoothed them along the insides of my thighs, and she put a knee on the mattress, lowering in. My heart skipped along faster, thumping a quick rhythm.

Her soft lips pressed to the spot where my leg joined my body, teasing me, and a quiet whine bubbled out of my mouth. I'd done enough waiting. I'd been a good girl, hadn't I? I deserved to get my reward. A wicked chuckle drifted from her like she was a mind reader, and then she finally closed in.

"Oh, thank you," I gasped.

Her tongue swirled over my clit, shooting sparks of pleasure down my legs. It felt so impossibly great, but at the same time, my body hesitated as I lurched toward release. I'd been fooled twice now with stalled orgasms, so she was going to have to work for it.

I slipped a hand into her fire-colored locks, holding her mouth to me and not caring if she was going to slap my directing hand away. She almost always straightened her hair with a flat iron, but it looked nice when she left it naturally curly too. I was a little obsessed with her hair, and a lot obsessed with my relationship with her and Silas.

But . . .

Not in an emotional way. They had each other for that, and honestly, I had very little in common with either of them. Regan and I worked at the club and were both bisexual, but that was it. I was a free-spirited dancer, who wore provocative clothes, never fit in, and stopped trying to years ago. She hid behind the buttoned-down accountant lifestyle, unless she was at the club. While Silas was a creative type, our similarities ended there.

I was submissive down to my bones, and she and Silas couldn't stand the idea of giving up control. So, our "relationship" was about sexual enjoyment and power exchange. And that worked great for both of us.

The relationship was open on my end. I could date if I wanted, but I had better odds of Ryan Reynolds leaving Blake Lively for me—or her doing the same—than finding a man in Chicago who was totally cool dating a girl who fucked strangers for a living.

It was fine. I'd accepted it and could always go cry into my stacks of money if I got lonely. But I never did.

Well, I *rarely* did.

Her tongue was frantic, whipping at me, and the full, intense sensation of my orgasm barreled at me. I sucked in a breath, writhing beneath her sinful mouth as I clutched at the sheets. Any second now, she'd make good on her promise and deliver a toe-curling orgasm.

"Regan," a male voice rang out from the bedroom doorway. "What the fuck?"

chapter SIX

TARA

Regan jolted and turned to glance over her shoulder.

If the gallery ever went out of business, Silas could always get a job at the blindfold club, because the guy was huge. He worked out a lot, was covered with ink, and had an imposing presence. His hulking form was squeezed in the tight, dark doorway, but I could make out the scowl twisted on his lips.

"You started without me?" He delivered his pointed question as he stepped deeper into the room. I was naked, but his gaze was focused on her.

"You told me I could."

"Yeah, but I didn't think you would."

Regan flashed me a devious smile and stirred two fingers over my clit, making me contract from the acute bliss. "I'm getting her warmed up for you," she said, just before putting her mouth back on me.

"Fuck," I groaned under my breath. Her hands were set on my thighs, and I grabbed them, lacing our fingers together. I needed to hold onto her as I bucked with satisfaction.

Now that he was here, everything was complete. Regan and Silas were a matching set. Like her, he was fucking hot.

I'd always gone for the big, beefy guys, anyway. The epitome of manly men. Once I'd realized I was bi, I discovered the inverse was true of women. I loved the feminine, girly girls. Dresses and high heels and red lipstick.

He grabbed the sides of the gray t-shirt he was wearing and stretched it up over his head, casting it to the floor. Next, he focused on the belt at the waist of his jeans, eager to shed them and catch up with me. His hair was shaved on the sides and long on top, and as he pushed the jeans down, his soft brown hair fell into his eyes.

"Why do you still have clothes on?" he asked.

Her mouth paused only to speak the annoyed words. "Because I'm busy."

He raised an eyebrow at her tone. Like her, he was a Dominant, which made for an interesting dynamic. They had figured it out, she told me when we'd first discussed the arrangement, but adding me in every once in a while gave them the opportunity to top at the same time. As a unit.

I'd only had to think about their offer for a second. Not one Dominant, but two? Two people focused on my pleasure was a pretty sweet gig, and being with them was intoxicating. Outside of the bedroom, we were friends. I didn't give them control of my daily life, and they weren't interested in it either. But in the bedroom? I submitted eagerly to every command they gave.

A single woman willing to have threesomes with an established couple is called a unicorn—because supposedly they don't exist—but couldn't the same be said of this couple? Women typically didn't like to share their men. Even though emotions weren't a part of it, Regan had no problem letting Silas fuck me.

Sometimes, she got off on it.

My "relationship" with them satisfied all our needs. Mutually beneficial.

An enormous tattoo sprawled across Silas's chest and down his arms, and as he stepped behind her and put his hands on her hips, the pattern in the ink moved along with the flex of his muscles. She was still dressed, and he had on a pair of boxers, but he tugged her back against him, grinding his hips into her ass.

"Get naked," he ordered. When she froze, and he realized his mistake, he tacked on, "Please."

He had to move when she backed off the bed, so he came to me. The mattress shifted as he climbed onto his knees, and I tried not to roll into him as he knelt beside my head. He palmed himself through his boxers—black ones with tiny maroon dots.

There was a glint of silver when he lowered the waistband. He was long, and thick, and still the only guy I'd been with who was pierced. I liked that. Just another thing that made our relationship special. His hair fell into his face once again as he looked down at me.

His voice was quiet and yet still firm. "Give me your hands."

Regan was nearly undressed, and I only caught a glimpse of her undoing her bra before I presented my wrists to him. His artist hands were rough with callouses, brushing against my skin as he pulled my wrists up, crossed them together, and pinned them to the bed in one grip. He used his other hand to hold himself steady as he dragged the tip of his rapidly hardening cock across my lips.

I opened my mouth and let him slide deep inside, and

kept my gaze locked on his. If I didn't, he'd order me to look at him while I sucked his cock. He moved his hips, slowly retreating and then diving inside again.

A moan tore from the back of my throat as a wet, lush tongue returned to my clit. She was a flurry of activity, sucking and massaging. She used all the tools she possessed to get me there. My eyelids went heavy and my vision hazed. The orgasm swelled, and then burst open, setting off fireworks of sensations.

Silas grinned as he watched the orgasm roll through me, leaving me shuddering and breathless on the sheets. He slowed his thrusts to a stop, maybe letting me enjoy the pleasure, or maybe he just liked the way it looked, his dick buried between my lips while he held me down.

When it was clear my climax had passed, he retreated and sat back on his haunches, my wrists still trapped in his hand. "No buyers tonight?"

"The deal fell through," Regan answered quickly. Maybe a little too quickly.

"Yeah?" He shot her a hard look, which was . . . strange.

I lifted my head to peer at her. She was perfectly nude, all pale skin and a smattering of freckles across her chest. Just inside of her shoulder, there was a black, circular tattoo. Silas's patterned mark on her.

Her tits wavered as she set her hands on her hips. "You want to talk about the club now? That place you hate?"

His gaze flicked to me with concern. "I don't hate the club." But then he stared at her, rolling his shoulders back. "I just hate that you work there."

She clenched her teeth and sucked in a breath through

her nose. I could see all the things she wanted to say but was holding back. This was the only argument I'd ever known them to have, and she definitely didn't like me hearing it. If they'd asked me, I wasn't going to weigh in, but in my mind? The club was where Regan got to be who she really was.

"Can we not right now?" she said.

Silas let go of my hands and turned his full attention to her. "You know, last time a deal fell through, I got a call you were in the emergency room."

Oh. Shit. That explained the look he'd given her. Last year, Regan had been strangled by a client and nearly killed before Julius was able to stop the guy. There'd been break-downs on multiple fronts, the other girls had told me, since I hadn't been working that night.

There was worry streaked across his face, and I couldn't stand it. "Nothing like that ever happened before."

"And nothing since," she added softly. "I can handle my-self, but I'm safe, I promise you. The second that changes, I'm out of there."

She climbed onto the bed and pressed herself to his back, wrapping her arms around him. Her pale, feminine hands broke the pattern of dark ink on his chest. He sighed and covered her hands with his own, melting into her.

My chest tightened watching them. I didn't get lonely, except for moments like these. Sex and love were something I'd separated a long time ago. You didn't need one to have the other.

But that also didn't mean I didn't think about both, or want to have each.

"Sorry to be a buzzkill." He shifted to see her better. "I

shouldn't have said anything."

When she kissed him, he lifted his arm over her head, put it around her, and pulled her to his side. The kiss deepened, and the tension in the room dissipated. Desire flooded in its place, pressing down on me. And apparently her too, because she broke the kiss long enough to cup the back of my head and direct me to him. To service my doms and get him ready for her.

We couldn't have painted a better picture of our relationship if we'd tried. Silas and Regan as equals and me at the bottom.

It was exactly where I wanted to be.

chapter SEVEN

TARA

I'd never danced on the stage at the Pritzker Pavilion, so today's dress rehearsal would be the first time. The outdoor theatre was in the center of Millennium Park, just steps away from the Cloud Gate sculpture we Chicagoans always referred to as "The Bean."

The walls framing the covered stage were stunning. Rolling waves of shining metal bending toward the skyline behind it, as if someone had used a massive can opener to peel them back. Red seating filled the slope leading toward the front of the stage, and the area behind the seating was a long, grassy lawn. If the seats were full, there was plenty of room to take in the show from a blanket or lawn chair.

Hopefully, people would. The showcase tomorrow night was free, and the weather forecast couldn't have been better. September in the city was usually great, but with an outdoor amphitheater, we'd still lucked out on dodging rain.

As I made my way down the concrete walkway that led to the backstage area, I glanced at the ChiComm logo being projected on the stage backdrop. It was the city's first year doing a showcase from the performance community. There'd be everything . . . sketch comedy, dance, live music, all for charity.

The orchestra area in front of the stage was bustling with people who were arranging music on stands and warming their instruments. All our practices had been with recordings, and I couldn't wait to hear the orchestra in person tonight. Live music pushed me to take my dancing to a new level.

It was just as busy in the wings backstage, and I couldn't find Elena. I checked the time on my phone, making sure I wasn't late. My friend's email had said six, and it was ten till right now.

"Tara," she called out, weaving her way through the crowd of people exiting the stage. "They want to move our spot in the schedule. Any chance you're warmed up?"

Being a dancer meant things were fluid. You had to be ready for anything, like learning a new eight-count of choreography minutes before performing it. I spotted an empty place just beside the stage and hurried to drop my bag there. "I walked fast from the CTA station, but I still need to stretch."

When she nodded, her rich, dark hair gleamed in the stage lights. Like me, she'd pulled her hair up into a top-knot, but wayward strands were curling at the nape of her neck.

My best friend was two years older than I was. She was super cute, with an infectious smile, and deep, expressive eyes you could see all the way from the back of the theater. We'd met during my audition to be a dance major at Indiana University, and after I'd been accepted, she'd become my unofficial mentor.

We were quite a pair. I was a tall, white girl with a long neck and the perfect frame for ballet. She was a compact Latina with great boobs, a four-pack stomach, and a sexy round ass. Even though we wore the same outfit—a black crop top with long, lacy sleeves and matching black bike shorts—it looked completely different on us.

I lunged down into a kneel and began to stretch my hip flexors, looking beyond her to the rest of our group already on stage. Elena had cobbled together all the guest instructors she'd had at her studio over the last three years, wrangling us into performing for publicity. She didn't need help keeping the lights on at her business, but she tried to offer dance scholarships and reduced-cost lessons to the kids who couldn't afford it.

I'd been lucky growing up. My affluent parents back in Iowa didn't understand why I liked dancing, but they picked up the bill. Dance classes and costumes and travel for competitions added up fast, and that shit was expensive. They griped and whined, but I never gave it up, and eventually we all just accepted I was the black sheep of the family.

"I still can't believe Nadine's here," I said. "She's so awesome."

Elena grinned. "What, her? That bitch was thrilled to come out of retirement."

Nadine was easily the biggest star in the last two decades to have come out of the program at Indiana, and she'd danced with the Pacific Northwest Ballet until last year. The girl didn't draw a single bad line with her body, and her turns were to die for.

I envied her. I got amazing lift on my jumps and could make complicated leaps look effortless. But turns were my weak spot. My execution of pirouettes caused directors to sigh and stick me in the back of the group.

It kept me from landing a spot in the corps of the Chicago Ballet Company, which had been my dream since the first time I'd laced up my pointe shoes.

Negative thinking helps no one, an old coach's voice echoed in my mind. I shook my head as if I could rattle the thought away, and it seemed to work.

I probably didn't stretch as much as I should, but everyone was waiting on me, and as soon as I felt good enough, I pulled off my sneakers and hustled onto the stage, tossing quick *hellos* to the rest of our group. Elena was at the edge of the stage, bent over to chat with the orchestra conductor, and as I took my place, she straightened.

"He's going to give us a four count in before they'll start," she said, hurrying to her spot opposite me. She settled and went motionless.

"One," the conductor started, "two, three, four . . ."

Off we went.

Elena had asked me to choreograph the piece, and I'd done my best to play to our strengths. There were six of us, coming from a range of dance styles, but I'd tried to creatively combine the fluidity of contemporary and hip hop with the precision of tap and ballet. Nadine was the star of the piece, but we each got our own moment to shine. Mine was a soaring leap where the group caught me mid-air.

Some sections of the music, we were each doing our own thing, complimenting each other, but as the music swelled, we came together as a unit in perfect synchronicity. As I performed, a thin sheen of sweat coated my skin and my pulse quickened to match the intensity of the orchestra.

My moment was coming up, and I was amped.

Our circle rotated, and I spun out upstage, which would give me room for a running start. As I made my approach, Elena turned her back, took a knee, and put her fist on the stage, becoming my ramp.

We'd practiced this all week. We'd done it until we felt comfortable enough we could execute it in our sleep. Elena was a powerhouse of muscle, and I knew I wouldn't hurt her using her as my springboard. The group was downstage, waiting for me, confidence in their eyes. They wouldn't let me fall.

The orchestra built to a crescendo, fueling my run, and I put one foot flat on her shoulder blade, vaulting up to the sky. I wanted jaws to drop tomorrow night when I did this. I wanted to fucking fly.

And I did.

I soared as if I'd been shot from a cannon, giving me more than enough time to do a grand jeté before turning midair to land safely on my back in my group's awaiting arms. I heard the gasps of people watching from the side of the stage as I fell into the net of arms, and a smile peeled back my lips—

Only for it to freeze. I'd been caught, but I had too much energy. I'd come in so hot, that when I landed . . . I *bounced*.

I rebounded right out of their hold, and was falling again, only this time it was off the end of the stage. There weren't practiced dancers to catch me now, just the back row of the orchestra pit.

Shit, shit, *shit*!

I pinched my eyes closed, bracing myself for the pain I wouldn't be able to avoid.

Only instead of landing on cold, unforgiving ground, I hit something fleshy and warm. There was a thunderous crash. Music stands went flying, people gasped and scattered, but the pain I was certain was coming . . . didn't.

Arms cradled my body, saving me.

The music petered to a stop, some orchestra members ahead of others.

My eyes flew open. All around, there were panicked faces and people shouting.

"Are you okay?" someone said.

I couldn't answer them, because the only thing I could do was stare at the man whose lap I'd crash landed in.

He was devastatingly and utterly gorgeous.

His silver eyes focused on me, his sensual mouth quirked, and his dark eyebrows were pulled together with concern. I was pressed against his chest, and he didn't seem to be breathing, which was interesting. I wasn't breathing either—I'd forgotten how. The sight of him was that distracting.

It was chaos around us, but I ignored it.

There was a short, dark beard along his jaw. It accentuated the long curves of his cheekbones, and I thought about running my fingers over the grit of his whiskers. It was probably a side effect of the adrenaline, but I wanted to nibble on his sensual, full lips.

Instead, I gripped fistfuls of his shirt to pull myself upright, and Jesus fuck, the guy was ripped. His chest was a plate of muscle. Was he security? How the hell had he made it into the orchestra pit so fast?

"Are you all right?" His voice sounded strange. It had a lilt to it I couldn't place.

"Yes," I whispered. And no. When I tried to escape, he only tightened his hold, and the submissive in me melted. How long could I stay in his lap before it became weird?

He wasn't convinced and gave me a skeptical look. "You sure?"

"I'm okay," I said. "You?"

The corners of his mouth hinted at a smile. "You might have given me a startle."

"She's all right," the conductor repeated, loud enough for everyone to hear. There were sighs of relief from the crowd that had gathered, and my dance troupe on stage.

I tore my gaze away from the stranger who was still holding me and surveyed the carnage around us. Folding chairs had been overturned and music stands knocked sideways in the crush to escape. A large string instrument lay on its side, its neck bent at an unnatural angle and wood splintered around it.

My voice was filled with dread. "Whose cello is that?"

The man followed my gaze and drew in a long, sobering breath. "It's mine."

For a second, I couldn't accept it. The major disconnect in my brain said there was no way this sexy beast of a man played a delicate, refined instrument like the cello. He looked far more likely to crush skulls than hang with Yo-Yo Ma. It wasn't the bow he still gripped in his hand that convinced me, but the way he stared at the broken instrument like it was a dead lover.

Oh, no.

In order to save me, he'd sacrificed the carefully crafted instrument of wood and strings that probably cost a small fortune. I scrambled out of his lap, flooded with guilt. "I'm so sorry," I blurted out. "I'll pay to fix it."

He peered up at me with a strange look, almost as if he were sadder I was out of his arms than about the broken cello at his feet. "What?"

"Your cello. It was my fault, I shouldn't have . . ."

The words died in my throat as he stood from his chair. He was even more impressive now, towering over me. The guy was like a tree. Thick and sturdy, and something I'd be happy to climb all over.

"It was an accident," he said. "I'm right glad you didn't get hurt."

I wasn't imagining it, there definitely was an accent there. New Zealand? Something vaguely British. Like he needed anything else to make him *more* appealing.

"Grant!" A man nearby reached for the cello but stopped as if he realized just in time it was infected with the plague. His tone was consolatory. "Oh, no."

The mountain of man who'd been referred to as Grant slid his gaze back to me. I'd just destroyed his precious cello, not to mention his night. He should have been upset or even angry. Instead, he simply stared at me. It was like I was a puzzle he was trying to decipher.

Around us, the orchestra members put back the chairs and stands my stage dive had disrupted. The conductor came down off his platform and scurried over to us. Well, more to Grant.

"Fredrick and Sons string shop," he announced. "Over in Streeterville. He'll give you a loaner while he repairs." He checked his watch. "And I think he's open until eight."

"I'll go with you," I said instantly.

Both men looked dubious, but Grant gave a sad smile. "That's really not necessary."

"It's the least I can do." It was clear he'd need more convincing. "Please, I feel awful about it. Let me help."

"That's a nice offer," the conductor interrupted, "but just so you know, a repair like that isn't going to come cheap."

"It's not a problem." I gazed up at Grant with pleading eyes. It was foolish to basically write a blank check, but this enormous cello-playing man with an unplaceable accent was fascinating. Now that he'd caught me, I was sure I didn't want to get away. "Grant, is it? I'm Tara. Give me a few minutes to finish up, and we can talk about it on the way to the shop. Deal?"

There was hesitation, but he finally spoke. "All right."

Blood roared in my ears. I was imagining it. Seeing things that weren't there, because I was all hyped up on adrenaline. That wasn't desire in his eyes . . . was it?

"Okay, good." A thrill zipped through me. "Can you help me back onto the stage?"

chapter EIGHT

GRANT

It had been the look of horror on Daniel's face and his frozen conductor's baton that gave me an inkling something was wrong. I paused my bow mid-stroke and looked up, only to see a body flying toward me.

The reaction was pure instinct. I heaved my cello out of the way and rose from my seat, bracing my arms to slow the woman's fall. She landed safely but hard, driving me back into my seat, and it was a miracle neither of us had gotten hurt. A split second later? She would have ended up skewered on the scroll of my cello.

As soon as I realized she was all right, the rest of my mind began to function again, taking in how beautiful she was. Her eyes were wild, no doubt from shock, but I was sure they were vibrant even when she was calm. They were as bright and blue as a cloudless summer sky.

Her hair was darker at her temples from sweat, but the messy bun of blonde hair on the top of her head was golden. Her nose was pert and cute, leading down to her cupid-bow lips. She was the prettiest girl I'd ever seen.

And her body . . . fuck, this girl did not disappoint. It wasn't the right time to assess her, but the male part of me was very happy to have served as the landing pad for this sexy woman.

In fact, none of this situation was bad—not until I saw my cello. It gave me the same feeling as taking an opponent's head to the solar plexus. I clutched my bow so hard, it was surprising it didn't snap in two.

It took a moment to absorb the image of the splintered neck, the strings no longer taut over the fingerboard, before I remembered I was prepared for this. The cello was valued at nine thousand dollars these days, but my parents had paid considerably more back when they'd bought it for me. Which meant I always carried instrument insurance.

Tara didn't need to know that just yet, though. She'd offered to go with me to the shop, and I wasn't going to pass up the opportunity to get to know her better. The girl was beautiful, sweet, and there wasn't a ring on her finger. My cello was broken, but maybe fate had rewarded me for that and literally dropped her in my lap.

I stood beside my chair, and as she climbed up on it, she put a hand on my shoulder to steady herself. She probably didn't need it for balance. Maybe she'd done it as an excuse to touch me. Then up she went, onto the stage to join the group of women waiting anxiously for her.

There was a quick conversation after she confirmed she was okay, and my mouth fell open when one of the girls told Daniel they wanted to start from the beginning.

They were going to run through it again? Would they take out the stunt that had sent Tara flying offstage?

I should have collected my busted cello and put it in its case. I should have looked up the number for Fredrick and Sons on my phone and called to tell them I was coming. But instead I stood beside my chair with my attention on the stage and watched her dance.

It was all I could do.

There was another girl who seemed to be the focus, but my gaze kept returning to Tara. She drew me in. Her narrow waist, her long legs, her flat stomach, and the way she moved . . . I was in awe. And I was probably projecting, but it seemed like she was looking at me as she danced.

Before, the leap she'd done had gone horribly wrong, but there wasn't a speck of hesitation in her eyes as she attempted it the second time. The girl was fearless. She bounded across the stage, flew high into the air, and dropping perfectly into the other dancers' hold. It was seamless the way she rolled out of their arms and back onto her feet, transitioning into the next movement.

I watched the performance all the way until the final pose. She was a siren, disarming me, and as soon as I figured out the song was over, I made my way backstage to where I'd stowed my case.

Making the phone call to the music shop wasn't hard, but putting the damaged neck back into the case was, and I grimaced at the unnatural twang of strings. I tucked the bow into its sleeve, put it away, and then snapped the clasps closed on the case lid.

While I waited for her to finish, I mapped out a course of action. The main objective was to invite her for a drink after the cello situation had been handled, but I'd also settle for her phone number. Tara was deep in discussion with the short, dark-haired girl who seemed to be in charge, and when she said something, Tara laughed.

I wished I had been standing closer, so I could

have heard it.

The group of women dispersed, and she raised her index finger to me, signaling one more minute. It was so she could go grab her bag offstage, and when she reappeared, she had one sneaker on and was hopping her way into the other.

"Okay, I'm ready." She sounded winded, but . . . happy? She'd enjoyed dancing, and I understood . . .I had definitely enjoyed her dancing. She reached out a hand. "Help me down? I'd like a controlled descent this time."

It didn't feel like I was overstepping, since she'd asked for it. I reached up, put my hands on her waist, and lifted as she jumped, guiding her down to the ground. When she landed, we were chest to chest, my hands on her hips. I fought the urge to run the pad of my thumb over the bare skin just above where her shorts ended.

Tara was an absolute smoke show. Her already quick breathing grew more erratic as she stared up at me. I had a twinge of relief. This attraction between us—I wasn't the only one picking up on it.

But I couldn't stay here all night with my hands on her waist, no matter how much I wanted to. The shop closed soon, and I had to try out the loaner piece. I reluctantly released her, bent, and grabbed the handle of my case.

"How are we getting there?" she asked. "I don't have a car. I took the CTA."

"I don't either, and as fun as it is to take this beast through the turnstiles, I was going to call a Lyft."

She nodded and immediately dug out her phone.

I wanted to do the gentlemanly thing and offer to cover the cost, but decided I was okay letting her pay for our ride.

It could be what absolved her of her guilt when she found out I'd file an insurance claim, and she was off the hook. Much better to pay a bill for thirty bucks than three thousand.

"Make sure it can seat three," I said. "The case doesn't fit in most trunks."

We walked out of the pavilion and headed toward the rideshare pick-up spot, weaving our way through the tourists collected around The Bean. There must have been a tour group, because it was packed with Asians. It was like running the gauntlet, trying to get through them.

A camera was abruptly thrust toward me. The white guy holding it looked pale and sweaty, like he wasn't feeling very well. "Do you speak English?"

I blinked. "Yes."

"Uh, great. Can you help me out, man?" He didn't wait for me to respond, he just set the camera in my hand and fiddled with the settings knob on top. As soon as he was satisfied, his voice dropped to a hush. "Take a bunch, okay? Thanks."

I set down my case and tossed a *"what're you gonna do"* smile to Tara. She grinned back and turned her attention to the nervous-looking guy. He hurried to join his girlfriend who was posed in front of the large, mirrored sculpture, the Chicago skyline reflected in it.

As I peered at the digital screen on the camera and made sure they were framed right, the guy stuck his hand in his pocket. What was he doing?

"Oh," Tara said quietly, her tone soft and warm. She gently nudged my shoulder. "Start clicking."

But the guy wasn't holding still. Or even looking at the camera—

Ah. Now I understood. I pressed the button, snapping as many pictures as I could before the girlfriend figured out what was happening, before the nervous guy got down on a knee and held up a ring. The shutter on the camera was fast, so I caught each moment. How her face crumbled with happy tears. How she nodded yes, too overcome to say anything after he asked her to marry him. And how he slipped the sparkling ring on her finger.

There was a smattering of applause from the tourists nearby as the newly-engaged couple kissed, and I kept photographing it, all the way until he started walking toward me. He didn't look nervous now. He looked like he thought he was the luckiest guy in the world.

"Thank you so much," he said, grinning.

"Of course." I passed the camera back to him.

"No, for real. I've been trying to find someone to take the pictures for the last five minutes, and I needed a guy who'd get what I was doing. You're the first American couple I've seen."

"Congratulations," Tara said.

"Thanks!"

I picked up my cello case as the guy strode to his fiancée, excited to see how the pictures had turned out.

"Are you?" Tara asked as we resumed walking, this time at a faster clip.

"Am I what?"

"American?" She said it casually, as if she were merely curious.

"Yeah." I chuckled. "Much to my family's disappointment."

"Meaning?"

We came down the concrete steps leading toward noisy

Michigan Avenue as I thought about how to answer. "My family has always looked down on Americans."

Her expression went guarded. "Oh, yeah? For what?"

"This is my South African family, not me. I've always been the outsider compared to them. I'm the black sheep." We'd reached the curb, but when I said that, she glanced up from her phone in surprise. Was that recognition lighting her eyes?

My wealthy and white South African parents had spent their entire lives at the top of the class hierarchy. Their status was so engrained in their personalities, they were unbearable.

I hesitated before answering. "They think Americans lack culture, that they're unrefined."

Tara raised one perfectly arched eyebrow. "I'm sure that's true for some people. But I also know people with a dollar to their name who have more class than people in the penthouses on Lake Shore Drive."

I couldn't agree more. It was just one of the many reasons I'd left Johannesburg.

She gestured toward the black SUV with the purple Lyft light on the dashboard. "That's us."

I needed to keep it light and steer the conversation away from my family. "You know someone who has a penthouse on Lake Shore Drive?"

She pulled open the car door and gave me an enigmatic smile. "Actually, I know several."

chapter NINE

TARA

Our Lyft driver was amused when Grant put his cello in the passenger seat and buckled it in, and I was pleased about it too. It meant Grant and I would ride together in the back seat and it'd give us time to get to know each other better. Although the drive wouldn't take long.

"South Africa, huh?" I said. "I'm sorry, I would have guessed New Zealand."

A smile tugged across his lips. "That's at least better than guessing Ireland."

"Wait, is that real? Someone thought your accent sounded Irish?"

"Oh, I get all the bloody awful guesses. Australian the most, which . . . all right. They're similar. But I don't understand when people ask if I'm Scottish or Irish, or . . . from New Jersey."

I snorted. "New Jersey, oh my God."

The car pulled out into traffic, and I fiddled with the strap of my seatbelt. How was I going to play this? God, I hadn't flirted in so long, I was sure to be terrible.

"So," I drawled, then corrected to not sound like a fool, "you don't look like a guy who plays cello. How'd that happen?"

His expression hinted he'd told this story many times, but still enjoyed it. "Growing up, my parents despised rugby.

All sports, really. Me—being the black sheep—of course it was all I wanted to do. So, I struck a deal. They'd let me go out for rugby if I took up the cello." His blue eyes gleamed. "I was sure I'd fucking hate it."

It was more statement from me than question. "But you didn't?"

He massaged the back of his neck, probably so I wouldn't see the faint bashfulness in his expression. I almost didn't because his thick bicep was sexy and distracting. "Well, I did at first, mostly to spite them. Then my tutor told me I was awful."

I gave him a skeptical look. "And this made you like it?"

"I'm competitive by nature, so I had to prove him wrong. Once that was done, I found out I could compete for first chair." He shrugged. "There was always some new challenge. I was doomed."

I laughed. "Poor rugby. It lost out to the cello."

"No, I still do that. Actually, I've got a match next weekend in Detroit."

"Oh," I said. *Oh, yes,* my body said. I knew nothing about the sport, other than the sexy-as-fuck men were built like brutes and just my type. "You play professionally?"

"No, it's Division One. That's a step down from professional." He forced a casual tone, but I heard the longing beneath. "I enjoy it very much, but I'm not meant to play at that level."

Meaning no matter how much he'd wanted to, it hadn't happened for him. Well, I knew all about that, didn't I? I shifted subtly closer to him in my seat, wanting to be near.

"It's the same with me and ballet," I admitted. "I tried for a while to make a career out of it, but it wasn't in the cards."

His eyes turned warm in understanding. "What do you do?"

I knew the question was coming, and yet I still wasn't prepared. Instead, I stalled. "You mean, when I'm not landing on hot cello guys?"

Surprise glanced through his face at my unexpected compliment, and the warmth in his expression heated further. It made the air in the car go thin.

The rest of society told me I should be, but I wasn't ashamed of what I did. It was the oldest profession, after all. I wasn't stupid. I'd had the conversation enough times with a potential partner to know exactly how it was going to go, down to the moment everything ended.

I wanted one night of . . . possibility. One evening free of the other person's hang-ups and judgement clouding their perception of me. I could take my pleasure now and feel guilty about it later.

"High-end sales," I said. It wasn't a lie. "You?"

"I'm a line producer on Channel Five, the morning news." He leaned back in his seat and cast an arm on the window sill, looking comfortable and confident and *very* inviting. "It sounds a lot better than it is. I went to school to be a journalist. This was the closest media job I could get."

"Do you do on-air stuff?"

"No. I plan the segments, the focus pieces, those sorts of things."

"Do you like it?"

"Well enough. I don't like getting up early, but otherwise, yeah. I'm never going to be a morning person." A smile hinted at the corner of his lips. "It's not as enjoyable as, say, a hot dancer falling on me."

I grinned.

But the car ride was much too short.

The shop was on the corner, and violins hung in rows in the windows. I stood on the curb, peering up at the sign overhead that looked original to the building, while Grant pulled his cello case from the front seat.

The door had an actual bell on it, and it rang pleasantly when we went inside. Warm, lacquered wood was all around because every square inch of the music shop had some sort of string instrument. The place seemed empty, but at the bell, a man appeared from a door near the back.

He had to be ninety, but he was a spry looking thing, and absolutely adorable. "Broken cello?" That was the matter-of-fact greeting he gave Grant. "Put it on the counter so I can take a look at it."

He wore glasses on a chain around his neck, and while Grant did as asked, the man cleaned the lenses on his shirt and slipped them on. I wandered toward the back of the store, half listening as I looked at the rack of sheet music.

The shop owner made a tsk-tsk sound. "What a shame, this is a beauty. You got insurance on it?"

"Yes, sir."

I paused. "Insurance?"

Grant's mouth skewed to the side. "This cello's the most expensive thing I own."

It was like the shop owner only noticed me now that I'd spoken. He tipped his head down and peered at me over the tops of his glasses. "Is she with you?"

"Yeah," I said dryly. "I'm the one who broke his cello."

His gaze flew from me to Grant, and his tone was accusatory. "What'd you do?"

Grant's shoulders pulled back in confusion. "What?"

"To make her mad enough," the man motioned to the counter, "to make her do this?"

"No." I fought back a laugh. "We don't know each other. I'm just the dancer who fell on him, and then offered to pay for the repair."

Now it was the man's turn to look confused. "But he has insurance."

I crossed my arms over my chest and gave Grant a sharp look. "Yeah, he failed to mention it."

Rather than look guilty, he flashed a shit-eating grin. "I told you it wasn't necessary, and you said we could talk about it on our way here."

Which we hadn't. There was mischief in his eyes. Yeah, he knew *exactly* what he'd done. Was I upset about this? No. Not in the slightest, but I wasn't going to let him off easy either.

"I guess it didn't come up, huh?"

"I'm sorry about that." Although he didn't seem sorry at all. He looked rather proud as he strolled over. "You could let me buy you a drink to make up for it."

I playfully narrowed my eyes at him, but who was I kidding? I was thrilled. "I suppose we could do that."

"If you're done hitting on her," the shop owner said to Grant, "I put the loaner over there for you to try out." He tossed a gnarled hand toward a chair in the corner, a cello in a stand beside it.

Grant left me by the sheet music and went to retrieve his bow from his case before moving to the chair. Pinpricks of excitement trickled down my spine as he picked up the instrument, sat down, and readied his bow. His thighs were large and powerful, parted around the beautiful cello.

I hadn't realized I was going to get to hear him play, and suddenly I was dying for it.

It was quite the juxtaposition to see this hulking bull of a man handle the instrument so delicately. I wished I were that lucky cello in his hands, lingering between his legs. He set his fingers against the neck, and it made me want those same fingers on the same place on my body.

The first slide of his bow over the strings, and I was done for. A single long note was all it took.

His gaze flicked to mine and he resettled in his chair, his face going serious. He knew he had an audience and wanted to perform for me. I got that. It was the same thing I'd done at the pavilion during our second run-through.

We drew in the same preparing breath before he started. And then he did.

The sound was mournful and rich, and it made me ache. I was riveted to my spot on the carpet in the tiny store, and the noise from the busy road went silent. Like all the cars outside had stopped just so they could hear him play.

His bow gliding across the strings was hypnotic, as were his fingers sliding down the long throat of the instrument, vibrating the string to produce a wavering note. It was all too much. Too beautiful to watch or listen to. It hurt to breathe.

Was it the same for him? His gaze drifted from mine and became unfocused. Either he was concentrating or lost in the music.

I'd surrendered to it instantly. The power of it made me want to dance, to express the beauty of the sound with the movement of my body. The choreography filled my head as the muscles in my calves contracted, wanting to rise into relevé. They yearned to leap.

The energy building inside me was frantic, desperate for release, and kept me from recognizing the music at first. I'd heard it before. I *knew* it . . .

Holy.

Fucking.

Shit.

I pressed my hand flat to my heart, covering the spot where an invisible fist had struck me. "Is that Coldplay?"

His bow ceased, the music stopped, and why the fuck had I said anything? Because that was the last thing I wanted.

"Yeah." His chest rose and fell quickly, like he was chasing his breath. "I played it at a friend's wedding."

With the absence of his music, the store became ordinary. The colors weren't as rich, and the polish on the violins didn't gleam as brightly. It was like the sun had disappeared behind a cloud. I still felt it lingering, even after it had gone.

I didn't want to disrespect the sound that had filled the shop, and my voice was hushed. "That was beautiful."

He dropped to match my quiet tone. "Thank you."

The shop owner came over, and the men discussed the setup on the loaner, but I couldn't listen. My body resonated like one of the strings he'd played, and my mind buzzed with ideas.

I'd come with him to get his cello repaired with the goal

of getting to know him better, but now I had an additional goal. I wanted him to play during my audition next month. Live music not only brought out my best side, it made the audience more receptive. With Grant performing alongside me, how could the judges resist sending me on to the next round?

We'd have to practice together. He'd have to play the beautiful song for me over and over again. Maybe there'd be long nights involved . . . The more I thought about it, the more excited I became.

I needed him, and I wasn't going to take no for an answer.

chapter TEN

GRANT

There was a restaurant across the street from the music shop, and once I had all the paperwork filled out for my insurance claim, Tara and I ventured over.

"Do you want to go home and change?" I asked, eying her tight shorts and bare midriff. The long-sleeved costume was dark lace and accentuated her curves. I didn't mind one bit the way she looked, but I also wanted her to be comfortable. Plus I was hoping for an excuse to drop off the cello at my place, change into different clothes myself, and meet her somewhere.

It'd feel more like a date that way.

She pulled the knot of blonde hair on the top of her head, tightening the loop so it wouldn't fall. "Nope. I don't care what people think. It's their problem, not mine. And I don't really have time. I've got a . . . thing later."

It was a Friday night, so the restaurant was busy, but the counter at the bar was mostly empty, and we took three chairs—one for each of us, and one to lean the large black cello case against.

She ordered a gin and tonic, and I ordered beer, and while we waited for the bartender to pour our drinks, Tara's gaze zeroed in on me. "Do you like performing on your own?"

Naturally, I did. "Solos are usually awarded through

competition."

"Oh, right." She crossed her arms, leaned on the bar, and smiled knowingly at me. "Your competitive nature."

"Yes," I said, answering her question in earnest. "I like performing solos." It was the way she'd looked at me when I'd played for her that left me completely disarmed. It made me willing to be vulnerable. "I learned early on in my life," I said, "to take every chance I got to be in the spotlight, otherwise I wouldn't be seen. I'm the youngest of three kids, and the least successful."

By a lot. My oldest brother, Joshua, had started his own company, and Pieter was a doctor. Even growing up, I'd struggled for our parents' attention. I didn't get the same high marks in school my brothers did. I didn't beat my father in chess like Pieter, or get into the prestigious Michaelhouse school like Joshua. My brothers cast such big shadows, I rarely got to be in the light.

The bartender set our drinks down in front of us, but Tara ignored hers, her eyes going wide. "I get it. I have two older sisters, and let me tell you, if I ever need to feel inadequate or like I'm wasting my life, I just spend five minutes with them, and problem solved." She made a face then reached for her drink. "Let's forget about that. Since you love competition so much, have you heard of the show *Dance Dreams*?"

I was halfway to taking a sip of my beer but paused. "Uh, can't say I have."

"It's sort of like *The Voice*, but for dance. People who make it on the show are put into groups, and they compete against each other every week."

A weird sensation prickled across my neck. It was

awareness that she was telling me this for a reason, and I wasn't sure how I was going to feel about that reason. I also didn't want to admit that although I worked in television, I rarely watched it. "Oh," I said, because I had no idea what else to say. "Reality television?"

"Yeah. Before you finish putting on that face of full-blown judgement, I should probably tell you I'm planning to audition for next season."

My dubiousness faded. "You should. You're a brilliant dancer."

Her tone was pure amusement. "You do know that piece I performed today wasn't supposed to be interactive, right?" She leaned over, gently nudging me in my chest with her shoulder. "But thanks."

It was strange how comfortable she was. Not just in what she was wearing, or what she said, but how friendly her gestures were. I'd been in the States for ten years, and it still struck me how different the culture could be. American women often felt . . . distant.

But perhaps I'd been dating the wrong women.

"I haven't told anyone," she said, like the thought just occurred to her, "that I'm planning to audition. You're the first."

"Why's that?"

Her soft eyebrows pulled together, creating a crease between them. "I don't know. Maybe because telling people makes it harder. It makes it real." She ran a fingertip absentmindedly along the rim of her glass. "Pretty much everyone who auditions is going to be straight out of high school or in college. I'm twenty-eight. The cutoff age is thirty." Her blue eyes were full of hesitation. "I don't want to be one of those fools who's delusional about their chances."

"Tara, there's no way. When you were dancing, I couldn't take my eyes off you."

She laughed softly. "That's because you want to get in my pants."

I struggled not to drop my beer. Since she'd offered it . . . "Well, you might not be wrong about that." Her directness wasn't just a huge turn-on, it took the guessing out on whether she was interested. "But you were the best one up on that stage, and if you don't know that, you're crazy."

"You're sweet, but those kids are going to give me some stiff competition. The guy who won last year? He walked away from a principal spot in the New York City ballet." She swiveled her seat until her knee was subtly against my thigh. "Any chance you want to help me?"

My dick stirred, which was ridiculous. She was barely touching me, and not in a sexual way. I struggled to keep my tone even. "Help how?"

"The Coldplay song you played . . . 'The Scientist.' I was already planning to use it for my audition." She blinked her big eyes at me, and they were filled with hope. "If you played it live, it'd give me an advantage. I'd stand out from all the other hopefuls."

I couldn't process what she was asking. "You want me to go on a reality TV show with you?"

"No, I want you to *compete* with me on a reality TV show."

I delivered a tight smile. "I see what you did there."

"Oh, Grant." Her expression was devious, and she set a hand on my knee. "You're not the only one allowed to use manipulation to get what they want."

Her touch filled my body with static.

It wasn't the first time a woman had come on to me with an agenda. I was a handsome guy, who played rugby and had an accent the girls declared sexy. I was a status to claim in college. Even Morgan had me questioning her motives about our relationship since I had some control over how much on-air time she got.

But this was a first—a woman who wanted me for my ability to play the cello.

It was strangely refreshing.

My parents would be horrified at the thought of me being on reality television, and that helped pique my interest.

"Full disclosure," she said, "there's no guarantee my audition would make it on TV. They could just use a highlight, or not show it, or I might not even make it that far in the rounds."

"How many rounds are there?"

"Last time they came to Chicago for casting, they started with groups. I guess they lump all the dance genres together, they pick the music, and everyone dances at the same time, freestyle. If the producers like what they see, then there's an interview. And from that, the top thirty or so are selected for solos. Those are filmed in front of the judges."

Her hand was still on my knee, heating through my jeans, and she gave me a squeeze.

"One of the kids at my friend's studio auditioned last year. She said fifteen hundred dancers showed up, but I bet this year there'll be more."

Just based on math, the odds weren't in Tara's favor, but I'd seen her dance. It'd be a crime if she wasn't in the top, and the idea I could help get her there was appealing, enough so that I considered saying yes without all the details. "When is it?"

"It's like a month away. October fourteenth."

I pulled out my phone, scrolled to my calendar. "That's a Saturday." She could tell from my tone that was a problem, and I elaborated. "It's rugby season. I have a match at three."

It hurt to see her crestfallen, but there was no way I was going to miss a match. I played sick or injured, or whatever obstacle was thrown at me. I couldn't play to win if I wasn't there. Plus, if one of the other players said he couldn't make it because he was auditioning for some TV show, I'd lose my shit.

"Is it in town?" she asked, trying to stave off disappointment.

"Yes."

"We could be done by then."

She did her best to sound convincing, but I wasn't fooled. "I know how television works. Unless it's live, shooting always falls behind schedule."

"How long does a game take?"

"A match is eighty minutes, plus ten minutes at the half. With penalties and the clock stopping on injuries, it's around three hours."

"Oh." She deflated, her shoulders slumping.

"Don't misunderstand, I'd love to help you, but I don't want to let my team down."

Her expression was resigned as she stared at her drink, but I could see her mind working. She didn't want to give up, and I admired that.

"Right." She brightened abruptly. "How about we play it by ear, then? If I make it to the judges by the time your game starts, I can ask to go last, and maybe you can come back after."

"That sounds like a long shot."

"It's better than no shot." She grinned. "This whole thing is a long shot, so what do you say? You want to take a chance with me?"

I wanted to, in more than one way. I gazed at this beautiful woman, who was looking back at me like I could be her hero. All I had to do was say yes.

"Sure," I said, and when excitement lit up her face, I felt ten feet tall.

chapter ELEVEN

TARA

After Grant paid for our drinks, he asked to see me home, and we shared a cab to my apartment. He left the meter running with the taxi driver and carried the loaner cello while he walked me to the main door.

I slipped my key in the top lock and let him follow me into the entryway. With the sun down, and my dance costume, it was cold outside in the wind, and I had the strong suspicion he was going to want to kiss me goodnight.

When it came to sex, I didn't mind an audience, but a first kiss was different, far more intimate, and I didn't want the skeevy cab driver watching. He'd been eyeballing me in the mirror most of the ride here.

"Thank you for the drink," I said, ambling my way toward my front door. The apartment building was like a condo. It had two floors with two units on each side, and a large set of stairs running up one wall. I was on the ground floor and gestured to my door, tucked at the end in the shadow beneath the stairs. "That's me."

Grant walked beside me, matching my hesitant pace, like he was as unsure as I was about what happened next.

I hadn't truly dated in three years, which meant I hadn't had a real kiss in that amount of time. Yes, men kissed me sometimes at the blindfold club, but that didn't count because those were empty, meaningless things. Silas and Regan's kisses didn't count either. Those were about pleasure, not emotion or connection.

I'd gone three long years without romance, and as I stood on my front doormat, I was suddenly painfully and achingly aware. It made my voice falter. "And thank you for saying yes to—"

"Have dinner with me tomorrow night."

The submissive in me responded with all she had, eager. "Yes, sir."

A confused, slightly embarrassed smile flicked across lips as he propped the cello against the wall. "Sorry, I didn't mean for that to sound like an order." He raked his fingers through his dark hair, and when he finished, he leaned in, setting his palm flat against my door, right beside my head. Even though his thick arm trapped me in place, his dominating body language wasn't threatening.

It was fucking inviting.

His tone softened until it was buttery smooth. "Can I take you out after the performance tomorrow?"

Would that be leading him on? I'd love for this thing between us to go somewhere, but what were the chances he'd allow that when he found out what I did every Friday and Saturday night?

What I wanted and what I knew I was supposed to do were in conflict, tearing me up.

"I need to tell you something," I said, hesitating. "I'm seeing someone else, but we're not exclusive."

"What does that mean?" It was like someone pressed pause on him. "You date other people?"

"I can, if I want to."

He considered it for an agonizingly long moment, before his expression firmed up. "Then, have dinner with me."

Breath halted in my lungs. His response was unexpected and exciting. "I already said yes," I whispered.

He licked his lips as his eyes went heavy, and he moved in for the kill.

I'd expected the soft, tame kiss of the musician, but got the power and intensity of the rugby player instead. His mouth crushed onto mine, and the force pressed me back into the door, where my bare skin kissed the cold wood. The palm from his other hand was warm on my hip, and he brushed his thumb across the line of skin above the top edge of my shorts.

The sensation sizzled. It forced me to swallow a breath.

Grant's lips moved against mine, his tongue asking for access, and I gave it willingly to him. My heart was beating just as fast as it had been the last time he'd had his hands on me, only now it wasn't from adrenaline.

It was from desire.

He shifted his stance, dragging his hand down the door with a quiet squeal, and put his weight into me, letting me feel the powerful length of his body against mine. I sighed into his open mouth, slipping further down into my submission. The more he took, the more I was eager to give.

His tongue caressed mine with a slow, lush slide. It was sensual and passionate, and heated the marrow of my bones. I fucking wanted him. I wanted him so badly, the ache flared from head to toe, strongest between my thighs.

We were secluded under the stairs, and the hallway was silent, so it must have made him bold. Or maybe he was like

me and didn't mind if someone came in and became an audience. As his kiss grew more consuming, his palm eased up
the length of my stomach until he settled on my chest.

I had on a sports bra, flattening my breasts to my body,
but still—I felt every stroke of his fingers as he kneaded
and sought out the hard tip of my nipple beneath the layers of fabric. I moaned when he found it and teased with a
gentle pinch.

His kiss went off center, brushing against my cheek as he
whispered, "Should I send the taxi away?"

Yes.

But, wait, no.

I had an appointment with Mr. Gold tonight, and if I
missed it, there would be consequences. He was the wealth-
iest client at the club and could always take up with a new
girl, though I doubted it. He'd been my regular for more than
a year and was rather attached. He'd made several offers to
both Julius and me to buy my exclusivity, but I'd had to remind the billionaire not everything was for sale. Definitely
not my will.

Also, variety was the spice of life, and all that shit.

The consequences I feared were the ones that came from
the hard side of a paddle, the sharp bite of a cane. I'd had
to cancel on him once when I'd gotten sick, and he'd made
me regret it. It was the only time I'd ever reached the limit
of what I could take. That night, I'd questioned if his money
was worth it.

Every night I got on the table, it was my choice. The moment it stopped being enjoyable, I knew I was done. I honestly hadn't expected to last as long as I had.

I wasn't ready to risk everything for one night of fun with Grant, no matter how good he looked, or felt pressed against me, or how his kiss tasted. Tomorrow I'd tell him everything and see where we stood.

"I can't," I said softly.

"Okay." He dropped a final kiss on my lips, lingering there. "Maybe tomorrow."

"Maybe," I echoed back. It all depended on how he handled the situation.

* * *

I arrived early to the club, hoping to talk to Regan, but when I entered the lounge, she wasn't there.

Julius must have noticed I was looking for her. "Regan called in. She's got a migraine."

"Oh, no," I said. She'd been doing so well and hadn't had one in months.

"Yeah," he said. "But I got Nina to cover for her tonight."

I kept my face plain, disguising my jealousy. It wasn't that I disliked Nina. She was nice, and beautiful, and everyone loved her. It was just that I was a girl, and it was simply impossible for a group of women not to have some bullshit drama. At least having Julius in charge kept the cattiness in check.

Nina and I were the unelected queens of this place, battling for the crown. We never talked about it outright, but the competition between us simmered below the surface. Who was better looking. Who brought in more money. Who had the most repeat customers. I was beating her in at least two categories—I had Mr. Gold. But she was beating me in the category of life, because Nina had a boyfriend. A legit one, who didn't mind what she did for living. Of course, he probably didn't take issue with it because Scott Westwood was a porn star and fucked other people for money too.

Nina had found an attractive guy, who loved and supported her, and had been blessed with an eight-inch cock. Man, sometimes life was totally unfair.

I nodded hello to Nina as I strode across the girls' lounge and set my purse on a makeup table, digging out my phone. The rest of the women were chatting with each other, some of them already in their robes, ready to see clients.

If Regan had a migraine, it meant Silas would be around, taking care of her. I fired off a text message.

> Tara: Julius said she has a migraine.
> How is she?

> Silas: Better now. I shot her full of Imitrex two
> hours ago and she's sleeping it off.

> Tara: Oh, good.

As their submissive, I was supposed to communicate everything. I didn't need their permission, but I didn't keep secrets.

> Tara: I have a date tomorrow. Just letting you
> guys know.

> Silas: With who?

> Tara: Someone I just met.

Silas: Girl or guy?

Tara: Guy.

He didn't respond immediately, so I set the phone down and surveyed the room. I always liked this place. The lounge was elegant, reminding me of an upscale hotel lobby. The furniture was nice, and the lighting subdued. It was comfortable, but also a little sexy.

It had been designed by Joseph, the creator and original owner of the club, and when he'd sold it, Julius didn't make many changes. Nothing was broken, so why try to fix it?

Taylor sashayed into the room on a pair of four-inch stilettos and a dress that probably restricted her breathing, but I had to give it to her. The girl was a knockout, with or without clothes.

My phone buzzed on the counter.

Silas: Are you working tonight?

Tara: Yes.

Silas: Text me when you're done. Regan might be up and we'd like to talk.

I pressed my lips together. What did that mean? If they told me they had a problem with me dating, then our whole arrangement was going to change. It'd probably come to an end. That was something I didn't want. I loved what we had.

I glanced at the clock on my screen. I'd have to get going because Mr. Gold was probably already in the building, drinking scotch in his private room, and my ass didn't want to keep him waiting.

Tara: OK, will do.

chapter
TWELVE

TARA

My frustration with Mr. Gold was reaching critical mass. He used to rush through negotiations, eager to get his pants around his ankles and shove his cock in my face. His wife didn't give blow jobs, he'd told me on numerous occasions.

But tonight, it had seemed as if negotiating with the sales assistant was his favorite part. Like it was some fun game for him to haggle with Nina, and I was simply a product he could take or leave. He'd forgotten I was the one with final say on the purchase price, so when his offer came in too low, I reminded him with a firm, "No."

He scoffed, downright offended. I couldn't see beneath the blindfold, but I pictured his sour face and his hands on his hips, pouting like a spoiled brat, even though he was sixty. That was, assuming he was the man I believed him to be.

Henry Katzenberg. The second richest man Chicago. He'd inherited his father's enormous wealth, terrible looks, and even worse personality. He needed constant validation on the way he fucked me, the size of his mediocre dick, and how often he got me off. It demanded all my performance skills to sell those fake orgasms.

He talked constantly during sex. I endured stories about his private jet, his dozens of vacation homes spread across the globe, and the celebrities he had dinner parties with. He cared so damn much about what other people thought of him, fuck, it had to be exhausting. And it was ironic. He cared what I thought, but that didn't mean I mattered to him.

Sure, he wanted me to see him exclusively, but it wasn't because he enjoyed my company. He thought I was the best-looking girl at the club, and I was owed to him. And he didn't want to share his toy with any of the other boys.

I listened to his footsteps as he stomp-paced the room and I tried not to smile when he tossed out a new, higher offer. He was probably going to make me pay for forcing up the price, but he was an idiot. All those nights of him throwing his wealth in my face meant I knew what he could afford. Plus, I wasn't going to put up with his shit for the same price I could get from some other guy on the waitlist, who probably was less of an asshole.

"I accept," I said.

Nina hadn't made it out of the room before I heard his belt buckle jingling.

As expected, Mr. Gold was pissed and took it out on me, using his favorite weapon of all—his words. Humiliating me made this small man feel big. It was the ultimate power trip, but the joke was on him. He could call me every dirty, foul thing he dreamed up, and I still wouldn't care. He meant nothing to me, and neither did his words.

My skin was so thick, it was damn-near bulletproof.

He settled in on bitching about the condom he was forced to wear. "Why do I pay all this money and still not get to fuck you how I want, huh? It's bullshit."

It wasn't bullshit. Lord only knew where else he'd stuck his dick, and I didn't want whatever venereal disease he might have. Rather than tell him that, my tone was flat and firm. "Club rules."

He got himself so worked up, he came a lot faster than he meant to.

As he threw out the condom and did up his pants, I lay on the table, staring into the black satin of my blindfold, ready for him to be gone. In fact, I was ready for him to be gone for good. No amount of money made my time with him acceptable anymore.

"We're done here," I said.

He sounded annoyed. "I'll leave when I'm ready."

"Don't schedule any more appointments with me."

All noise stopped. "What?"

I choked the lie out in a syrupy-sweet voice. "I've enjoyed our time together, but I think it'd be better if you found someone new."

"I don't want someone new." His footsteps brought him closer, and I instinctively moved away from the sound, as much as my restrained hands would let me. Gone was his smug, arrogant tone, replaced by an apologetic one. "I was a little mean tonight, and perhaps I went too far, but you know I didn't mean it. I'm not even thinking when half the stuff comes out of my mouth."

He was a goddamn liar, but he was too big of a client to say anything. Besides, maybe one of the other girls would want his money. I didn't believe for one second he hadn't meant what he'd said. The way a man talked to you on the table, when he knew there'd be no consequences, when he thought he owned you . . . it was his truest, most unfiltered self.

"I understand," I said. "But, I'm sorry, I'm not interested in doing this again." I left off closing it with 'sir' because that was a level of respect he couldn't earn, no matter how much money he had.

"I can tone it down." There was an edge of desperation.

"Thank you for the evening." I opened and closed my hands rapidly, sending out the club distress signal. Upstairs in his office, Julius and the sales assistants monitored each room on closed-circuit cameras, and now that I'd sounded the alarm, it would only take ten seconds before someone came to my rescue. "Goodbye, Mr. Gold."

I stood under the awning outside Regan's apartment door, staring at the panel of buttons on the side of the building, and tried not to feel nervous. After Mr. Gold had been escorted to the payment room, I cleaned up, got dressed, and discovered a text message on my phone.

> Silas: She's awake. Come over when you're done.

The feeling of dread chased me the whole ride over to her place and worsened as I hesitated by the building intercom. If they were going to forbid me from dating, our arrangement would be over.

I stabbed the button with a finger, and a few seconds later, the main door buzzed.

Silas was waiting for me in the open doorway to her

apartment, but I couldn't read his expression. His icy blue eyes were a puzzle I couldn't solve. He stepped back, allowing me to come inside, and shut the door behind me.

The lights were off in the room, and a few candles cast their flickering glow up onto the walls. If I hadn't known better, I would have thought this was romantic, but it was likely for Regan's benefit. The scentless candles provided just enough light for Silas without aggravating her migraine.

She sat on the couch, wearing a sweatshirt, flannel pants, and her hair twisted back into a ponytail, in stark contrast to my silk shirt and sequined skirt. There were dark circles under her eyes and her makeup-free skin was pale, but she still looked beautiful.

I kept my voice soft. "How are you feeling?"

"Better," she said.

My gaze flicked to Silas for confirmation. Regan was tough. She didn't like being vulnerable or perceived as weak. But he nodded, wordlessly telling me it was the truth. "You want something to drink?" he said casually.

"No, thank you." All I really wanted was to know why they'd asked me over. I'd worked tonight, and she wasn't feeling well, so doing a scene didn't seem to be on the menu.

"Silas said you have a date tomorrow," she said. "Does the guy know where you were tonight?"

Fuck. She went straight for the jugular. I shifted my weight on my feet, uncomfortable in my guilt. "No, I haven't told him yet. I was going to tomorrow."

"What'd you tell him about our arrangement?"

I stared at the carpet. "I, uh, haven't done that either. I told him I was seeing someone, but it wasn't exclusive." I frowned. "I just met him today."

Her tone was measured. "How?"

"At rehearsal for the ChiComm thing. He plays the cello."

I wasn't going to give her much information, because Regan could be ruthless. She could read people in an instant and knew everything about everyone. Her accountant personality made her obsessed with data, and she dug into people's backgrounds, including mine.

Regan gave the word 'thorough' a whole new meaning. It was great at the club—not so great in my personal life.

I wanted Grant to remain the man I hoped he was, just for a little while. If he had unpaid parking tickets or a kid from a previous marriage, I wanted to give him a chance to tell me.

She leaned back against the couch, and there was a crack in her façade. She looked nervous. "We like what we have with you, Tara."

My breath caught in my throat.

She bit down on her bottom lip, her confidence crumbling faster now. "Is there something you need that we can give you?"

Her question punched the air clean from my lungs. They'd called me over tonight, not to demand my submission, but because they were worried they were losing me.

I went to her, kneeling beside the couch at her feet. "No," I said quickly. "What we have is great." I swallowed hard, needing to be honest. "What you guys have with each other . . . it's just, sometimes I want that for myself."

I probably should have said I *needed* it, rather than wanted.

There were four positions in the hierarchy of a dominant/submissive relationship. As the sub, my wants were at the bottom, but my needs? Those were at the top, more important than anything else.

My first dominant's voice echoed through my mind. Joseph had drilled the phrase into me. *Live the hierarchy.*

"I need this." I gave her a soft smile. "But don't worry. I expect him to bail as soon as he knows everything."

She considered my statement. "Let's say you tell him, and he's okay with it. Would you let us meet him?"

I sat up straighter. As much as I wanted Grant to accept all of me, I lived in reality. "He won't."

"But if he did, could—"

"Sure." There was no way Grant was going to be fine with it.

Pleasant surprise darted through her expression. She hadn't expected me to agree. And when I gave an inch, Regan took the whole fucking mile. Her shoulders straightened as her power swelled. "Can we make a request?" When I nodded, she added, "Can you not sleep with him until we've had a chance to meet him?"

My pulse quickened. "Is this . . . a rule?"

The atmosphere in the room began to shift as it filled with sexual tension. Silas's voice was full of seduction. "If you would like it to be one, it can."

She matched his tone. "We could give you all kinds of rules."

I was flooded with heat. It was a new way for Regan and Silas to control my pleasure, even when they weren't in the room. They dangled their dominance like a carrot on a stick, and I was willing to follow.

"No sex," I rasped. "The same rule for when I'm with you too, then." That was only fair. "How about . . . other stuff?"

She sat forward, gently placed a hand on my face, and pulled me close, her warm breath wafting over my skin. "You need us to define the rules?"

I nodded, my face moving under her grip.

She grinned and kissed me, but it was hard and controlling. And so fucking hot. "Silas can show you what you are and aren't allowed to do."

His tone was powerful and absolute. "Stand up. Face the wall and lift your skirt."

chapter THIRTEEN

TARA

As I rose to stand, my knees wobbled beneath my silver sequined skirt. Not with fear, but with excitement. I put one
foot in front of the other until my nose was to the closest wall,
then gripped the sides of my skirt, dragging it up slowly.

The paint color was a bland beige, even more drab in the
low candlelight, and since it was all I could see, it wasn't that
different than when I had on a blindfold. I'd have to rely on
my other senses to experience the scene.

There was a sound of soft skin meeting soft, damp skin.
A kiss. Silas had delivered one to Regan on his way to me.
She rustled on the couch, probably settling in to watch the
show. My body was tight with anticipation as I held the
skirt bunched at my sides, my ass exposed in my simple
black thong.

The warmth from his body told me he was right behind
me, and I drew in a shuddering breath. How was he going to
touch me? Silas and Regan both liked to be aggressive, but
the few spankings he'd given me had been more in the heat
of the moment, driven by lust or the desire to quickly correct.

The idea of him slapping my ass and me counting the
strokes seemed wrong for him. It was more Regan's style.
But since she was out of commission for the evening, would
he pick up the reins?

He put a hand on the small of my back and eased me forward until I was actually pressed to the wall and had to turn my head so my cheek could rest against the hard, painted surface. With my entire length leaning against the wall, it pinned my skirt in place around my waist.

Before he'd opened his gallery, he'd worked construction, and he had the rough, calloused hands of a laborer. He wrapped them around my wrists and pulled my hands from my waist, lifted them up over my head, and pressed them to the wall. He didn't tell me they needed to stay there, because he didn't have to. As he let go of my wrists, he smoothed his hand down my tattooed forearm, his fingers trailing slowly over the curves and lines of the ink, admiring his art on my body.

Fuck, it was erotic. This simple touch brought the memories back in a rush. His needle dragging over my skin while Regan's tongue slid between my legs. He'd had to strap me down to hold me steady, because I couldn't hold back my orgasm, even as they'd both ordered me to.

I sighed against the wall, and since I couldn't see anything anyway, my eyes fell closed.

Silas gathered my long hair in his hands, twisting it into thick rope, and then used it to tug my head back. It wretched a gasp from my lungs and sent tendrils of bliss down my legs.

His breath was hot on my neck as he leaned in. "This," he whispered, "is okay." He pressed his damp mouth to the tender skin just below my ear, and goosebumps burst on my arms. He kissed, and sucked, and nipped at the side of my neck, and he made a sound of enjoyment when I shivered in response.

There was a sharp smack as he slapped my ass, then immediately gripped the stinging cheek.

"Also, okay." His deep voice wasn't loud, but it filled my ear. It seeped into my mind, and I squeezed my eyes shut tighter, focusing on the sensation of his rough hand holding me.

He hooked a finger under the string of my underwear and jerked it down over my hip, then did the other side. The scrap of fabric, damp with my arousal, slid down my legs and dropped to my ankles.

My moan was long and filled with need when his fingers skated between my cheeks and headed down between my thighs, discovering how turned on this demonstration was making me. He pressed his fingertips to my clit and rolled one tiny circle.

"He can touch you like this. Would you like that?"

"Yes." I imagined it was Grant's thick fingers plucking at me like the strings of his cello, and the line between men blurred. I was sure it'd feel different between the artist and the musician, but right now I pretended I had both.

I moaned into the side of my arm when Silas pushed a finger deep inside me.

"But he can't do this." He sounded so powerful, it hinted there'd be hell to pay if I broke the rule. "Only Regan and I get to do this." He pulsed his finger in and out of my greedy body, and my gasps for breath matched his tempo. "Understood?"

"Yes, Sir." I etched my nails against the wall, clawing for something to hold onto while I moved my hips, riding his finger. My arms were tired and tingling, but I held my position. I wasn't going to give Silas a reason to stop.

But he did.

I sobbed my disappointment as he withdrew, but it died in my throat as he dropped to his knees. Oh my God, was he going to—

He planted a giant hand on either side of my ass, peeled me open, and buried his mouth in my pussy.

"Oh, fuck," I groaned.

"That's also off limits," Regan said from her perch on the couch, watching as her boyfriend ate me out. It was filthy and hot, and good lord, I didn't want this scene to end.

The stroke of Silas's tongue was wet velvet. Warm and lush, and the muscles low in my belly clenched with pleasure. I bucked back into his face, wanting more contact, and when my skirt started to fall, his hands were there, keeping it out of his way.

Blood raced through my veins, spreading fire as I built toward orgasm. My legs quivered while his tongue probed and teased. If I had use of my hands, I would have reached back to grab a fistful of his hair and hold him to me, riding him until I came all over his face.

But I obeyed, leaving my palms pressed to the wall, my lower body trembling and threatening to give out. His tongue moved slower, distracted as his fingers searched for the zipper at the back of my bunched-up skirt.

He found it. It inched down with a soft *vrrrp*, and he drew back, letting the sequined fabric fall to my silver heels.

"Turn around."

I spun in place, leaving my arms up so the backs of my hands and shoulder blades were flush against the wall. Now that I had things to look at, I wasn't sure where to focus. Did

I lock eyes with Regan and hold her gaze while she watched Silas fuck me with his mouth? Or did I give all my attention to the dominant leading me through the scene?

He made the decision for me. Silas stood, seized the hem of my shirt, and dragged the silk up. There was nowhere else to look but at him. In the candlelight, the angles of his face were more pronounced, more attractive. The white silk disrupted our gazes for a moment as it passed over my head, and he flung it away. I leaned back against the wall, heaving air into my body, and his attention went to the rise and fall of my chest. Or perhaps the white lacy bra I wore. "Take it off," he demanded. "And then hands at your sides."

I did, and when the bra fell to the floor, I was completely naked. His gaze skittered over my bare flesh, and I felt it like invisible fingers, touching me everywhere.

He didn't seem affected, not in his expression, but his quiet, uneven voice gave it away. "This is allowed." When I swallowed a gulp of air, Silas stepped up to me, cupped my breasts, and dropped a kiss on my lips. "So is this."

I had permission to stand totally nude in front of Grant. He could touch me and kiss me, but nothing more. It was cruel, almost evil, to give us some leeway. It meant temptation would be difficult to overcome.

It was strange to kiss Silas. He was a good kisser, but it was completely different than the one I'd had with Grant several hours ago. Silas's kiss was like dancing too close to the fire—hot, but risky. Regan was there watching, which flavored his lips with danger.

His palms slid over my breasts, teasing my hard nipples for a moment, and then coursed downward. It was so he could undo the snap of his jeans and drop his zipper. He moved so fast, it didn't register what had happened until his hand was hard on my shoulder, pushing me down and my knees into the carpet.

Yes. The longer we played this game, the more eager I was to check things off the list. Were hand jobs allowed? He dug his pierced cock out of his boxers, and as soon as it was free, I closed my fists around it, squeezing and twisting down his length.

"This?" I whispered, staring up at him with hopeful eyes.

He flung his hands up on the wall to support himself and peered down at me, his gaze burning. It was more growled than spoken. "No. You can touch him everywhere *but* here."

It was only for Silas. I was disappointed but also . . . not really. It was fun to pretend that these rules would apply, but they never would. Grant would walk as soon as he found out he'd have to share.

Silas closed his fist over mine, stilling me. Was I doing it wrong? Did he need it harder? No—he'd done it because he had another rule to define. He steadied himself and pressed the tip of his dick to my lips.

"Only me," he said. "Say it."

"Only you—"

When I parted my lips to speak, he took advantage and drove as deep inside my mouth as he could get. I backed off until my head thumped against the wall, giving me no escape.

His thrusts were aggressive, plunging all the way to the back of my throat and forcing tears into my eyes, but fuck, how I loved it. A sound of rich, dirty satisfaction came from him, and it was my reward. Pleasing someone else filled me with ecstasy. It was a different kind of orgasm. Muted, but deeper and longer.

I choked as he pushed right to the edge of what I could take, and he retreated. Saliva trailed from my mouth, spilling over my kiss-swollen lips, and dribbled on my chin. I didn't wipe it away. I left the glossy mess on my lips and smiled up at him, ready to try again.

He was hard as steel, and wide enough it didn't take long for my jaw to ache and my tongue to grow tired of swirling over him. I couldn't hear Regan over his grunts and quiet moans of enjoyment, but I imagined she had a nice view. Silas's undone jeans hanging across the tops of his thighs, the muscles in his tight ass flexing as he thrust into my mouth.

She stirred on the couch. Was she touching herself? Taking off her clothes and going to join us? I pushed my way down as far as I could go on his cock, moving my head side to side to try to gain a few more centimeters.

"Fucking yes," he groaned. "Take it."

I tried, but my gag reflex protested loudly, and I backed off, gasping for breath.

Regan was standing by his side, her head leaning on his shoulder, and was transfixed by his cock buried between my lips. She didn't just approve of this, it got her hot, and her voice was hurried with excitement. "Such a good girl."

I went back to my task with newfound enthusiasm, created by her praise. I sucked until it carved hollows in my cheeks. I pumped my tight fist along with my mouth, working him over until the muscles in his neck flexed and strained. His whole body shuddered, and a deep groan rose out of him as he came, thick liquid pooling in my mouth.

I swallowed it back with a smile, savoring how the bob of my throat made him flinch with sensation. His gaze down at me was intense, but pleased, and I stayed on my knees as he pulled on his pants and zipped up.

Regan strode toward the ottoman, put a foot on the edge, and shoved it out into the center of the room. It skidded across the carpet, drawing his attention. They communicated with a look, and then he bent down, hooked me under the arms, and lifted me.

I didn't get my feet under me before he tossed me onto my back on the tufted ottoman, so hard I bounced and an "*ompf*" came out of me. I giggled at the ridiculous noise, but he was entirely serious, and I sobered quickly as he dropped with a thud to kneel at the end of the ottoman. He scooped me up by my knees and jerked me to the edge, shoving his face in my pussy.

"*Yes,*" I gasped.

Regan knelt beside him, watching us with parted lips, breathing as fast as we were. Her hand wandered over my breasts, massaging me as his mouth worked aggressively to take me right to the brink.

My heart was beating a thousand miles a second, and I struggled to find air. Everything was spinning and blurring as the pleasure closed in.

"Yeah," he urged between frantic strokes of his tongue. "Get there."

His order flung me past the point of no return, out of control. I gasped, seizing as bliss rocketed through my core. It was a lightning strike of ecstasy, vaporizing everything away.

She wore a delicious, dark smile, and it sent an aftershock

of pleasure down my spine. I hadn't just pleased him . . .

I'd pleased them both.

He lingered until the last of my orgasm faded, before sitting back and kissing Regan. I remained splayed out and naked on the ottoman, lying under their supervision.

"It wasn't a full demonstration," she said. "No anal either."

I laughed. "Yes, Mistress."

She was into anal play, but as far as I could tell, that was all. She probably didn't like being that vulnerable. As a group, we hadn't gone down that road yet. The arrangement was still new and exciting enough.

When the kiss between them ended, she focused back on me. Her expression was soft. "Start with us, before you tell him about the club." She tucked a strand of hair behind my ear. "If he can keep an open mind about this, then maybe . . ."

I gave her a smile that said she was kidding herself. "Yeah, right."

She shrugged. "You never know with some people."

Nine months ago, I'd asked Regan to take me home and let me play with her and Silas, sure I'd be shot down and end up embarrassing myself. Look where I was now.

Maybe she was right.

Maybe I'd get lucky enough to find my own unicorn.

chapter
FOURTEEN

GRANT

After the concert was over, I took the loaner cello back to my apartment, changed out of the black dress shirt and pants I wore for the orchestra performance, and into jeans and a navy button-down.

I'd told Ruby I had a date tonight, and she'd been adamant if I wanted to hook the girl, I'd have to make sure I showed off my arms. She'd informed her boyfriend Kyle she'd rather receive a forearm pic over a dick pic. It was infinitely sexier, according to her.

As I rolled the sleeves back to my elbows, I chuckled to myself. When it came to Tara, I'd take every advantage I could get.

When I arrived at the restaurant, a trendy place in Wrigleyville, Tara was already waiting. She flashed a nervous smile, but I almost missed it because whistles blew loudly in my head.

Her blonde hair was pulled up into a high, sleek ponytail, creating a stream of gold silk down her back. Her black, long-sleeve shirt was opaque and just see-through enough to make out the shadow of her black bra.

The neckline. Jesus. I couldn't catch my breath or stop staring. The shirt flaunted her skin and her cleavage and her fucking *perfect* tits. Below, black leather pants with a dull shine, and she was statuesque in stilettos heels.

The girl oozed sex, and as I strode toward her, every male eye in the room watched me with envy, or downright jealousy.

"Shit, Tara. You look fucking amazing."

Her shy smile was replaced with a full-out grin. "Thank you."

Her gaze raked appreciatively down my body, and had I imagined her pausing as she lingered over my arms? No, she'd definitely focused on them. *Good call, Ruby.*

Our table was ready, and we were seated deep in the center of the open restaurant, which was noisy, but not terrible. The constant conversation going on at the busy tables around us made it feel somehow intimate.

We ordered wine, and by the time it arrived, I realized she had barely said a word. I'd dominated the conversation, and as soon as the server finished taking our dinner order, I was going to correct that.

"I've been going on nonstop since we sat down." I was acting like a fool, flustered by her. "I'm sorry."

A soft smile graced her lips. "You shouldn't be. I like listening to you."

It was surprising how nice it was to hear, but I needed to change topics. I wanted to know more about her. "How did your performance go?"

"It went good. Were you worried I was going to end up in your lap again?"

I'd be very happy if you were in my lap right now.

"I'll be honest—I held my breath. But it sounded like it went brilliantly. There was a big reaction from the audience."

She looked pleased, but then her gaze dropped to her

wine. Something was off. She seemed different tonight. Unsure. Where was the confident woman from yesterday?

"Are you all right?"

Her attention snapped back to me, and my anxiety grew. Her expression was strained. "I need to tell you something."

It was the same phrase from yesterday, right before she'd revealed she was already in a relationship but wasn't exclusive to the guy. Instinctively, I braced for the worst. Now was when she told me she had an open marriage, or needed money, or that she believed Nazis were just misunderstood.

I tried not to sound skeptical. "Okay."

"I want to tell you a story, but first, I have a question. How do you feel about sex?"

I blinked. "Uh, I like it?" How was I supposed to answer that? "I like it quite a bit, but maybe you want to be more specific."

A tense laugh drifted out of her before she turned serious again. "Do you think it's possible to separate it from emotion? Like, does sex need to be an emotional experience every time you're with someone else?"

A warning siren wailed in the distance, telling me to choose my words wisely so I didn't come off looking like a guy who was into meaningless fucks. I wasn't. But between girlfriends in college, I'd had plenty of one-night-stands, and I was a man. Whenever the opportunity presented itself and a girl was interested, I usually didn't turn her down.

"No," I said. "Sometimes, sex is just sex."

She nodded in agreement. "You don't have to be in love, or really even in 'like' with the other person every time. Don't get me wrong, with the right person? Sex is powerful and meaningful. There's nothing else like it. But sometimes, it's just about having fun and feeling good, right?"

Was this a trap? It felt like a trap. I hesitated before answering. "Right."

"You look terrified," she said. "I'm doing this all wrong, but what I'm getting at is, can people be in an emotional relationship, let's say in love, and never have sex?"

"Of course."

It was the answer she wanted to hear, because her eyes charged with energy. "So, would it be possible for people to be in a relationship when it's the opposite of that? Sex without love or emotion?"

My mouth went dry. "Is that what you're looking for with me?"

She let out a tight breath. "We'll have to circle back to that." She snatched up her wine glass and took a long sip, leaving me to wonder where she was going with this.

Did I want a purely sexual relationship with Tara? No. I'd want more. I'd want everything. But if sex was all she was willing to give right now, I'd take it without complaints and do my best to make her interested in more.

She licked her lips as she set the glass down, and her blue eyes clouded with an emotion I didn't understand. Apprehension?

"Story time. Like you, I was the black sheep of my family." Her gaze fixed on me. "So, when I couldn't fit in, I decided I'd stand out instead. If everyone was going to go right, I'd go left. It's why I started dancing."

I understood what she meant. I'd grown up in a different hemisphere, but so much of my life had been similar. There'd been fights I'd gotten into over stupid shit, all just to get noticed. To make sure my voice was heard.

Her mouth twisted into an ironic smile. "Joke was on me, though. A lot of the time ballet is about blending in, matching the people around you. Anyway, when I got to college, I met this girl." Pink tinged her cheeks. Either she was embarrassed, or the wine was warming her up. "She was smart, and funny, and kind of bossy. Like, in a sexy way, and . . . it was confusing. I always tried to be unique, my own person, so I couldn't tell if I was actually into her, or if it was just—I dunno, me *trying* to be into her. Because it was different, you know what I mean?"

"You thought it wasn't real."

She nodded. "Like, all the cool girls at the time said they were bi. They weren't. They were just playing at it. For most of them, it wasn't sexuality—it was a trend."

There was a clatter of silverware at the table next to us, but I didn't give it any attention. I only wanted to hear what she was going to say next.

"I didn't act on it. I was afraid to go down that road if it wasn't true. I didn't want to hurt anyone, and I didn't want to get hurt either." Her posture changed as she kept talking. She relaxed, tension leaving her shoulders. "About three years ago, I auditioned for the Chicago Ballet Company. It was my third attempt. I told myself if I didn't get accepted, that was it. I was done trying to be a professional dancer."

Even though I knew how it was going to end, I still had hope that her story would go another way.

"After it was over, I went to some random bar to get shitfaced. I'd spent my whole life trying to be seen, but that night? I wanted to be fucking invisible. I didn't know what I was going to do with my life, or who I was anymore."

I opened my mouth to say something, but she lifted a hand, signaling she had more to say.

"This guy comes over, and suddenly I'm telling him my sob story, whining to him over the drink he bought me." She looked amused. "Not unlike what I'm doing right now. So, we have this long conversation about everything. I told him I'd spent the last twelve years of my life doing what other people told me to do, moving how they wanted, and now without a director, I was lost. To a man like Joseph—that's the guy's name—hearing that was, like, the greatest thing ever."

"What?" I scowled. "Why?"

She swallowed hard. "Because he's a Dominant." The word hung, suspended between us. Tara toyed with the napkin on the table, tracing the edges with her fingers, hinting at her nervousness. "You know what that means?"

"Yeah," I said quickly.

I didn't get into details with Ruby, but I knew she lived the lifestyle, and it was good for her. She had issues with her temper, and Kyle helped her keep it under control. McAsshole had a history with Ruby that made me wary of him, but his positive influence on her was undeniable.

"I'm submissive." Tara declared it with ease. "After a month with him, it was clear I was bisexual. Girls, boys, I like them all . . . as long as they're the ones in charge."

Beneath the table, I balled my hand into a fist. The idea of her with another woman was so hot, I had to do something to distract from my basic instinct. *This isn't about you. Don't make it about you.*

I thought my reaction was good. I wanted her to feel comfortable, but I must have failed. Her breathing picked up, and her gaze darted away from mine, which made me just as nervous as she looked. Did she think I wasn't cool with this? Because I was. It was brave that she'd told me.

"Tara, I think—"

"I'm in a relationship." She spat it out like she'd been holding it back and it escaped by pure force.

I flinched, even though I'd heard her. "You mentioned that."

"Right, but it's an unusual one. That's why I told you all this, and why I asked if you thought it was possible to be in a relationship that excludes emotion."

I fought to process what she was saying, "You and this guy, it's just a sexual relationship?"

"Not a guy. It's a couple."

A *couple*. Her and a guy and a girl. My curiosity kicked in, overriding everything else and I asked it genuinely. "How does that work?"

"They're together and very much in love. I'm their third. I care about them, and they care about me, but it's a respect thing, not emotional."

I picked up my glass of wine and drank, not so much because I was thirsty, but so it would give me a chance to organize my thoughts.

"They're my doms," she continued. "Because of where I am in my life, I don't date. I like what I have with them, and up until recently, I thought it was all I needed. But if the right person came along, I'd . . . well, things would change."

Wait a minute. I set my wine down, but my fingers

remained on the bell of the glass. "What are you saying?

"I like you, but I don't know you well enough yet. If you're just looking to get laid, I'm afraid I can't help you."

"You have your doms for that." The second it was out, I wanted to take the shitty comment back. I hadn't meant to be so plain, but it felt like I'd already lost the chance to date her before I'd known I was competing, and I was a sore loser.

Thankfully, she didn't seem offended. "Yes, exactly."

"And what if I'm not just looking to get laid? I asked you to dinner—"

"A lot of guys think dinner's a prerequisite." Her expression dared me to say otherwise.

I wasn't going to, because she had a point. "Fair enough, but you didn't answer my question."

She sat back in her chair and evaluated me critically. "I'm not allowed to sleep with you, but we could get to know each other and see if there's something here."

My eyes went as large as the head of a timpani drum. "What about them?"

"I won't be fucking them either."

Was this crazy? I had to say it out loud to make sure I was understanding it. "So, you propose we date, but not sleep together."

She nodded. "Yeah."

"And your couple would be stuck in a holding pattern."

"Unless I decide to end it, yeah."

"Or I don't make the cut, and you go back to them." I shoved a hand through my hair, probably making a mess of it. "It sounds like they're getting the raw end of the deal."

"There are other ways for me to please them."

"How?"

"I could give them control over us." Her eyes were full of seduction. "If you were into that sort of thing."

Beneath the table, my dick twitched. Her sexy voice instantly made me into a lot of things, including considering her strange offer. I knew nothing about this couple, other than one evening with me had her considering leaving them. If this couple and I went head-to-head, how could I not win?

"I know this is a lot," she said. "I'm super excited you're still sitting here after I laid all this out. But . . ." she took in a deep breath, pushed up her shirt sleeves, and leaned on the table, "there's something else I have to tell you."

My gaze locked onto the beautiful tattoo crawling along her forearm, and my heart stopped.

Bloody. Fucking. Hell.

chapter FIFTEEN

GRANT

Without thought, I reached across the table and grabbed Tara's wrist, gently pulling her arm toward me and pushing up her sleeve. I stared at the tattoo in disbelief.

Like an idiot, my first reaction was to scan the restaurant as if Julius was going to appear from nowhere and throttle me. He'd warned me to stay away from his club, giving me a thinly-veiled threat. Yet, here I was, sitting across from the woman I'd tried to buy a night with. I was chilled with a cold sweat of panic.

My second reaction was a flood of memories. What Tara looked like naked and bound to the table. How the ice cube melted and slipped from my fingers. How she'd tasted. I ran the edge of my thumb over a curve in the ink, and her eyes hazed. My sweat turned from cold to hot, my body overwhelmed.

My third reaction was anger. I glared at the scrolling tattoo and grew mad. Not just at the patterned artwork, or the way I couldn't seem to let go of her, but at myself. How hadn't I noticed it before? Fuck her sleeves. And why hadn't I recognized her? It was amazing what a difference a simple blindfold could make. I wanted to put one on now and go back in time to when I was blissfully ignorant.

Ignorant.

She hadn't really told me what she did for a living, but judging by her expression, that confession was up next. If she didn't tell me, and someone saw us together right now, I could claim I didn't know. It was a stretch, but it could work.

It could save me.

"Do you like it?" she asked.

Wires were still crossed in my brain. "What?"

An incredulous smile warmed her lips. "My tattoo? You're, uh, petting my arm."

"Sorry." I was finally able to pull away. "It's beautiful."

"Thank you." She straightened in her seat, her expression filled with longing. Like she wished I hadn't stopped touching her. It was the same for me. Wait, no. I needed to put distance between us.

The server appeared with our dinners, and we stayed silent as the plates were set down. I stared at my burger, no longer hungry. How was I going to keep her from telling me?

"I don't need to hear more," I said as soon as the server departed. When her face twisted with hurt, I felt it sharply in my chest. Shit. I had to fix it. "What I mean is, thank you for being honest with me. I bet it wasn't easy, and I appreciate it. But I . . . need time to absorb all this."

"Oh," she said, confusion running visibly through her. "Okay, but—"

"Does anything have to be decided right this second?"

"No, but I should—"

"Perfect. I'm starving," I lied. "We can eat first. You said you wanted to get to know each other better. Let's do that."

She was submissive and liked when the other person was in charge. That was good. I liked taking the lead, and right now, I'd do my best to steer her away from revealing the whole truth.

I picked up my burger, readying to take a bite. "Tell me about the *Dance Dreams* audition."

"Um . . ." She struggled to pivot that rapidly. "What do you want to know?"

"What do you get if you win?"

"The whole show? It's a cash prize and a contract with a talent agency, but I won't win. I'm too old, my turns aren't good enough, and it's a popular vote system. The audience is mostly women, so guys are more likely to win."

"But if you can't win, why do it? What's the goal? Exposure?"

She nodded. "That, and to get to work with some amazing people. I really like choreographing, and I'd fucking love to see other people's process."

"What's yours like?"

"My process?" Her eyes lit up, and internally I breathed a sigh of relief. I had her hooked now. "I used to be really structured. I'd write out the eight count sections and map the whole thing from start to finish, but lately I've been improvising. I put on the music and let it tell me how the piece should go." She picked up her fork and speared a leaf of her Caesar salad. "That's how I'd like to do it with you."

I paused. "With me?"

"I can get rehearsal space at my friend Elena's studio. Just let me know when your cello is fixed and what days and times work with your schedule."

The audition seemed like a very bad idea now, but I didn't want to leave her stranded. "I'm pretty busy. Can I send you a recording?"

"Sure." She lifted a teasing eyebrow. "But my routine won't be as good, and I thought you were a competitor."

I was. And this girl was killing me.

I couldn't have her. Not as a girlfriend, or a lover, or even as a friend. I didn't scare easily, but I also wasn't stupid. What would happen if Julius caught me? I didn't want to find out.

"One session," I said. "I'm usually done around two on the weekdays." I'd be careful and make sure we stuck to the task at hand. As soon as it was over, I'd have no choice but to ghost her.

My curiosity ate at me, though. Did the couple she was with know she worked at the blindfold club? And if so, why was it okay for her to fuck strangers for money, but not me?

Because it's about power.

I was jealous of them. If things were different, I would have stepped up to the challenge. It was two against one, and I loved a good underdog fight. It made the victory even sweeter.

Somehow, Tara and I made it through the meal without straying back to our original conversation, and although we were friendly, there was tension hovering over us. She was probably worried I was judging her, which I wasn't. I was worried about slipping and confessing that the brief night we'd shared three weeks ago had been one of the hottest things I'd ever experienced.

Not to mention, I'd spent months trying to get a lead into the story of the club, and Tara could bust the thing wide open for me. That was, if I was the kind of guy who was willing to use her like that.

I wasn't . . . was I?

"I'm not going to hear from you again, am I?" she asked when the check arrived. "I'm too weird for you."

I snatched up the bill as she reached for it. "No, not at all. You're exactly my brand of weird."

"If you say so." She didn't believe me. "Okay, where does that leave us?"

There was a huge lie wedged between us, and I was the one who'd put it there. I swallowed thickly. "Hanging out and not sleeping with each other—I guess that makes us friends?"

She pressed her lips together. This wasn't the answer she hoped for, but it wasn't a total loss either.

"Okay," she said finally. "But friends split the bill, Grant."

Monday morning, I was drinking my second cup of coffee when a production assistant came scurrying up to me, her eyes wide with fear. "Morgan needs to see you."

"What's going on?"

"Wardrobe put her in a size eight dress."

"Shit," I muttered and drank the rest of my coffee in two huge gulps. "Where is she?"

"In makeup."

I tossed my paper cup into the garbage and checked my watch as I made my way toward the makeup department. I'd need to handle this quickly. If she was in tears, we might not have enough time to fix the damage, and I wasn't going to put her on-air with a runny nose and mascara smudged under her eyes.

Morgan was seated in the chair in front of the bright mirror, white napkins tucked into the collar of her dress to protect it while the makeup artist brushed powder on her forehead. As soon as the artist saw me, she stepped back, shoved her brush into her apron, and gave me a knowing look.

"I'm gonna grab some coffee," she said.

The woman didn't want to hear the upcoming conversation, and I couldn't blame her. I certainly didn't want to be having it . . . *again.*

Morgan's gaze found mine through the mirror, and she grabbed the armrests of the chair, pushing up to stand. "Grant, finally. Look at this dress."

It was hard to miss because it was a bold yellow. Wardrobe liked to put her in happy colors because it was a morning show, and the short dress was cute with scalloped edges. The color was good on Morgan. Her skin looked tan and her blonde hair was a softer hue, complimenting the dress color instead of clashing with it.

She pinched the dress at her side, her pretty face filled with irritation. "It's huge on me."

It wasn't. There was barely a millimeter of fabric between her fingers. "I think it looks fine."

"Fine?" Her face flooded with alarm.

"Great," I said quickly. "It looks great."

She turned to face the mirror and reevaluate, her expression dubious. "I just want clothes that fit me. I mean, I've never been an eight in my life."

Except I'd instructed the wardrobe department to switch out the labels of her dresses before fitting. The sizes seemed to be arbitrary. One brand's size four could be a two or a six in another. What difference did it make what was on the label? I'd never understand why it mattered so much to her, but then again, she was Morgan. Everything mattered when it came to appearance.

I pinched the bridge of my nose as I mustered up the strength. "It looks perfect to me. It's very flattering."

"Yeah?"

"Yes."

Satisfied enough, she lowered back down into the chair. Crisis averted, I turned to leave—

"Wait," she said. "How are you? How was your weekend?"

My lungs tightened in my chest. In our professional life, the breakup had gone as well as one could hope for, given that she'd sent nudes to half of the guys we worked with. It was a miracle she hadn't been fired, but it might have been part of her plan. She craved attention, and it didn't matter what kind.

"It was fine." I used a clipped tone to show her I didn't want to have a conversation.

She ignored my signals and asked it casually. "What'd you do?"

I narrowed my eyes. I knew what she was doing. Morgan didn't care what I'd done—she was fishing for me to ask about her weekend. Whatever she was excited to tell me about, I wasn't interested. It was ridiculous I had to constantly reassure her on her looks, and I was fucking tired.

"I went on a date."

There was a spike of surprise followed by jealousy in her expression that she unsuccessfully tried to disguise. "Oh?

With who?"

"A girl I met. A dancer."

Morgan's mouth fell open. "You went out with a stripper?"

"What? No, ballet. We met when I had an orchestra thing."

The sunny yellow dress wasn't enough to brighten her frown. "You're dating a ballerina?"

It was petty to want to hurt Morgan, but I couldn't help it. Her betrayal still stung, and I wanted her to feel some discomfort too.

"Yes," I lied and then switched to the truth. "You should see her dance. She's absolutely beautiful."

Morgan looked the way she did when the teleprompter stopped working. A vacant smile was frozen on her face, but her eyes were pure panic. I left her like that and went back to the set, needing to do some actual work.

Justin, my boss, was talking with one of the anchors, but when he saw me, he waved me over and dismissed the anchor. His stern expression made the coffee in my stomach churn.

"Grant, we need to talk about your segment proposals. What is going on with you? You're all over the place." He put his hands on his hips, and his tone was serious. "When you first came on, your stuff was so edgy, but now you're giving me nothing but fluff."

My stuff had been *too* edgy, he'd lectured. Frustration boiled inside me. There was no pleasing this man. "It's a morning show. You told me to tone it down and that viewers love fluff."

"They do, but we have to find a balance, otherwise we become a joke. I can't have that."

"Of course not."

"Tell me you've got something good in the works."

Unease crept over my skin. I knew I should keep my mouth shut, but it spilled out anyway. "Maybe."

Interest piqued through him. "Yeah? What is it?"

"It's not ready." I tried to walk it back. "It could be nothing."

He scowled. "Well, let's hope it's something, because people aren't going to keep watching if we're giving them nothing. You understand what I'm saying?"

"Yes."

I didn't love my job, but I needed it, and if I didn't give Justin something he could work with, he wouldn't keep me around. Then, I'd have to find a new job or go crawling back to my wealthy family in Johannesburg.

Neither option was appealing, and I wasn't going to let it come to that.

"Next thing I turn in will be huge," I said.

"Excellent." He brightened. "That's what I wanted to hear."

chapter SIXTEEN

TARA

Elena's studio was a converted warehouse, and she'd kept the industrial feel but softened it up with cornflower blue paint and warm white pine floors. I loved the space. It was enormous, but the windows let in tons of natural light, which bounced off the mirrored wall. The dark colored ceiling was lit by strands of hanging globe lights, and their reflections glowed on the gloss of the highly-polished floor.

She'd scheduled me for an hour at three p.m., fitting us in before an after-school hip hop class. I'd have the entire dance floor to myself—other than the chair I'd set up over to one side for Grant.

Elena had retreated to her office, and the studio was silent.

I went to the ballet barre on the far wall and stepped through another warmup routine to keep my muscles loose, ignoring the clock over the mirrors. It was already ten after three, and wasted time was rushing by. I needed to prepare myself for idea that Grant, my "friend," had flaked on me.

The only time a guy told me he just wanted to be friends was after we'd fucked. He'd gotten what he wanted, and the friend status was delivered so he could make a quick exit.

But I hadn't slept with Grant.

Not yet, but I was pretty sure he'd hop into bed with me if I offered. It was all very confusing. Dinner with him had gone better than I'd expected, but also worse. I had no idea where we stood.

I glanced up at the clock. 3:12. Well, that told me enough, didn't it? I sighed and walked across the dance floor to retrieve my bag. I could hook my phone up to the speaker system via Bluetooth and start choreography with—

The front door whooshed open, and there was a loud bang as the side of Grant's cello case cracked against the doorframe. "Sorry," he said, although there was no one at the front desk.

Had he just apologized to the door?

His dark hair was tousled, either from the wind or his nervous hand running through it, and his shoulders lifted on his rapid breath. Had he run here? Carrying his big-ass cello case?

Looking at him made me as out of breath as he was. Goddamn, he was fine. He had on jeans, a dark gray hooded sweatshirt, and a look of anxiety as he peered around the front room, searching for something. Probably me.

"Hey, there," I yelled. "Did you get lost?"

"My Uber driver was bloody awful and dropped me off on the wrong block. Sorry I'm late." He strode down the open hallway and onto the dance floor, lugging the cello like it weighed nothing. For being such a big guy, he could move fast. It probably came in handy when he played rugby.

"It's okay." I gestured to the folding chair I'd set out for him. "Do you need to warm up?"

He marched over to his spot, set down the case, and popped open the latches. "I only need a minute."

"Okay, cool." I could stretch some more while waiting.

"Also, hi."

He stopped for a moment to give me his full attention and a genuine smile. "Yes. Hi."

I stared at him, gawking like a lovestruck teenager. Wasn't I supposed to be doing something? Oh, right—stretching. I went back to the barre and rested my hand lightly on it, while lifting my working leg.

I snuck glances at him while he fiddled with the cello and made adjustments. Which looked great—I couldn't tell it had been broken or repaired. The wood was smooth and a deep honey brown.

I continued my stretch, extending my leg up, pushing energy out all the way through my pointed toe. He played a few notes, and I sighed deeply at the haunting sound.

"All right," he said. "I'm read—"

I turned my head toward him, curious what had made him stop mid-sentence, and a thrill coursed down my body when I realized it was me. I stood straight, one leg planted on the floor and the other lifted to the sky, creating a perfect vertical line. Was he admiring my flexibility? His eyes were lidded, heavy with desire.

Friends, my ass. Friends didn't give each other looks that said they wanted to bend them over the ballet barre and fuck them senseless.

Grant cleared his throat and adjusted. "Uh, I'm ready."

I moved to the center of the floor. "I only need the first two minutes of the song."

His bow dipped down as he looked surprised. "Why?"

"Because the judges never need more than two minutes to make a decision." I'd worked with some directors who only needed thirty seconds.

Less if there was a pirouette in the routine.

I shoved the thought away. Time was precious, and I wasn't going to waste it on negative shit.

"Hit it, maestro," I joked.

His phone was laying on top of his cello case, and he leaned over, tapping the screen. Piano music tinkled from the speakers.

"What—"

"When I did it for the wedding," he said over the song, "it was a duet. I have a recording of the piano I practiced with."

The intro was beautiful, but it didn't hold a candle to when he began to play. His cello created the melody, the piano the perfect accompaniment. The rich sound flooded the studio, blanketing everything from the floor to the rafters.

My eyes wanted to watch him play, to follow the gentle seesaw of his bow over the strings, but my heart and body needed to dance. I turned away from the mirror so I wouldn't watch or judge my movements, and let his music carry me through the steps as if they had already been written.

Before this session, I'd created a general guide to work from. I knew what leaps I wanted to perform and where to place them. I had several ideas for level changes, but listening to the music helped me transition from one phrase to the next.

Grant played the same two minutes over again, and each time he started anew, I was in awe. It sounded better than the last. He didn't tire of playing it or ask me if I wanted to do it again. He just knew. I danced until I was breathless, my heart racing and soaring.

And every time I caught his gaze in the mirror, he was fixated on me.

"What's this piece for?" a female voice rang out when the music ceased. I glanced over at Elena, who must have come out of her office at some point to watch.

I wiped the beads of sweat off my forehead with the back of my hand. "Uh . . . so, I was thinking about auditioning for *Dance Dreams*."

Her lips parted in surprise, but she didn't say anything.

"Do you think it's a bad idea?" I asked. God, was I being stupid?

"No, no, not at all." Her eyebrows pulled together, making her look deep in thought. "But tell me about Hot Cello Guy."

Grant smirked, amused.

"I was going to audition with live music."

She'd been looking at him, but her focus snapped to me. "Will they let you do that?"

I shrugged indifferently, but it was an act. I didn't know for certain if they'd let Grant up on stage. "There's nothing about it in the rules."

He looked less amused now. "You don't know if live music is allowed?"

Her attention yo-yoed back to him and his accent. "Where are you from?"

"New Jersey," I said, refusing to shrink under his withering stare. "I told you it was a long shot. What's the worst that could happen? They say no, and I dance with recorded music."

"And I've wasted my day."

"That might happen, yeah." My voice was soft. "But I'll pay for your time, and even just having you there in support would be a huge help." After so many failed auditions, I'd begun to struggle with pre-performance anxiety. "I think they'll say yes, though. Who wouldn't to Hot Cello Guy?" I flashed a hopeful smile. "If they do say no, you could always go rogue and play it from the auditorium seats."

He considered my suggestion for a moment, and then his shoulders relaxed. "Guerrilla style cello."

I laughed. "Yes."

Elena folded her arms over her chest. "Assuming they let him perform with you, you've got another problem, then. Hot Cello Guy is distracting. I'm thinking about it from a judge's perspective. They spend all day watching dance solos, and suddenly there's this gorgeous motherfucker with his cello. Their eyes are going to that."

"If I haven't mentioned it," Grant piped up, "your friend seems cool."

Ever the director, Elena was too focused on the issue to respond to him. "He's going to upstage you, Tara. You'll have to put him behind the curtain, off the stage."

She made an excellent point, but I didn't want to hide him. "What if . . ." I started. The idea blossomed in my head and took shape.

Whatever expression I had, it filled him with visible unease. "What if, what?"

"What if I made him part of it? We put him center stage." The words sped out of me as I grew more excited. "He's static while I'm moving around him. I could even play off of him with the choreography."

"Yas, girl." Elena grinned. "It'll make you travel more too. That was going to be my next suggestion." She grabbed the back of Grant's chair and tried to move it, but he was still sitting there with a dubious expression. "Front and center, Hot Cello Guy."

He humored us, carrying his bow in one hand and the neck of his instrument in the other, while she dragged the chair to the center of the room.

"If I put my hands on you while you're playing," I asked him, "will it mess you up?"

"I guess it depends on where you put your hands." He'd said it with a straight face, but his eyes dripped with innuendo.

I was absolutely capable of putting my hands somewhere to make him lose control, but . . . I couldn't, could I? My body went tight at the thought.

"Uh, your shoulders."

He considered it. "As long as it doesn't affect my posture, that should be fine."

"Okay, let's try it."

Elena helped him sync his phone to the sound system as I walked through a few steps, plotting out my new routine. When we were good to go, I moved behind his chair and set my hands on his broad shoulders, my fingers splayed down his chest.

At the contact, he took in a sharp breath, like this simple connection was shocking. The crazy thing was I felt it too. I nodded to Elena to start the music. At the first notes of the piano, I began to move, trailing my hands across his body, separating from him just as he readied to play.

When his music started, I came alive. Every sound he produced was echoed in my body. I became his bow. I fluttered around him, trying to be the visual representation of the song.

He wasn't just directing me with his music, he made me his willing slave.

It was the shortest and longest two minutes of my life, and when he stopped playing, I ached for more. But Elena turned off the recording, and her expression wasn't at all what I expected or hoped for. She looked . . . dissatisfied.

"What's wrong?" I wanted to cry it at her but managed to keep a handle on it.

"Nothing. It's beautiful."

I wasn't buying it. "Then why are you looking at us like that?"

Her sigh was full of reluctance. "I have a suggestion, and I don't think you're going to like it." She glanced up at the clock, then back to me. "Never mind. It's not important."

I charged at her. "Oh, no, you don't. Spit it out."

"The song. It's so . . . safe. I mean, he plays it beautifully, and your technique, your choreography—it's all on point. But you're dancing classical ballet to a song that has a classical sound."

I was filled with dread. "It's a snooze-fest."

"No, I wouldn't say that. It's that the song is, like, serious." She dropped the pretense. "It's somber as fuck, and it's so not *you.*"

Holy shit. She was absolutely right.

The front door opened, and a group of kids came in, chatting noisily as they hung their backpacks on the hooks in the waiting area.

Which meant it was four o'clock, and I was out of time.

chapter SEVENTEEN

TARA

Grant had told me one session, and I'd just wasted it with the wrong song choice. All the highs I experienced while dancing only made the crash to reality worse. I turned away from Elena and Grant and stared at the floor, not wanting them to see how upset I was. What the fuck was I going to do?

He rose from the folding chair, his voice soft. "It's all right. We'll figure it out."

I hated how my eyes burned with tears. Three years ago, I'd closed the door on my dream, and with this audition I'd allowed myself to nudge it back open. I had one shot to prove I hadn't wasted my life foolishly chasing after it.

I was supposed to stand on the stage and show my family that success wasn't always judged by a paycheck or a job title. That art had just as much value as math and science.

I could feel Grant's gaze burning into me, and I turned to meet it.

His expression was determination. "I can learn a new song."

A breath burst from my body, making space for hope. "You'd do that?"

"Yeah." His lips lifted in a soft smile. "Of course I would."

My heart tripped over itself, and my knees went weak. I could barely stay upright in the onslaught of him. My words were a whisper. "Thank you."

He nodded.

The noise in the front room grew as more students came in, and it pulled us from the moment we'd shared. I scrambled to come up with a plan.

"Pizza," I announced abruptly. He looked at me like I was a crazy woman, and he wasn't wrong. "Come to my place," I said, "I'll order pizza, and we can talk about it. I mean, pizza solves everything."

"It does," he opened his case and gently lowered the cello in, "but I have training from five to seven."

For rugby. Like I needed a reminder of how insanely sexy he was. I readjusted. "After, then."

He considered it and smiled. "I'll be there around eight."

I wasn't a neat person. I didn't always make my bed in the morning, sometimes I left dirty dishes to soak in the sink overnight, and I didn't vacuum as often as I should. But it didn't take me too long to tidy up before Grant's arrival.

I had a laundry basket of clean clothes that never got folded, and as I hid it in the closet, I listened to Brad and Hector above me as they discussed their day. There'd been drama at Hector's job—two of his coworkers had been caught screwing in a vacant office behind a stack of old desktop computers. He told it like it was scandalous, and it made me giggle.

If only they knew what I did for a living.

I frowned. I still needed to tell Grant.

And I had no idea how he was going to react. What if I told him and he freaked? I liked him and didn't want him to vanish on me. Thinking about it made me nauseated.

While I waited for his arrival, I flopped down on the couch in my living room, tucking my legs underneath myself, and searched YouTube for new song ideas. Elena had been right. The Coldplay song was beautiful, but it didn't show off my personality, and that was just as important as dance technique if I wanted to make it as a contestant on *Dance Dreams*.

It was just after eight when Grant arrived. He must have showered after his practice because his hair was styled, and he had on jeans and a nicer sweater. Like he'd made an effort.

I'd touched up my makeup, but my clothes were casual. My jeans hugged low across my hips and rolled at the ankles, and I wore a tight black tank top. It ended below my waist and showed off a band of skin above my jeans, and as he stepped into my apartment, his gaze went from it to my cleavage. I quirked my mouth into a half-smile. Was I showing too much skin for him, or just the right amount?

"Hi," I said. "Come on in."

"Hey." He stepped across the threshold.

"How was training?"

"It was fine."

He turned his attention to my place. The living area was just my couch and an old steamer trunk I used as a coffee table. Beyond was the dining table and a wall with a built-in bookcase. The apartment was old. It had creaking floorboards and knocking pipes, but high ceilings and gorgeous woodwork. It had so much character, I gladly paid the steep rent and put up with having to call the super when things needed repair, which happened often.

"Wow," he said. "Your place is nice."

"Thanks. You want something to drink? Come on back to the kitchen, and I'll show you what I've got."

As I led the way, I stifled a chuckle. I hadn't meant for it to sound sexual, but it came out that way.

He followed me into the tiny room, stepping onto the black and white penny tile, and he was so big, he made the cramped kitchen feel even smaller.

"Beer, if you have it," he said.

I did. I'd bought it on my way home from the studio. I opened the fridge and grabbed a bottle, passing it to him. There were faint lines in the corner of his eyes, hinting he was tired.

I grabbed a beer for myself. "Long day?"

"Is it that obvious?" He twisted off the cap and drank. "At my job, some days are more of a challenge than others, and today was one of those days."

I attempted to twist off the top of my beer, but he set his down, took the bottle from my hands, and did it for me, passing it back. I nodded my '*thanks*' and leaned against the butcher block counter.

"Why was it a challenge?"

His expression was suddenly guarded. He didn't want to tell me? He sighed, just enough that I saw the subtle slump of his shoulders. "One of my responsibilities is planning the segments we do. The show runner hasn't been happy with anything I've brought him." He followed my lead and leaned against the counter opposite me. Since the kitchen was so tight, there wasn't much space between us, and I liked that. I hadn't had a man in my apartment in ages, and yet it was instantly comfortable that he was here.

"What's wrong with your stuff?"

His tone was frustrated. "It's not exclusive, or it's too depressing, or it's not hard hitting enough. He told me I need to bring him something big, or . . ." As he trailed off, he tore his gaze away from mine and took a long drink.

Ultra-competitive Grant didn't like losing, and it was obvious how hard this was for him. It was surprising he shared it at all, and I was touched.

When his gaze returned to me, he forced enthusiasm. "You don't happen to know about any big scandals I could use, do you?"

My heart launched into my throat, and it sped faster the longer he stared at me.

Three years at the blindfold club had made me a treasure trove of scandals. I knew which conservative politicians were cheating on their wives, which celebrities were dirty freaks like me. I knew several guys in the Chicago police department who looked the other way about how the club operated.

A few of them I knew *intimately*.

Now it was my turn to look away. I liked what I did, but the people I worked with? They were family, and I wouldn't sell them out for anything.

As the tense silence hung between us, my stomach became a jar full of fluttering butterflies. I was supposed to tell Grant what I did for a living. I'd had trepidation before, worried he'd bail on performing during the audition, or worse . . . that he'd judge me.

But now, how the hell could I explain I let people fuck me for money? If I gave him even a hint of the illegal club, I didn't trust him enough to leave it alone. I had little to gain from telling him, and everything to lose. I was so screwed.

I hated lying, but I'd had to do it a few times since I'd begun taking clients, and had no choice but to do it again now.

"Uh . . ." I said finally, needing to fill the silence. "No. No scandals." God, I couldn't have sounded less convincing if I'd tried. I had to deflect. "What do you want on your pizza?"

Was I imagining his disappointed look? It was only a flicker and then gone. "Anything, as long as it's not fruit."

"Extra pineapple, got it," I deadpanned.

He shuddered, and I grinned widely, relieved I'd been able to successfully move him to a new focus. I pulled my phone from my pocket and ordered the pizza from an app.

"Aren't you cold?" he asked, his gaze lingering over my barely-there top.

I shrugged. "I'm used to it." I'd spent so much of my life in skimpy dance costumes and cold theaters, I no longer noticed if the air was chilly on my skin. And if I were cold right now, it was a small price to pay for the way he was looking at me. His expression was barely concealed desire.

I gestured to the doorway that opened to the living area, and he nodded.

"Remind me what you do again?" When we crossed back into the main room, his focus turned to the bookcase. "Sales?"

My mouth felt sticky with the lie. "Yeah. High end wines."

His back was to me as I sat on the couch. He studied the titles and the framed photos placed on the shelves. "Like a sommelier?"

"Not really. More like a broker." I repeated the line Joseph had taught us girls over the years. "Specialty brands and exclusive labels that are difficult to find."

"Is there a lot of research in that?"

My pulse sputtered. I needed to get him off this line of questioning. "No, it's mostly negotiations. Can I ask you something?"

He turned to face me. "Sure."

"Why did you leave South Africa?"

He hesitated for a moment, as if deciding whether to answer, then strode toward the couch. He sank down beside me, one seat cushion away, plunked his beer down on the coffee table, and laced his fingers together, his forearms resting on his knees.

"My family has a lot of money and clout, but if there's one thing they really excel at, it's being racist."

I stiffened in surprise.

Grant's tone was matter-of-fact. "For my whole life, I thought it wasn't their fault. It was just ignorance. Everyone we were surrounded with was white. Neighbors, coworkers, their friends. They didn't know anything else."

I sensed more coming when he took in a preparing breath.

"My final year of school, there was this girl. She was beautiful and sweet, the smartest person I'd ever met, and she was black." He tilted his head toward me, and his blue eyes clouded with shame. "I was stupid. I thought I could just show them this wonderful girl and open their eyes. I asked her to dinner with my parents. She didn't want to go because, like I mentioned, she was smart. She knew what was going to happen. But I convinced her it was going to be all right."

My voice was tight. "What happened?"

"My parents were caught off guard at the beginning, but then we had a lovely evening. They were so nice to her, and really impressed with her plans for university. I remember thinking, 'I've done it. I've shown them something outside their bubble.'" He straightened and smoothed his palms down the tops of his thighs. "The first thing my mother tells me during the car ride home is that it had been the most uncomfortable dinner of her life."

It shouldn't have come as a surprise, but it did. "Oh, Grant," I whispered.

"There was nothing that girl could have done to change my parents' view. She could have fucking cured cancer, and still my mother would have preferred not to share a table with her. All because she wasn't white like we were." He snatched up his beer and drank before continuing. "I spent so much of my life trying to fit into the box they wanted to put me in. I had to leave before they did it. I applied to Randhurst University here in Chicago that same night."

"What about the girl?"

"She could have said she told me so, but she didn't. I think it made her sad to be proven right, but she understood why I had to get out." His smile was soft. "We're still friends on Facebook."

The conversation lulled for a beat as we both drank and contemplated what had been said.

"I'm sorry," I whispered.

"For what?"

"That you couldn't make them see."

He played it off like it was no big deal, but I could tell it was. "They don't see anything beyond themselves."

I knew all about living outside the box. "We're a lot alike."

He looked at me with an intensity that made the air go thin. "Except I'm a terrible dancer."

"I'm sure you're better than if I tried to play the cello." I put my beer down and pulled out my phone. "Which reminds me, I have some ideas."

"Yeah?" He brightened, ready to move on to a lighter subject. "Let's hear them."

I cast YouTube from my phone onto my TV and showed him the different videos I'd liked from earlier, but he watched with an unchanging expression. I couldn't get a read at all.

"Do you not like any of these?" I asked.

"No, they're fine, but I thought what I like doesn't matter." His face skewed. "What I mean is, Elena made it sound like the song was supposed to be a reflection of you."

"It is." I frowned. There was so much pressure riding on this choice, it was hard not to second-guess myself.

"These ones are all good. They're pretty."

"I feel a 'but' coming," I said dryly.

He looked sheepish. "I don't like them as much as what you were originally going to do."

"Well, shit." I stared glumly at the TV screen, my gaze focused on the YouTube logo in the upper corner. The couch shifted as he leaned over and stole the phone from my hand. He scrolled through the suggested videos, tapped the screen, and a new one began to play.

It was a room full of bright windows and a woman poised at a black grand piano. In front of that, a man was seated, a cello nestled between his knees. She began playing almost instantly, quickly followed by him. The song was wistful, even though it had a quick tempo.

It took several bars before I heard the lyrics in my head. "Is this 'Chandelier'? The Sia song?"

He nodded, but his gaze was fixated on the screen, watching the cello player's fingers leap up and down the stem, moving rapidly and with such precision, it was its own kind of dancing.

That thought was all it took for me to fall in love with the song, and the line about living like tomorrow didn't exist solidified it. The track was *perfect*.

I shot a hand out and latched onto Grant's arm. "This one."

Only he gazed back at me with a strange look in his eyes. Was that fear? "It's, um, kind of fast."

I sucked in a breath. "You can't play it?"

His shoulders went tight. "No, I'm sure I can." Although he didn't sound all that confident. "You're sure this is the one you want?"

I bobbed my head in an enthusiastic nod. "I'm visualizing it already." I looked at the caption of the video. "There's a link to buy the sheet music right there. Do you think we can get your friend to record the piano part for us?"

"Probably." He still looked nervous, though.

"Hey," I said, "if this one is too hard, we can—"

He raised an eyebrow, annoyed by my challenge. "It's not. I'll be fine."

"Okay, great." I couldn't contain my excitement. "I think this is going to be amazing."

The pizza arrived not long after, and while we were eating, Grant got a text from his pianist friend, confirming she'd be able to record the piece. I purchased the sheet music and emailed it to her.

I asked about rugby, and he spent a good ten minutes trying to explain the game to me, although I got hung up on the fact that there was a position labeled the hooker. How ironic.

Grant grabbed another round of beers from the fridge, and when he returned to the couch, this time he sat much closer. We hadn't talked about our date, or if he wanted to be more than friends, but all signs pointed that way.

Was not telling him about my job really that bad? We weren't sleeping together. I'd told him I was already in another relationship and couldn't be exclusive. I'd make sure to tell him the full truth before crossing any lines with him, once I knew I could trust him. Not just with my secret, but with everything else. Maybe even my heart.

So, he didn't need to know tonight. As long as we weren't fucking, what difference did it make?

I was aware the mental gymnastics I was doing to get what I wanted were astounding, and I should have felt guilty. Yet, as I stared at this gorgeous man who'd said yes to helping me, all I felt was desire.

Hot, needy desire.

He stared back at me through his long lashes, his strong jaw set, and seemed to feel it too.

"Can I get some clarification?" he asked, his fingers worrying the edge of the label on the bottle in his hands.

"About?"

He put down his beer and shifted so he was facing me. "You said we're not allowed to have sex," his voice dipped low and was smooth as liquid, "but what about the other things?"

Heat flashed up my body, warming my cheeks and kicking up my heartrate. "Like what?"

As he moved closer, the cushion beneath me shifted and caused me to lean into him. He cased my face in his hands, the callouses from his cello playing rough against my skin and making me soft everywhere else.

"I can kiss you." His eyes were deep and magnetic. "If you want me to."

"Yes," I breathed. *Yes*, my whole body screamed.

He blinked slowly and licked his lips in preparation. "Then, tell me you want me to."

Had he realized this was an order, and one I was more than happy to obey? "I want you to kiss me, sir."

It was his hands on me, or maybe it was habit, that had gotten me to tag the *sir* onto the end of it, but I suspected not. I wanted him to take, and I wanted to give. I needed to surrender to him.

And as he fused his lips over mine, that was exactly what I did.

chapter EIGHTEEN

GRANT

When Tara addressed me as *sir*, I flashed back to the night she'd been on the table. I'd wanted so badly then to kiss her, and now here I was, my lips pressed to hers.

I'd told myself that as long as I didn't fuck her, what I was doing wasn't bad. I was here with her because I wanted to be, not because I was fishing for a story. If it happened, that was just a bonus. I wasn't using her, and it was why I hadn't pressed her for more details when she'd given me the fake job description.

Part of me had hoped she'd come out with it when I'd prompted her in the kitchen, but I also didn't want to know, because I didn't want to explore my feelings. She was a prostitute. That idea was supposed to turn me off.

So, why the hell did it turn me on?

The kiss had started soft, even tame, but her sharp inhale of breath caused power to build in my bloodstream. It raced through my veins, heightening my awareness of her and dulling my senses to everything else.

I pushed my lips to hers, moving my mouth against her mouth, giving her what she'd asked for. I licked at her, urging her lips to part, and shoved my tongue inside, all while holding her face steady in my hands.

In no time, we were both grasping at each other, our

breathing ragged. I tilted her head, adjusting the angle so I could slide my tongue deeper inside her mouth and explore. When I drew a moan from her, I nearly lost control. Kissing her was fucking fantastic, but I wanted more.

"What else is allowed? I need to know the rules," I demanded. Her top was a V of fabric, slicing deep down her chest, exposing so much cleavage I wondered if I stared too long, I might go blind. I'd put my hands on her breasts the first night, and she hadn't stopped me, but this was before I'd known about the couple she was seeing, or who she was.

Everything had changed since.

No, that wasn't true. I still wanted her just as badly.

"No sex," she said between her uneven breath. "Including oral."

It was impossible to know which loss was more disappointing—going down on her, or her going down on me. I loved giving orgasms. Watching a woman come was amazing, and my tongue was my best option for making that happen.

I was pissed it had been taken from me and wanted to take something from them. "All right, but I have a rule for them. They can't kiss you."

She jolted. "Anywhere?"

"On the mouth," I amended. "They can't kiss you on the lips. That's mine now."

She shuddered as if the thought gave her satisfaction, and her fingers coursed through my hair, fingernails scratching against my scalp. I groaned and went back on the attack, plunging my tongue in her mouth, claiming what was mine.

When I'd been satisfied enough for the moment and let her catch her breath, I asked, "Can I touch you?"

"Yeah." She straightened abruptly, pulling back. "Everywhere—except you can't put your fingers inside me."

Irritation flared hot in my chest, and her nervous expression said she wasn't finished, either. "What else?"

She bit down on her bottom lip. "I can't touch you. Only over the clothes."

I narrowed my eyes to slits. This fucking couple had handicapped me almost completely, but the longer I considered it, the more appealing it began to sound. They thought they'd taken away her ability to give me any pleasure, but they were wrong. They'd protected her needs, and as long as I had the chance to make her feel good, that was more than enough. I didn't mind getting creative while going about it.

"I can't put my fingers inside you," I defined, setting my thumb against the seam of her rosy lips.

Her eyes flared with lust as she understood what I meant. She wrapped her fingers around my wrist and pulled my hand over her thigh, dragging it up between her legs. Her lips parted to speak, while she rubbed my hand over the crotch of her jeans. "You can't here."

She closed her wet mouth around my thumb and sucked, and the sensation shot straight to my dick. I swore a million words in Afrikaans in my head, and possibly some out loud. She made me crazy.

"Anything else?" I asked. She slowly shook her head, and as she did so, my thumb slid out of her mouth, trailing over her lips.

"Good." My voice was thick and powerful, and I coasted my hand over her neck, my fingertips gliding down through her cleavage until I gripped a handful of fabric at the center of her chest. "I can work with that."

I yanked her onto me until she straddled my lap, pulling so hard I heard the threads of her top ripping. Should I say I was sorry? Because I wasn't, really. I was too excited to test out the limits that had been put on us. I slammed my mouth against hers as I scooped my hands under her ass, holding her tight to me. She ground her body against mine, and it felt good enough for me to realize we needed a better location. I rose from the couch, lifting her with me.

We'd passed her bedroom on the left earlier when I'd followed her into the kitchen, and once I was on my feet, her legs wrapped around my waist, I stumbled that direction. It wasn't her balance that made me clumsy, it was the urgent aching inside me. Tara hung on, her lips attached to mine, her kiss never wavering even as I careened dangerously into the door to her bedroom.

It crashed against the wall. I took a hand off her only to turn on the lights.

The room had a bed in it, big enough for both of us. That was all I noticed as I carried her inside and dumped her on her back on the mattress, following her down. My dick was hard and throbbing behind the fly of my jeans, and I pressed it against her, swiveling my hips so she could feel every inch of me. Did she understand how badly I wanted her? I needed her to understand.

"I want to see all of you," I whispered against the hollow of her throat.

I didn't know if it was allowed, but thankfully she was immediately tearing at her top, struggling to get out of it. While she yanked it up over her head, I focused on the snap of her skinny jeans. Her taut belly quivered as my fingers brushed over her bare skin.

Her tank top must have been one of those with a built-in bra, because her breast spilled out of it as she hurled the top off. I rewarded her with another pump of my hips, dry-fucking her. Normally, I'd skip over simulated sex and get to the real stuff, but knowing we could only go so far made this action hotter.

She fucked men for a living, but she was with me by choice, and that fact wasn't lost on me.

I had her zipper undone, exposing the top of her lacy panties, but was distracted. I cupped her perfect breasts, one in each hand, and squeezed, sliding my thumbs over her pebbled nipples. She arched off the bed, stretching into my touch. Fuck, she was even more gorgeous than I'd remembered. Her skin was softer. Would it taste better too?

I slanted my mouth over hers, drinking in her moans while my erection stabbed between her legs. Could I make her come like this? Humping like teenagers with our jeans still on?

Whimpers rolled from her, matching the tempo I thrust into her. The hard grind felt so good, I clamped my teeth tight. It wasn't sex. There were clothes in our way. But what we were doing? It was fucking. Raw, and passionate, and intimate. We weren't joined physically, but we were connected regardless.

Tara clawed at my chest. "Off," she gasped, tugging at my sweater.

It only seemed fair since she'd shed her shirt. I grabbed a fistful of wool and ducked out of it, dropping it to the floor.

Her eyes warmed as she gazed at me, her gaze noting every muscle across my chest and the V of my hips leading below the waist of my jeans. Then, her fingers followed suit, tracing them. It sent shivers glancing down my spine.

As nice as her touch felt, I resumed my goal of removing her pants. After watching her dance this afternoon, all I could think about was running my hands over her magnificent legs. Her jeans were tight, and it was a bit of a struggle, but as soon as she realized what I was doing, she was there, helping me along.

I dropped the wad of jeans to the carpet with a soft thump, taking in the sight of her wearing only a pair of skimpy black lace underwear. I wanted to tug them off and bury my face in her lap. Run my tongue over her slit until she was panting, but it wasn't allowed.

I've already done it once.

I couldn't think about that, only what I was going to do tonight, right this moment.

Her blonde hair stood out against the gunmetal gray bedspread beneath her, and her skin was satin in my hands. I slid my hands over her bare legs, following the curve of her calves up to her knees, before pressing them open. I kept one hand on her while I undid my pants with the other, pushing the denim down until the bulge of my cock was only sheathed by the cotton of my thin boxers.

"Fuck," she hissed as I seesawed my erection between her legs. It was dangerous and exciting how close we were to breaking the rule, and I wanted to push it further. I was so curious. Would she be a good girl and stay true to her promise to her doms? Or would she beg me to fuck her, and I'd have to be the one to enforce the rule?

Jesus, I needed to know.

I hooked my fingers under the sides of her panties and jerked them down. She moved her legs, urging me along, and then she was completely bare, squirming on the bed before me, her parted legs trembling.

My gaze drew a line from her ankles up to her eyes, not missing the fact that her pussy was wet and ready. I wanted to sink two fingers inside her. Taste her again. Drive my cock so deep she'd claw up my back and moan for more.

Instead, I gripped her hip and pressed our bodies together, letting the heat of her soak into my boxers. Her eyes hazed before they drifted closed, and I found a pattern with my thrusts that left her swallowing enormous gulps of air.

My voice was so commanding, it surprised me. "I don't need to fuck you to make you come, do I?"

"No, sir," she replied.

Her hands gripped my biceps, holding on as I gyrated against her, gaining friction. She rose to match my rhythm, writhing against my painfully hard cock, searching for the spot that rubbed against her in just the right way.

Tension coiled inside me. The sensitive underside of my dick was cradled perfectly in the valley of her body, and I bit the inside of my cheek to distract. Tonight wasn't about me, and I needed to make sure she understood. My pleasure wasn't more important than hers. It was secondary.

She drenched the fabric covering me, and I clenched a fist on her breast, squeezing a pointed nipple toward the ceiling. It seemed insane to have to hold back, given what we were doing, but satisfaction flooded through me. It felt good riding her like this.

No, that was an understatement. It felt amazing.

I swallowed a difficult breath and refocused. Since the night at the blindfold club, I'd imagined a hundred times what she'd sound like when she'd come, and now it was time to find out. I dropped to a knee at the edge of the bed, slapped two fingers against her clit, and pressed my lips to the inside of her knee.

"Oh!" Her fists went white-knuckle on the bedspread.

As my kiss marched along the inside of her thigh, she tried to scoot away from me, but I wasn't going to allow it. I nudged my fingertips back and forth over her swollen clit and let the sensation pin her to the mattress. She was close. At least as close as she'd been when I'd gone down on her at the club.

I was vicious as I rubbed her, stirring faster and faster, all the while my mouth crept along until it was at the spot her leg met her body. I was so close, she could probably feel my hot breath against her damp skin.

Her voice brimmed with panic. "Grant."

"Shh," I whispered. I had no intent of breaking her rule, but every intent of making her balance on the edge of worry. Danger made things more attractive, and I'd use it to my advantage.

I created a seal with my lips and began to suck at the delicate skin that was only an inch away from where I was stroking her. The harder I sucked, the more she bucked and writhed. It probably wasn't all that comfortable, but she was a submissive. A little discomfort likely gave her a thrill.

"We can't," she whined, but her hips moved, rocking with

the furious caress of my fingers.

I broke the seal of my lips and admired the dark red mark of my work. Tomorrow it'd probably be a purple-blue. "I'm not doing anything wrong," I said. "Just letting them know I was here."

"Oh, fuck," she groaned.

The concept was too much for her, and she broke open, her body convulsing with waves of bliss.

Yes. Satisfaction poured through me as she came violently. It rocked her body like an earthquake. Gasps and moans flowed from her, each one giving me more power and a pang deep in my belly. I wanted to come and let the pleasure carry me to the same place so I could join her. But just listening and watching her was enough.

More than enough.

The orgasm wracked her body like an electrical shock, and a grin spread across my face. I held my fingers firm to her, feeling the pulse vibrate through her clit, the contractions slowing until I couldn't sense them anymore.

I climbed to stand, smoothing my palms up her legs, over her belly, and cupped her tits. She sighed with enjoyment as I kissed each nipple, swirling my tongue over the hard buds.

"I want to see it," she whispered. "Can I watch you jerk off?"

The corner of my mouth pulled up into a lewd smile. She couldn't touch me, but this was a good compromise. I straightened, and as my huge shadow fell on her, her blue eyes teemed with anticipation.

Down I tugged the waistband of my boxers until they cut across the fronts of my thick thighs, letting my cock spring free. I had a big build and the right proportions all over. I tightened my fist around the head and pushed down my length, all the way to the base. Her gaze followed the stroke of my hand as if mesmerized.

As I pumped up and down, she swallowed so hard it was audible, and her lips parted so she could drag in a deep breath. Her eyes flared with lust, while her hands balled the comforter beneath her. Pleasuring myself felt good, but watching her response to it was infinitely hotter.

Plus, my palm was dry. It didn't slide easily along my skin—

Tara must have known. She sat up and put her hands flat on my chest, causing me to pause. It was to get me to hold still. Her focus stayed on me as she leaned forward and angled her face downward. Her lips pursed slightly, all so a long strand of saliva could drip from the tip of her tongue and onto my dick.

It was pornographic. Filthy.

Exactly what I needed. I pumped my fist, lubing myself with her saliva, moving and twisting faster until the slick sound of me fucking my hand filled the room. She looked transfixed, her eager gaze bouncing from my hand to my face and back again.

"This is what you wanted?" My voice was like gravel, punctuated by sharp breaths.

"Yes." Her tone was pure excitement. "It looks so good. I wish I was the one doing it."

"Yeah?" Heat was a bubbling cauldron in my center, threatening to boil over. "You want to slide your hands all over this cock? Pump your fist on me and make me come?"

She nodded, looking deadly serious. "I'd put it in my

mouth first. Work you over until you couldn't hold off another second."

Fuck me. The picture she drew in my head took me right to the edge. I jammed my hand in her hair at the back of her head and tugged, forcing her to look straight up at me. It was rougher than I'd ever been, but the limits put on us seemed to bring out something primal in me. Or perhaps it was the competition with her doms.

Maybe it was a combination of the two.

"I'm going to come," I growled.

My grip in her hair was fierce, but she didn't even wince. Her expression was determination. "Do it."

I squeezed my fist so tight, it was right on the edge of being too much. My fingers strained and ached, all the muscles in my arm flexing as I moved at a blistering pace. I even thrusted my hips subtly, giving me the final push to get there.

Her eyes widened as she realized what was going to happen. "Oh, God. *Please*," she cried. She arched her back, shoving her tits forward, giving me permission.

Ecstasy burst from me, leaping onto her creamy skin, painting ribbons across her curves. I groaned as I came, shuddering with each pulse. Satisfaction throbbed through me, not just physically, but at the sight of my cum dripping off her chest. I'd already marked between her legs, but this claim was darker.

"*Fuck*," I grunted, pumping through the final spurt until I was spent. I relaxed my fists, the one on my cock and the one in her hair, and she flopped back on the bed, an enormous smile decorating her face.

All those years of playing rugby meant I had thighs like

tree trunks, and yet when I looked at her it made me so weak, I could barely stand. Tara's satisfied look was my undoing. It made me slow, and it wasn't until her smile froze that I realized something was off. There was a sound from overhead.

Clapping?

"Yes, girl," a disembodied male voice said.

My gaze flew up and focused in on the vent in the ceiling. "What the hell was that?"

She let out a deep sigh, and as she scrambled off the bed, her tone was sheepish. "My upstairs neighbors must have heard us."

They weren't in the room with us, but it sort of felt that way. I cast my gaze upward once more as I pulled my boxers and jeans up. I'd wanted to enjoy the moment with her longer, but they'd killed the mood.

She rose onto her tiptoes and dropped a kiss on my lips. "I'll be back in a minute."

Tara sashayed naked into her bathroom, shutting the door behind her, and the second I was alone, guilt needled at me. I'd intended to take things slow with her. Convince her I was worth giving up this other couple for. Instead, I'd tossed her on her bed, stripped her naked, and dominated her, fueled by competition.

I buttoned my jeans, fished my sweater off the floor, but as I pulled it on, the open drawer beside her bed caught my eye. Something pink and chrome was inside, and I was sure it ran on batteries. She hadn't said anything about her doms ruling out toys, and an evil grin spread across my face.

This could be so much fun.

In the bathroom, Tara ran the faucet, no doubt cleaning

up. I strode toward the nightstand and tugged the drawer open further. What else did she have in there besides a vibrator?

A black, leather-bound book was the answer, with a red ribbon tucked between the pages, marking her spot. My curiosity compelled me to investigate. I knew it was wrong, but all I wanted was a peek. Was it a book of poems? Scripture? A day planner?

I glanced at the bathroom door. The water was running and gurgling in the sink. I peeled back the cover and thumbed through the handwritten pages, each dated in the upper-righthand corner. It was a diary?

My pulse raced as I scanned one of the paragraphs. It was more like a ledger.

Jesus Fucking Christ.

I paged through it, my mouth going dry and my body numb. Judging by the dates, Tara had recorded every night she'd worked at the blindfold club. The book contained more than two years' worth of entries, all written in black ink and her feminine script.

My curiosity screamed to find my entry, desperate to know what she'd thought, but as I flipped through the pages to get to it, the water cut off in the bathroom. I slammed the cover closed and fumbled with the drawer to get it closed.

The bathroom door swung open with a creak and her voice was heavy with suspicion. "What are you doing?"

"Trying to figure out how to turn this on," I said. I snatched up the vibrator and turned to face her, forcing myself to look nonchalant. "Your drawer was open, and I saw this, and unless it's against the rules, I thought I could use it on you."

She had put on a simple baby blue robe, and when she zeroed in on the vibrator in my hand, her expression heated. "They didn't say anything about it being against the rules."

"Good." My chest expanded on my deep breath. "Then take off that robe and get on the bed."

chapter NINETEEN

TARA

It was overcast and windy, and I pulled my leather jacket closed as I made my way across the grassy field. I'd meant to get here before the match started, but time had gotten away from me. I climbed up on the metal bleachers, which were half full of spectators, sat down, and peered out onto the field.

To my untrained eye, the rugby match looked like chaos. It was a pile of brawny men in mud and grass stained uniforms piling on each other. A weird, oblong football was chucked between them, but unlike American football, it was never passed forward.

Ten minutes in, I thought I had part of the game figured out. Fifteen minutes in, I was hopelessly lost. Sports were weird.

What I did understand was the effect Grant had on me. He wore the Lions uniform—all black, with shorts and a fitted athletic shirt stretched across his broad chest. It was like he was composed entirely of thick, powerful muscles.

My body clenched as I thought about the last time I'd seen him. He'd put my vibrator between my thighs and sucked on my tits until I'd come so hard, it'd taken me more than a minute to catch my breath.

He was . . . surprising.

And fucking *exciting*.

I'd expected him to be bolt when I'd laid out Silas and Regan's rules. Instead, he'd taken it in stride. Better, really. The day after he'd come by my place for pizza, he'd sent a text message asking if he'd left a mark on the inside of my thigh.

I sent him a picture of the hickey.

His response was I should send it to Silas and Regan. God, how this guy turned me on.

"Hey, new girl. You want a macaron?" a female voice asked.

I turned over my shoulder to look at her. She was a cute brunette, maybe a few years older than me. She had on thick, dark-rimmed glasses and held out a Tupperware box. Inside, colorful cookies were stacked in rows.

They looked great, but I wasn't in the habit of taking food from strangers. "Thank you, but I'm okay."

She didn't seem offended as she closed the lid and set the box beside her. "The same people come to these matches every week, so we all know each other. But I haven't met you before. I'm Ruby." She thrust her hand out for a handshake, which I accepted. "I'm with that one," she said, gesturing to the field. I followed her long, manicured finger toward the player, and my heart dropped to my toes.

She was pointing at Grant. He was standing on his own from the pack of his teammates, his hands on his hips, while the officials nearby discussed something. There was no mistaking who she'd singled out.

I wasn't exclusive to him, so I had no right to judge. And I'd never asked if he was seeing other people, but now I really wished I had. Because this hurt much more than I expected.

I hadn't told him I was coming to his match today, wanting to surprise him. He hadn't seen me yet. Was there a

154 | NIKKI SLOANE

chance I could slink out of here without him seeing?

Ruby didn't notice, or I did a good job of hiding my sinking feeling from my expression, because she kept talking. "Which guy are you here for?"

How was I supposed to answer? I stared at him as he awaited the call, his face flushed and chest moving rapidly with his hurried breathing. "Uh . . ."

Then he spotted me, doing a double-take. His expression warmed with pleasant surprise, and he lifted a hand in a wave. I had no choice but to wave back.

"Oh." A wicked smile twisted on Ruby's lips. "Of course. You're Tara, right? I should have recognized you. Grant definitely has a type."

"What?" There was a lot to unpack in her statement, and I wasn't sure where to focus first. He'd talked about me? And he had a type?

"Blonde and beautiful? We've been friends since college, so I've seen all the girls through the years."

It came from me without thought. "Friends?"

Her mouth dropped open as she realized the meaning behind my question. "Yes, just friends. He dated my sister a long time ago, so he's like my brother."

"Oh." Relief washed through me, loosening the tension in my shoulders.

"It's nice to meet you."

"You too," I said.

She crawled over the bleacher seat and plopped down right beside me without an invitation, and I stifled a laugh. She couldn't have been more obvious. Ruby was the nosy friend who wanted all the details about the new woman in

Grant's life.

Whatever the penalty was, it had been sorted out, and the players moved back into their huddle.

I couldn't hold the question back. "He mentioned me, huh?"

She flashed a knowing smile. "Oh, yeah. You're the first one he's talked about since Morgan." My blank expression must have forced her to explain. "His last girlfriend? They lived together for a while, until he kicked her ass to the—"

Her voice lost its power at the end, as if she realized at the last second she probably shouldn't have said anything.

"He kicked her out?"

She looked embarrassed. "I should probably let him tell the story."

We watched the men, their feet churning up the grass as they tried to drive toward the end. Awkwardness hung in the silence between Ruby and me, and it must have been too much for her.

"It's not bad," she said. "Well, I mean, it *was* bad." She sighed and pressed her fingertips to the center of her forehead, rubbing the crease there. "She sent a bunch of nudes to their coworkers. I didn't tell you that."

"Wait, *their* coworkers?"

"Yeah, Morgan's the on-air weather person."

Nudes. To his coworkers. I couldn't wrap my head around Morgan's motivation. "Why?"

Ruby shrugged. "Because she's not too smart, or has self-esteem issues, or who the hell knows? That girl was the worst. So high maintenance."

She wasn't subtle as she scanned my clothes, taking in

the ripped jeans and combat boots, and she seemed pleased. I looked edgy and comfortable, and anything but high maintenance.

We spent the first half of the game chatting in between the plays. It was helpful having her there to explain what was going on, and I made sure to keep the conversation focused on her, so she wouldn't ask what I did for a living.

She was an attorney, as was her boyfriend. In fact, she'd been the one to help Grant with his US citizenship a few years ago. Ruby had a foul mouth, a direct personality, and rage-baked fabulous macarons. I'd eaten two of them before the break at the half, and it took even less time for me to decide I liked her.

Throughout the game, Grant would sneak peeks my direction, and each time he did, my pulse skipped. Oh, I was in trouble. I liked him way too much, and it meant several things had to happen.

I'd have to take him to meet Silas and Regan. And I'd have to tell him about the blindfold club, which was a huge risk. Not just for my audition, or our relationship, but for my friends and coworkers. Unease swelled, and I calmed it by reminding myself there wasn't a rush. Grant was playing by the rules right now, and maybe even enjoying them.

It was better if I waited until the audition was done. Then, if he chose to walk away, I'd at least have that.

Two more weeks of lying to him.

I scowled and forced myself to not think about it. Hopefully, he'd forgive me.

When the game ended, he grabbed his gear bag off the bench and bounded straight for Ruby and me. His team had won, but I got the feeling his glowing smile was more about me than anything else.

"You came," he said. "That's awesome."

"You're the first girl who's done that," Ruby added. "Besides me."

The spectators around us stood and gathered their things, leaving the stands. I stood as well, leaning close to him. He was covered in a sheen of sweat, patches of mud with bits of grass, and athletic tape around his knees.

"Hey." My voice wavered because I had thoughts about ducking under the bleachers and fucking him right then and there, the rules be damned. "I wanted to see you play."

His eyes lit up. He liked hearing that. "What did you think?"

"It's a lot like dancing, except for the part where it's completely different." I smiled. "It was . . . interesting." Late in the game, he'd ended up at the bottom of a pile and came up with a bloodied lip. "You okay?"

"This?" He pointed to the scrape on his lip. "It's nothing. I'm fine." He grinned widely, like he enjoyed the pain. Was he a masochist? I could understand. I wasn't a huge pain slut, but in the right setting and with the right Dominant? I was into that.

He glanced at Ruby, and his expression turned to concern when he saw the enormous box of macarons. "What's happened?"

"Relax," she scoffed. "Nothing's wrong. Kyle asked me to move in with him, and I'm testing out his oven. You and your guys get to be my guinea pigs."

Over his shoulder, several of his teammates milled about,

stealing anxious glances at Ruby. Or more likely, the box of cookies in her hand.

Grant straightened. "You're moving in with McAsshole?"

"Have I mentioned how much he loves that nickname?" she said, her voice flat. "And *maybe* I'll move in with him. If his oven sucks, he's moving in with me."

He shifted his bag from one hand to the other and tossed a look at the crowd of guys waiting. "Well, go on, then. Rogers is hoping you brought the lemonade ones again."

She did, and I agreed. The lemonade cookies were delicious. She nodded and left us, hurrying toward the players. As soon as she was out of earshot—

"You don't like her boyfriend?"

Grant made a face. "I like him all right. They broke up once, and he was bloody awful to her, but that was a long time ago. He's good to her now, but I like to give him shit so he knows I haven't forgotten."

That had to be intimidating for her boyfriend. Grant wasn't a small guy, and after watching his game, I knew firsthand he had no problem being aggressive.

"What are you doing now?" he asked. "I've got to get cleaned up first, but you want to hang out?"

The invitation was innocent, but his eyes were not, and the muscle in my center clenched. "Actually, I was hoping I could ask for a favor. My sister texted me this morning. She's in town for a business thing and wants to grab dinner tonight. Wanna come?"

Surprise filled his face. "You want me to meet your sister?"

"What I really want is you to save me from my sister, but yeah." I grasped the sides of my leather jacket I wore over my skimpy top and held them closed. The sun couldn't be seen through the overcast clouds, but it was setting, and it was growing colder by the minute. "It's going to be boring. I won't blame you if you say no."

He peered down at me like I was being silly. "Of course I'll go."

I stepped up to him and picked a few blades of grass off his shirt sleeve. It was mostly an excuse to touch him. I slowly lifted my gaze to meet his, filling my voice with seduction. "I promise to make it worth it later."

He dropped his bag with a thud and slid his hands around my waist, pulling me tight against him. He lowered his mouth to mine, and his kiss was intense. If his lip was bothering him, he didn't let on.

Warmth spread from his kiss, lighting up my body and drawing a sigh.

It was over too soon. As we parted, he whispered in my ear, "Worth it already."

GRANT

I had four more stops on the El before I'd reach the restaurant when Tara texted me.

> Tara: I'm at the bar. I already need a drink and she's not even here yet.

> Grant: On my way, be there in 10.

I pocketed my phone and tightened my grip on the strap hanging from the ceiling as the train wound through a curve. I'd gotten several text messages from Ruby earlier telling me how much she liked Tara. I was still blown away she'd come to my match this afternoon.

By herself.

I'd never been able to convince Morgan to come. The closest I could get her to watching rugby was the film *Invictus*, and only because it had Matt Damon in it.

Once again, I kicked myself for not seeing the warning signs earlier with her. Thinking with my cock instead of my brain was never a good idea. At least I didn't have that issue with Tara.

Well, not completely. We didn't fuck in the traditional sense, yet there was a ton of heat and sex between us.

But there was also the lie. I'd been told to stay away from the blindfold club. I couldn't claim ignorance if I admitted I knew she worked there, and I didn't know how she'd react when she found out I'd been her customer once. What had she thought about that night? Was I just a faceless john to her, or had there been a connection even then?

There was a black ledger in a drawer in her apartment that could tell me.

Curiosity killed the cat, remember?

I wasn't going to do that to Tara.

If Morgan had wanted to post her nudes to Reddit or some porn website, I probably would have been fine with it. The worst of her betrayal was the invasion of our privacy. She hadn't asked before inviting strangers into the intimate side of our lives. She'd taken that choice away from me, and I still struggled to move past it.

The restaurant was only a few blocks over from the stop, and I found Tara at the bar like she'd said, a mostly empty drink in front of her. She looked so happy to see me, I couldn't help but wonder if she thought I wasn't going to show.

"Big surprise, Erin's running late," she said. "We should get a table now. She promises to be here, like, eventually."

We didn't have to wait long to be seated, and after I'd ordered a drink, Tara folded her arms and leaned on the table, crushing the menu beneath her elbows.

"Did you get a copy of the piano recording? Francine sent one to me, but—"

"Yeah, I got it."

"It sounds great, right?" Her anxiety over her sister's arrival seemed to be forgotten, because Tara was full of bubbly energy. "How's your part going?"

"Fine," I said quickly.

She bobbed her head. "Awesome. Elena can fit us in on Monday, the same time as before."

"This Monday?" Unease twisted my gut. I wasn't ready to perform the piece for anyone, let alone her, but pride made it impossible to say that out loud. "With training and my match today, I haven't had a lot of time to practice."

Her energy deflated somewhat. "Oh. Yeah, I know it's not a lot of time, but the audition is in two weeks." She forced a carefree smile. "If you don't think you have time and it's easier, let's just do the Coldplay song. It's not a big deal."

There was no way I was letting her down. "No, I've got it. I can't do Monday, though, I've got an appointment with Mr. Fredrick."

"The repair guy? Is something wrong with your cello?"

"No." My voice was tight. "It's nothing. I wanted some help with my technique."

Her eyes went wide. "You're taking lessons?"

"Like, one lesson," I mumbled.

She looked stunned, and for a moment, she was speechless. Was she even blinking? Her voice was just loud enough to hear over the din from the rest of the tables around us. "You're taking lessons . . . for me? You didn't have to do that."

I drew in a deep breath. "I want it to be perfect."

Her eyes went soft and warm. She was moved. But before she could say anything else, her expression shifted and her shields went up. A woman came to the table and hung her purse on the back of the empty chair beside me.

"No, don't get up," she said as Tara made a move to stand. "Sorry I'm late."

Tara's older sister wasn't a hugger, it seemed. The

resemblance was clear, but Erin was a brunette, and it was like someone took all of Tara's features and dialed them up to 'severe.' Her nose was sharper, her shoulders wider, her face gaunt. Her blue eyes were dull and shrewd.

"Hi," she said, glancing from Tara to me. "Who's this?"

"Grant Kruger," I said, holding out my hand.

"Erin Vannett." Her attitude was all-business as she shook my hand aggressively then pulled out her chair and sat. "Did you wait to order?"

"Yeah," Tara said, studying her sister critically. "It's good to see you." Although her tone and expression said otherwise.

"I'm glad this worked out." Erin was barely paying any attention to her sister. Instead, she glanced around the room, looking for the server. "I'm starving. Did you order an appetizer?"

Our server must have sensed her, because he came over immediately. Tara and I sat in silence as her sister ordered a salad and asked for half of the ingredients on the side and had detailed instructions about how she'd like it prepared.

A salad.

Maybe Tara was right, and her sister was a monster.

When we'd ordered and she relieved the server, Erin focused on her sister, giving a smile so big it felt like a production. "How are you? What's new? Dad said you're still doing the sales thing."

"Yup."

Erin wasn't satisfied with that answer. "How's that going?"

"Fine." Tara's gaze connected with mine for a split second, and it looked strangely like she was offering an apology. "How's work for you?"

It made sense soon after because Erin spent the next twenty minutes talking about herself. We listened dutifully as she told us all about her job as a project manager and how she was steadily climbing the ranks within the company. It wasn't until after her salad arrived that she took a breath.

"So," she said, pushing her salad around with a fork to ensure it was correct, "Grant. What do you do?"

"I'm a line producer for a local morning show."

She paused, probably just now hearing my accent. "Where are you from?"

"Ireland," Tara said, and I smiled.

The inside joke wasn't just lost on Erin, it seemed to annoy her. "What?"

"South Africa," I said.

"Oh, wow. Interesting." She dipped a bite of lettuce in her cup of dressing. "And you two are dating? Or just friends?"

Tara's voice was sure. "We're together."

I lifted the corner of my mouth in a smile. I liked how she'd confidently stated it.

Erin's gaze shifted toward her sister. "You're into guys again?" She lobbed the comment at me under her breath, like it was a funny secret she was letting me in on. "She went through a phase where she dated girls."

Tara raised an eyebrow in displeasure, and her tone was patronizing. "Yeah, a phase of bisexuality that will unfortunately last the rest of my life."

Her sister set down her silverware. "Why do you have to be like this? No one cares if you want to be gay." She sighed with indifference. "Just pick one and be gay if you want. Or be straight. It's really not that hard."

My jaw nearly hit the table.

Rather than get upset, a smile curled on Tara's lips like she found the whole thing hilarious. "You're right, it's totally a choice. I wasn't born like this, I chose it." Her tone was affected. Too bright and fake. "Just like you—you weren't born to be a self-centered asshole. You wake up every morning and make the choice to be that way."

Erin rolled her eyes. "Oh my God, calm down. You know what I meant. I'm just saying it's confusing for us, and it's not necessary. Mom and Dad are okay if you want to be a lesbian. You don't have to pretend to be straight for our benefit."

Tension coiled in my back. Tara didn't seem upset by her sister's callous attitude, but the male part of me was hardwired to want to protect. I didn't want to see her get hurt, and although it wasn't my place, I couldn't stop myself. "She's not pretending, and I'm sure who Tara chooses to date has nothing to do with you, or your family."

Tara pushed her plate back. She'd lost her appetite, and judging by her irritated expression, her patience too. "I think we should get the check."

Erin's shoulders snapped back, and her tone was incredulous. "You want to leave? All because I told you I was okay with you being a lesbian?" Her expression patronized. "Okay, that makes sense."

"But I'm not a lesbian," Tara snapped, waving the server down. "I'm bi. Just like I told you I was at Lacey's wedding, and the last time I was home, and at least three other times. I've tried to explain it, but I'm just . . . tired. I'm bi, Erin. I'm sorry if that's confusing, but as Grant mentioned, it's not actually about you."

Her sister stared at her salad, pouting, and it reminded me of the car ride home with my parents. No amount of effort was going to make Erin understand, because deep down, she didn't want to.

Tara asked the waiter to bring the bill, and when he headed off, Erin leveled a gaze at her younger sister. "I guess I'll get the check."

"What's that supposed to mean?"

"You work in sales."

Fire burned in Tara's eyes. It was so hot, it was a miracle it didn't burn her sister to ash. "You're unbelievable. You think I don't have money? I guarantee I make more in one night than you do in a whole month."

Erin paused. "One night?"

Tara stood abruptly and dug her wallet out of her purse. "What was the reason for this dinner?"

"What do you mean?"

She shot her sister a plain look. "Why did you want to get together? What's happened that you needed to tell me about?"

Erin's gaze darted away, caught. "Lucas asked me to marry him."

As I rose from the table, my gaze dropped down to the diamond ring on Erin's hand. It barely fazed Tara. She dropped several twenties on the table. "Great. Congratulations." Her gaze lifted to me, and her expression was loud. It screamed, "Let's get out of here."

"Nice meeting you," I said, but it was a hollow, throwaway comment. I took Tara's hand in mine as we headed for the exit.

When we made it out the door and onto the sidewalk,

she pulled me aside, tucking us up against the building, her face serious. "I work at a private club. It's very exclusive, with a high member fee, and on Friday and Saturday nights we do tastings. That's what I meant when I said I make more than her in a single night."

"Oh," I said, playing along. She hadn't really lied, she'd only omitted the larger truth. "It's Saturday. Do you have to work tonight?"

"No. I had a client who got a little too friendly with me, so my boss and I thought it was best if I took the next two weeks off."

Alarm prickled across my skin. "Is everything all right?"

"Yeah, it's fine. It wasn't a big deal."

"If this guy made you uncomfortable, why are you the one being punished?"

She reached up and cupped the side of my face, her thumb just outside the scrape in the corner of my mouth I'd gotten in my match. "I'm not. It's a paid vacation. I needed a break anyway so I can focus on the audition. My boss is in a tough spot. He doesn't want to lose the guy because he's a good customer—it's just the guy only liked dealing with me."

I didn't like it, but I could understand. I wanted Tara all to myself too.

Was that true? It was more in the emotional aspect. The idea of her fucking other people strangely didn't turn me off. It made my heart beat faster. Made me break out into a sweat. It got my cock hard. Last night I'd thought she was working at the club, and the part that bothered me the most was that I wasn't there. I wasn't included.

Her doms had forbid us from fucking, and she'd said the

168 | NIKKI SLOANE

same applied to them . . . but what if it didn't? The idea of her with a woman was exciting, so that wasn't a problem. And the idea of watching her with another man was hot, but could I actually handle it? I was so damn curious.

"I just want you to be safe," I said, stepping closer and sliding a hand onto her hip. "I like you, and you told your sister in there that we're together."

Pink tinted across her cheeks. "Was that okay?"

"Are you fucking kidding?" I slid my hand down until it was on her ass and squeezed. "Yes."

She looked thrilled, but I saw deep in her eyes, there was guilt too. Was she thinking about what was unsaid between us? I didn't want her to. Hopefully, after the audition, she'd be ready to tell me. She'd trust me enough to not think I was using her to get a story.

I bent my head, bringing our lips together. The kiss was slow and sensual, totally different than one we'd shared before. It came from passion and intimacy, rather than pure lust.

When we parted, her eyes were unfocused and dazed, but she blinked it away. Her voice was sultry. "You want to come over?"

Every part of me said yes, some places more enthusiastic than others. But there was something I needed. "Can I meet you over there? I have to go get something first." I'd let her assume I meant I was stopping by my place to pick it up.

"What is it?"

I gave a coy smile. "A surprise."

"Is it, by chance, shaped like a cello?"

I laughed. "No."

Her expression went dubious. "Okay, then. I guess I'll

see you soon?"

I grinned widely. "You sure will."

chapter TWENTY-ONE

TARA

When Grant arrived, he wasn't carrying his black cello case, but a simple brown paper bag, the top folded down. Had he bought liquor? Whatever was inside, it didn't seem to be bottle shaped.

"Hi," I said, eyeing him as he shrugged out of his coat and hung it on my coatrack. "What's in the bag?"

His smile was devious, and hot, and I felt a dull throb between my legs. He held the bag down at his side. "Mind if I grab a beer first?"

"Sure."

He set it on my dining table as he strolled toward the kitchen, leaving me standing in the living room to study the package for a hint of what was inside.

"You want one?" he called from the kitchen.

"No, thank you." I'd poured myself a big ol' glass of wine after dinner with my sister—I'd earned it.

He reappeared, beer in hand, and moved to the couch, the bag forgotten. He sat and stared up at me expectantly, and I realized this was a game. He was testing my curiosity, but this was a game I'd win easily. I sauntered over, sank down beside him, and a pleased smile drew across his lips.

"The couple you're seeing," his tone was light and conversational, "how did you meet them?"

"At a mutual friend's wedding." It was sort of the truth. The first time I'd played with Regan, I'd been working at the club, on the table and blindfolded. Silas had bought an evening with me—but for her—and he'd watched without participating. I hadn't officially met them as a couple until Payton's wedding.

Grant's expression was unsure, and it was a strange look on him. "I don't mean to pry, and you don't have to answer, but I'm curious. Whose idea was the arrangement?"

I appreciated that he'd waited this long before bringing it up. I was sure he had a million questions. "It's okay. The arrangement was their idea, but the first time we had a three-some? That was mine."

"Really?" It was a question from him, but more of a statement. If he was surprised, it didn't show.

My tone was straightforward; I didn't have any shame about this. "I told her she was hot, that her boyfriend was hot, and I wanted to go home with them."

His Adam's apple bobbed on a thick swallow. "How was it? It must have gone well enough, because—"

I grinned. "Oh, yeah. It was great. I mean, I was nervous the whole time she was going to change her mind, or things would get weird, but they didn't. And honestly, that's part of what made it so exciting. It was a little bit dangerous. Not in a physical sense, but emotionally."

It was clear he wanted to know more, and I didn't mind sharing. He seemed so open to everything, just like me.

"So, a few months later, she asked me over to her place to play again. Since they're both Dominants, it's fun for them to be able to top at the same time." I nestled in under his arm and set a hand on his thigh. "We don't get together often. We're all busy, and three schedules are hard to work with."

"But you enjoy it when you do."

"Yeah." I traced a pattern on his jeans with my fingertip. "For a long time, I thought sex had these really strict rules I had to obey, like one partner, a committed relationship, man and woman. Then I met Joseph. He showed me the only rules I have to follow are the ones my Dominant gives me. If I don't like those rules, I go find a different dom."

"You like their rules, then."

A half-laugh bubbled out of me. "I don't love their no sex rule right now, but yes." I wasn't working at the club for the next two weeks, and I wasn't sleeping with anyone. It was going to be a very long fourteen days. Possibly longer.

He smiled, only with his eyes, saying he agreed. His voice dipped low. "Is it strange if I say I think about you with them . . . a lot?"

I sat up and swiveled on the couch cushion to face him. "In a good way, or a bad way?"

His eyes were charged with desire. "Good."

It wasn't surprising. It was the classic male fantasy—two girls and one guy. But it was still nice to hear, that he was fantasizing about me.

"I think about watching while you go down on her." His breath hitched. "I think about watching while he's fucking you."

I gasped. In his fantasy, I had assumed he was the guy participating in the threesome, swapping himself for Silas. But, no. He was there *watching*.

Grant imagined himself as a voyeur.

Before I could say anything, his hands were in my hair, holding me still as his mouth claimed mine. "I think about you coming on his cock," he spoke in between rough, dominating kisses, "and what that would look like."

Jesus, his words lit me on fire. I'd never heard anything so erotic. This was another concept I'd let society trick me into thinking was a rule. Men didn't share their women. Yet, here Grant was, telling me the idea aroused him.

It turned me into liquid.

His lips burned a line down my throat, and I couldn't slow my heart down. It was beating so hard in my chest, as if it wanted to break out and get closer to him.

"I follow their rules, and you follow mine," he said. "You like that, right?"

Oh, how I did. I thought it was fan-fucking-tastic.

When I nodded, dark satisfaction streaked across his face. "Take everything off. Once that's done, go open the bag."

To illustrate his command, he sat back, stretching one of his powerful-looking arms across the back of the couch, settling in so he could watch.

I sucked in a breath and tried not to stumble to my feet. I was clumsy with anticipation. Excited to be naked and eager to solve the mystery of what was in the bag. The desire was to follow his order as quickly as possible, but also to please him, and his heavy gaze said he didn't want me to rush.

Off came my shoes and socks, dropping to the floor in a hurried thud, but as I reached for my top, I slowed my movements, peeling the fabric up one inch at a time. I exposed the raspberry colored bra I'd changed into before Grant's arrival. The demi-cups were cut so low my tits almost spilled over the top. They jiggled a little as I undid my jeans and pushed them down.

The air in my apartment felt weighted. It was heavy to drag in and out of my lungs as he watched me strip, and although I wasn't exerting myself, I was quickly out of breath. The room was hot and cold, and charged with electricity.

I kept my eyes focused on his while I undid the clasp at the back of my bra. He watched the straps as they slipped down my arms and fell to my bare feet. He also seemed to be short of breath, because his chest rose and fell rapidly, mirroring mine.

It was strange how the more naked and vulnerable I became, the more powerful I felt.

His expression was lethal as his gaze tracked the descent of my matching raspberry lace panties. I flushed with heat, yet shivered under his intense stare. He admired me as fine art, a statue of sex and desire and hedonism, and I lingered for a long moment to let him look his fill.

But I also wanted my reward, and when he nodded, I turned on my heel and scurried to the table. The paper crinkled as I unfolded the top and peered inside. A laugh escaped me, and I pulled the package out to look at it closer.

It was a flesh-colored, eight-inch dildo, complete with balls and a suction cup at the bottom, encased in plastic. "Oh my God, did you go buy this after dinner?"

It seemed amusing to me until I glanced over at him. His eyes were dark, his expression sinful, and I sobered in an instant.

My voice fell to a hush. "I would have gone with you."

"I know you would have," he said. "Open it, wash it, and

bring it to me."

Every muscle in me clenched. Grant had said he'd never been in a Dom/sub relationship before me, but he had the authoritarian voice down cold. The edges of the plastic clamshell case bit into my fingers as I carried it into the kitchen. Scissors were grabbed from a drawer and used to cut along the edges. God, why did they make these packages so difficult and precarious to get into? I avoided the sharp edges of the cut plastic as I peeled the sides open and popped the dildo free.

I tried to be an adult about it as I ran the water in the sink and rinsed off the rather realistic-looking dick that included tiny veins along the shaft. It was soft, but firm, and according to the packaging . . . dishwasher-safe—top shelf only.

Once I was finished, the laughter in my head drained away.

I padded out into the living room to find him standing beside the couch, shirtless and barefoot. He'd turned off all the lights in the room except for the small, crystal chandelier that hung over my dining table. The prisms cast tiny rainbows across his chest.

Fucking hell, he was breathtaking. He was thick, and wide, and distinctly male. Powerful muscles stretched and corded around his frame, carving out notches and shadows, hard places beneath soft skin. I wanted to skate my tongue down his perfect chest, but he'd given me a command. I would obey it like it was the law.

I marched to him and offered the silicone toy, but he didn't take it from me. We had to paint quite the scene— me stark naked and holding out a fake dick, him still in his jeans and the printed waistband of his underwear peeking out the top.

"Do you want me to fuck you?" he asked.

I understood how he meant, and the word rushed out of me. "Yes."

There was a hint of a smile behind his lips as he took the toy from me and we fell deep into the scene. "Get on your knees and make my cock wet."

I hit the floor so fast, pain shot up through my kneecaps, but it was gone and forgotten as he ringed the dildo around the base with his hand, and positioned it directly over the fly of his jeans.

I peered up at him and made a production of licking my lips. This blowjob wasn't going to have sensation. It was all about the visual, and I didn't want to let him down. I could still bring him pleasure; it'd just be a different kind than I was used to.

His gaze was locked on mine as I parted my lips and dragged the tip of my tongue over the head of the cock. Of *his* cock. Was that why he hadn't asked me to go with him to buy it? Because he didn't want some purple, jelly, alien-looking dildo; he wanted one that was him?

We didn't break eye contact when I opened my mouth wider and closed my lips around the head. It didn't taste like anything, and the silicone was nice. It had a velvety soft feel against my tongue. I hollowed out my cheeks as I sucked, and Grant's eyes flared with lust. His shoulders lifted in an enormous breath.

Warmth bloomed in my chest. He didn't have my mouth on him, but he could see it and imagine what it would feel like, and it clearly gave him satisfaction to watch me slide further down the length.

"Fuck, that looks so good," he uttered.

I gave my own noise of satisfaction as I established a rhythm. There wasn't as much give as there was when going down on the real thing, and my jaw began to ache almost immediately, but it was a small price to pay to see how he enjoyed the show. He wound his free hand in my hair and cupped the back of my head, not to push, but to guide. To show me exactly how he wanted it.

I was thrilled to have his direction.

Like it was the real deal, I pulled off and wrapped a hand around his cock, pumping my fist up and down. The muscles in his jaw flexed. He was clenching his teeth, and the realization made me smile.

I gave him a final pass in my mouth, working my way as far down to his fingers as I could get, and then I was abruptly pulled to my feet, so fast it made me dizzy. Grant plodded the half-dozen steps to the dining table and stuck the suction cup right on the closest corner.

He stood beside it, turned his gaze until it was fixed on me, and held out his hand.

TWENTY-TWO

TARA

Air whooshed into my body as I swallowed a thick breath.

This was an invitation I wasn't going to refuse. I put one foot in front of the other, took Grant's extended hand, and let him jerk me up against him.

His chest was made of granite, and his embrace was so tight, he crushed my breasts between us. But even that felt pleasurable in its own way. Skin against warm skin.

His mouth possessed mine while his hands possessed my body. They caressed and teased, slipping over my skin, kneading my ass and cupping my tits, turning me on even more than I already was. Goosebumps pebbled down my arms as his lips brushed against the shell of my ear.

He turned me slowly in his embrace until I was facing the table. The dick was poised and ready for me, its tip curving up toward the ceiling. His cello-playing fingers trailed down my stomach, drawing a line down my body, all the way until he stroked them through my soaked pussy. I flinched with pleasure at his touch, every nerve in me a live wire.

His palm was warm on my left thigh, and as he slid his hand inward, he also urged me to lift my leg so he could ease my knee up onto the tabletop. I leaned forward, just enough to put my hands down and give me the leverage I'd need.

The height wasn't bad, and since I was at the corner, I

THREE *guilty* PLEASURES | 179

had room for my supporting leg. As I centered myself over his cock, there was rustling behind me and a zipper rang out. Then his bare chest was warm against my back, his hands grasped my hips, and he helped lower me down.

It wasn't as warm as he was, but the stretch felt amazing, and I welcomed the intrusion deeper inside me. A moan drifted from my throat as he pressed the rest of his body to mine, and I discovered he was naked. His dick was hard against my ass, while I descended further on his cock, and although the angles were off, and it wasn't actually him inside me . . . it *felt* like he was.

It felt like we were fucking.

"Oh," I sighed so softly, it was a ghost of a word.

His mouth latched onto the side of my neck, and one hand came up to cup a breast, the other hand staying firm on my waist. It was so he could guide me up and then ease me back down. The first gentle stroke of my body riding his cock, moving in time with him.

This one was louder from me. "*Oh.*"

Grant's grip tightened in both places, and he directed me to move faster. And faster. Until I was pumping my body on the table, fucking at the tempo he demanded from us. His dick was nestled between my ass cheeks, sliding in the valley there, and I balled my hands into fists on the tabletop, fighting against the sensations.

Because it all felt so good. The slick slide. His rough hand pinching my nipple. His hot mouth sucking at my neck.

As we fucked, my knee squealed against the veneer and the table leg hammered on the hardwood floor. Other sounds rose above it. The wet stroke of my pussy, our gasps of satisfaction, and my whimpers of pleasure. I reached a hand up and behind, fisting the hair at the nape of his neck, which was already damp with sweat. It caused me to arch my body as I clung to him, my chest angling upward, my breast high and undulating with reverberations as I rode the table.

His words were raw and aggressive. "You like it deep inside you?"

"Yes," I gasped.

He grunted his enjoyment and forced me down farther, right to the edge of discomfort. It was a challenge to take it, but I did, and after a few more pumps, I grew accustomed.

We fucked until my supporting leg shook and I was hopelessly out of breath, becoming a sweaty, panting mess. Moans mixed with whimpers and sighs.

"Would you like it," Grant asked, "if he fucked your pussy while I fucked your mouth?"

"*Yes.*"

And then his fingers were there, two of them sliding past my lips, pulsing in my mouth. It made it so easy to imagine. To picture Silas beneath me and Grant standing beside me, his dick buried so deep down my throat he would feel each swallow. I wanted to ask where Regan was during this fantasy, but his fingers kept my tongue still, so I imagined her facing me while straddling Silas's face, her tits in my hands.

I nearly came from the idea of it.

But I wasn't one of those girls who could orgasm from penetration alone, so I wrapped my hand around Grant's wrist and guided him to pull his fingers from my mouth. "I want to come," I whined. "Please, Sir. Make me come."

He knew exactly what I needed, because those wet fingers

instantly went down between my legs, searching for my clit. I shuddered, letting him know when he'd found it. The pads of his fingers flicked over me as his hips pressed to mine and forced me to fuck faster. Harder. Pleasure welled up, threatening to spill over. My heart skipped beats. My breath cut off as everything focused inward, then was sent flying out in all directions as I fell over the edge.

I cried out as I came, trembling so hard the table vibrated. His arms locked around me, holding me steady, and he feathered kisses in a line down my neck and the curve of my shoulder.

The orgasm rolled through in waves. The first peak was so strong, I couldn't feel anything but acute bliss. The second wave wasn't as powerful, and now I sensed the toy lodged deep inside me, giving my body something to clamp down on and throb against.

On the third wave, my heart started again. I was able to inhale new air into my lungs, bringing me gradually back to Earth. Jesus, that orgasm had been epic.

His kisses slowed to a stop as he sensed I was nearing the end of my recovery, and in the quiet, there was only our hurried breaths, synced as one, our chests heaving together.

Grant lifted me in his hold, raising me up off his cock, and backward until I had both feet flat on the floor. His dick was still hard, stabbing me in the small of my back, but he seemed content not to do anything about it right this moment. I turned my head blindly to him, seeking his mouth on mine.

Our kiss was a song, and the first verse was restrained and deliberate. Our lips moved, restlessly shifting to find the right angle and maximize our connection. We found it as we hit the chorus. The intensity picked up with the tempo, leaving me dizzy and struggling to stay matched with him. His tongue invaded, dominating the kiss, and just as my weak legs buckled, Grant was there, sweeping me up into his arms.

He stepped out of the clothes puddled around his ankles and carried me into my bedroom, depositing me on the bed, and switched on a lamp. I was naked, as was he, and I couldn't help but stare at all of him.

His dick was rock hard, protruding toward me. Physically, it wasn't that different from the one out on the dining table, but it was different in all the ways that mattered, because it was a real part of him. My hands ached to touch and stroke. I wanted to know what he tasted like.

But as much as I longed for those things, I also desired staying obedient, and in the haze of lust, it was hard to see anything beyond instant gratification.

"I'm worried I'm going to break a rule," I admitted, rising onto my knees on top of the bed. "I want to touch you."

He smiled softly as he touched himself, gliding his hand down his length. "You are."

I understood how he meant, that he was imagining my hand in place of his own, but . . . "No, I'm serious. I really want to touch you. May I?"

He stilled. A war waged in his eyes. He wanted this, but also to follow the rules. Was he stronger than I was? It wasn't a test, and I hadn't consciously meant to tempt him, but subconsciously, perhaps I wanted to know. How strong was his self-control? And if it was the same as mine . . . would Regan and Silas discipline us for breaking the rule?

I placed my hands on his shoulders and ran them down

his arms, following the flow of his muscles, but he abruptly stepped back. His expression gave nothing away as he turned and disappeared into my dark bathroom. What the hell?

My eyes went wide, and a shiver raced up my spine as he returned, the satin sash of my robe in his hands.

"Yes?" he asked, looking at the sleek, blue band of fabric he held, then up to me.

"Yes," I breathed.

I was in disbelief as he busied himself tying one end around my wrist. This guy wasn't just a unicorn, he was fucking *perfect*.

The knot was snug but not too tight, and he draped the sash behind my back, then focused on the other wrist. He left just enough slack between the knots, so my hands weren't pulled behind my back, but I couldn't reach forward either.

"How's that?" The dark timbre of his voice was sexy.

"Good," I whispered. "Thank you."

"You're welcome." He raked his gaze down my body, pausing on my lips for a moment, as if distracted and thinking about kissing me, but moved on instead. That same gaze traveled back up, slower this time, more deliberate. He was savoring me like this.

His palms were warm when he set them on my collarbones and inched them down. His fingers crept over the tops of my breast, brushed over my sensitive nipples.

There was an undeniable gravity to his voice. "Do you trust me?"

Hadn't I already proved I did? I'd let him tie me up—although these knots I could undo myself if given enough time. I answered genuinely. "Yes."

184 | NIKKI **SLOANE**

A satisfied smile burst on his face, but I didn't get time to enjoy it. He pushed me down onto my back, and with my hands tied, I was completely at his mercy as I fell. He softened the landing by holding onto my biceps, and once I hit the mattress, he dragged me to the edge of the bed.

My brain went blank with panic as he stepped between my parted legs, and his dick brushed over me. It might have felt good, but the alarms were too loud. My fists went white knuckled as I tried to reach for him, and the sash stopped me, digging into my back.

"Don't move," he ordered. "Stay absolutely still."

He grasped himself at the base with his thumb and forefinger and dragged the tip of his naked cock over my bare pussy.

"Oh my God," I groaned.

"This isn't against the rules, is it?" He sawed himself back and forth, rubbing over my clit and coating himself in my arousal.

My words were tight, because every muscle in me was tense, following his command. "It's a gray area."

He was *right* there. The slightest shift in angle and he could slip right inside.

But he didn't. He peered down at where we were touching, watching as he ran himself over my pussy, letting me feel the ridge at the tip, down to the grip of his fingers. It felt so impossibly good. It was horribly teasing, and probably something we shouldn't be doing, but—fuck—I loved it.

He sighed, and it was heavy with pleasure, which only made it feel better to me.

"Dangerous," I whispered.

His expression was smug and ruthless. "It's part of what makes it exciting."

He'd just parroted back to me the same line I'd given him while talking about my first threesome with Silas and Regan. It was as true now as it had been then. The risk of breaking the rule made the act hotter.

I was desperate to writhe, but I fought it back. The only movement he wrung from my body was the tremble in my legs. I couldn't stop that even if I tried.

"Could you come from this?" he asked, driving the head of his cock through my slit, repeating the motion endlessly. It was hard to focus. It was impossible to think about anything other than his smooth, soft skin rocking over mine and the erotic, electric current the friction created.

Heat was building at the base of my spine. I was already halfway to an orgasm. "Yes," I cried.

Grant slowed and gave the bed an evaluating look. Whatever he was thinking about, the decision was made, because he stepped back and helped me to my feet. "I want you on top."

Oh.

Yes.

It was tricky getting into position since I didn't have use of my hands, but I put my strong dancer's core to good use, and he was there, guiding me. He lay down on the bed, his head on the pillow, and I climbed on top of his lap. We let out a collective hiss of breath at the contact.

Now that I was sitting on him, his cock was pressed between my pussy and his stomach, and it meant he had full use of his hands. He seized my hips and directed me to rock on him.

The new position changed the sensation, and not in a bad way. I could feel more of him. The pressure was greater. I no longer had to hold still.

With this new freedom, I went wild. I ground my body on him, like I was trying to map his cock with my clit. He filled his hands with my breasts, sucking and biting at me while groans rumbled from his chest.

I humped him, squeezing my ass, flexing my thighs, do- ing whatever it took to get the speed my body desired to help get me off. I risked a glance down at his chest and saw the glistening head of his dick peek out between my pussy lips as I slid over him.

The sight was too much. My orgasm had seemed near, but it suddenly was right upon me. "I'm going to come."

"Fuck, do it," he encouraged, his voice rasping. This sexu- al act was taking its toll on him. The muscles in his neck were strained. Was he about to come too, but holding back for me?

A cry pealed from my throat as ecstasy slammed into me. I tried to stop riding him while the bliss rushed through, my clit overly sensitive, but Grant wouldn't have it. He clamped his hands on my waist and jerked me forward and back, heaving me over his cock.

Then he shuddered and let loose an enormous groan, his body jerking below me. Strands of cum shot out, flicking over his stomach and splattering his chest in short spurts. It was so fucking sexy, it prolonged my orgasm. I could feel every throb and jerk of his cock against me, and it gave aftershocks of pleasure.

One gasped breath, followed by another, and we began

to calm. We hadn't had penetrative sex, but used all of the same muscles, and felt spent. Grant reached up to cradle my face in his hands and pulled me down so I was leaning over him, my hair falling into his face, into our kiss.

As he tasted me, brushing his lips over mine, he put a hand on my wrist and worked the knot free, releasing me. I rolled off to lie beside him, undid the other knot, and propped my head up with an elbow on the mattress.

"No applause this time?" he asked, casting his gaze up to the ceiling.

"They're not home. Brad and Hector went out for a game night with their friends."

"Well, they missed out, then, because we were bloody brilliant."

I grinned so wide, it made my cheeks hurt. "You want to stay the night? We can repeat the performance in the morning for them."

He rolled his head on the pillow toward me. "Sleeping together is against the rules."

"Not *actual* sleeping."

He liked my offer a lot, judging by his expression.

He climbed out of my bed, strode into the bathroom, and grabbed a handful of Kleenex to wipe himself off. When it was done, he made his way back to me, but hesitated as he reached to pull back the covers. "Are you going to be able to control yourself, or do I need to tie you up again?"

I scoffed. "We'll be fine." But then I thought about it. I was satisfied now, and he was temporarily out of commission, but tomorrow morning he'd likely wake up ready to go. And I was always ready to go. I pressed my lips into a thin line.

188 | NIKKI SLOANE

"Okay, maybe you should put your underwear back on. Just to be safe."

He smirked, and it was that moment I realized how much I was willing to risk for him. I'd give up the arrangement with Silas and Regan if he wanted that. I'd do it in a heartbeat.

And if he wanted me to give up the blindfold club . . .

I was beginning to believe I'd do that too. Anything to keep him.

chapter TWENTY-THREE

GRANT

I wasn't ready to play the song for Tara until Wednesday, and even then, I was more nervous than ever. I'd practiced it a hundred times, first with the metronome, then my lesson with Stan Fredrick, and finally with Francine's piano recording.

Something wasn't right. I was missing the spark I usually had when I played, where I commanded the bow across the strings. Now I fought the music, struggled with finger placement. Currently, the song was making me its bitch, and unease twisted in my gut.

This performance was important to Tara . . . and she was important to me.

When I played for her, I wanted her to look at me the same way she had all the other times. I'd never seduced a woman with my music before. Tara had watched me play my cello with a dreamy expression on her face and desire burning in her eyes.

Her performance had a similar effect. Seeing her dance? The way she moved her body ensnared me to the point I couldn't do anything but watch. It made my heart stop.

Tara had been in my apartment twenty minutes, and I still hadn't reached for my cello yet. I'd stalled by showing her around—all five hundred square feet of my one-bedroom place—and then poured us some wine and asked about her day.

And then I stalled further by scheduling the final rehearsal at Elena's studio.

"Are you okay?" she asked once we were both seated on my couch, a glass in hand. "You're awfully quiet tonight."

Since the day she'd come to my match, we'd gotten so close. Between orchestra, rugby training, and learning her audition piece, it was difficult to find time to see her, but we talked and texted several times throughout the day.

Every day.

Which meant I'd put off the bad news long enough. I sighed. "I need to play the song for you, so you can decide what you want to do. I'm not sure you're going to be happy with it."

Her expression was dubious. Did she think I was being humble? I wasn't. I needed my performance to be perfect, and even my best run through the song wasn't close. I set my wine down, stood, and marched to the cello resting in its stand, snatching up the bow hanging beside it. The chair I'd play in was across from the couch, and as I sat and settled into position, Tara began to struggle out of her shirt.

"What are you doing?"

She flung the shirt onto the cushion beside her and hitched her fingers under the waistband of her skintight leggings. "I'm getting naked."

"I see that." My mouth watered at the sight of her tits, since the black bra she wore was sheer and see-through. "Any reason why?"

She'd taken off her heels when she'd arrived, so there was nothing to slow her down as she shimmied out of her pants, revealing her long, gorgeous legs. "I think it might help you."

"You mean to distract me?"

"No," she said. Her expression was determined. "I think you feel vulnerable playing for me. I thought this way we could be equal."

I was touched by her gesture, but she was insane. "You're underestimating the power you have when you're naked."

Her smile was lopsided, but she wouldn't be deterred. Her arms twisted behind her back, her bra was unclasped, and off it came. Her breasts swayed as she hooked her fingers under her panties and pushed them down over her knees.

Was I truly stupid enough to complain about this? If my stunningly beautiful and sexy as hell girlfriend wanted to listen to me butcher the song while she was nude, I should be grateful.

She crossed her legs, folded her hands into her lap, and waited dutifully for me to start. She looked regal, like a queen sitting on a throne rather than my leather couch, and although she'd taken off her clothes so we could be equal, we weren't. Our power exchange was flipped upside down, and I was off-balance with the lack of control.

When I was in charge, she liked to please, but it wasn't the same for me in this role. I wouldn't feel satisfaction at pleasing her—only relief that I hadn't disappointed.

I swallowed thickly, straightened my posture, and pressed play on the recording.

The piano intro was short. I had to start playing as soon as I heard the music, but as I struck my bow across the strings, my fear evaporated. The tight tension released from my shoulders and I relaxed into my movements, suddenly finding it easy to keep time with the hurried tempo.

Every note was echoed on her face. Her eyebrows lifted, and her lips parted, but she didn't seem to be breathing. Maybe she didn't want anything to interfere with the sound of my cello as it sang.

As I played, energy flowed from my fingers. It was exhilarating.

We passed the two-minute mark, but I kept playing along with the recording, having memorized the whole song just in case. Tara looked like she was hanging on every note in awe, and it was clear what had been missing from all those times I'd practice.

Her. Tara was the spark.

My spark.

Whoa. My brain told me to pump the brakes. It was much too soon to be thinking like that.

As I struck the last chord, she rose from the couch. The sustain on the piano faded to nothing and the recording ended, and in the new silence, her expression shifted. Her eyes smoldered and she stared at me like I was her trapped prey.

When she stalked forward, I hurried to get the cello back in its stand in time to make room for her. She climbed into my lap, draping her legs over me and shoving her warm hands up under my shirt.

Her lips tasted like wine and longing.

I wrapped my arms around her, pulling her deeper into the kiss, and in that instant, the power dynamic flipped right-side up. I was fully clothed, but she was totally nude and writhing in my arms from my hungry kiss.

How could it get any better than this? I felt like the Pied Piper, my music making her my eager slave. Would she follow me anywhere?

"It was beautiful," she whispered as I kissed the hollow of her throat, my mouth journeying toward her breasts.

"You're beautiful," I answered instantly.

She whimpered like the understated compliment was too much and leaned back, placing her hands on my knees. Her head tipped up to the ceiling, arching her body toward me, and it was miles of creamy, flawless skin. I trailed my palms up her sides and closed them around her breasts, holding her steady as I feasted, my mouth plucking at her hard nipples.

As I went from one to the other, "Should I play it again?"

"Only if you want me to break every rule and fuck you in this chair."

I chuckled wickedly against the curve of her breast. "That should make our next rehearsal quite interesting."

Her fingers laced together behind my head and pulled me until our foreheads were pressed together. Her words were weighted. "Thank you, Grant."

I inhaled a deep breath to match her sincerity. "The pleasure was all mine."

Time was limited, and Tara was too focused during rehearsal to make good on her threat of fucking me. She was a whirlwind as she danced, leaping and turning and sliding across the floor while I played.

Elena came out of her office to say hello at the start of practice and never left. She sat in the corner, her back against the mirrored wall, watching us. Watching Tara, really. I couldn't blame her. Tara was absolutely captivating.

When she'd performed it all the way through the first time, she looked over at her friend for critique. Elena pressed her fingertips to her lips, unable to say anything, but her eyes spoke volumes. Finally, she moved her hand down to cover her heart.

Her voice was hushed but powerful. "It's good. It's really, really good."

The smile that burst on Tara's face was enormous, and I was grateful I was seated when she turned and directed the smile at me.

We spent the rest of the hour perfecting the routine. She remarked that she wanted to do it enough times that she couldn't get it wrong.

The days before the audition were short, but it was likely because any time I got to spend with her seemed to fly by. I'd come back to my place, sweaty and tired from training with my teammates, and she'd arrive with dinner shortly after. I'd offered to buy, but the week leading up to audition she was on a regimented athlete's diet, and it was easier this way.

"Next week, we'll eat all the pizza you want," she said on Thursday night, after we'd just finished our chicken and steamed vegetables. I put the empty takeout containers in the trash as she surveyed me from the kitchen table.

"I'd eat it for every meal if I could."

She gave a half-smile. "I've had cold pizza the morning

after. You can keep it."

"Brilliant."

I sat back down and watched her drum her fingers absentmindedly against the tabletop. She didn't say them out loud, but I could read her thoughts. Less than forty-eight hours until the audition. I wanted to distract from her anxiety.

"What time are you planning to be at the theater?" I asked.

"Five. The doors don't open until eight, but the line will probably be a mile long."

"Would you like some company tomorrow night? We could go together in the morning."

"Just invite yourself over, why don't you?" Her eyes sparkled with amusement, only to turn sincere. "I would love that." She faked a stern expression. "But no shenanigans tomorrow. I need my sleep."

"All right." I lifted an eyebrow. "I'll have to get those 'shenanigans' taken care of tonight, then, I suppose?"

She laughed like she thought I was joking.

"Oh, you're serious, huh?" Her tone was playful and sultry.

"Get on the table."

I'd show her how serious I was. She swallowed so hard, I heard the click in her throat. Was she thinking about the blindfold club? How she would lie on the cushioned table and let anyone have her for the right price?

It defied logic that this appealed to me, but my body was simpler. The concept had blood rushing to my cock, which swelled in my jeans. I wanted our first night back. I needed to do it right, but now we had these rules preventing it. I'd disliked the rules at first, and then began to enjoy them. It forced us to be creative.

We'd fucked each other in every way imaginable, except for the ways that were expressly forbidden. And I would have done it regardless, but the rules made sure I took care of her pleasure and placed its importance over my own.

The table was plain black and something I'd probably picked up at IKEA years ago, but it was sturdy enough. It barely shook as she sat on it, her legs dangling, and her hands curled over the edge as she stared up at me.

As I undressed her, she let my hands roam and explore. There wasn't a spot on her body I hadn't already touched, but it didn't matter. Each time I was as eager as the first. I striped her of her shirt, bra, and jeans, but left the delicate pair of pink lace panties in place.

"Move back and lie down," I said, placing a hand in the center of her chest and pressing gently, until she followed my command. She shifted on the wood, settling into a position that was still probably a little uncomfortable, but she didn't complain.

My chest tightened as I gazed at her. My kitchen was well lit and boring, unlike the intimate, sexy club. She wasn't blindfolded, or tied down, or even completely naked. But it was close enough, and I struggled to keep focus.

"Don't move," I commanded.

I left her, my footsteps swift as they carried me into my bedroom and to the bottle of scented oil I'd bought on my lunch break earlier in the week. When I returned to the kitchen, she was exactly as I'd left her, prone on the table, her palms flat against the wood. I approached and stood by her side.

She turned her head to me, her gaze landed on the bottle,

and a coy smile warmed her lips. Tara approved.

I unscrewed the cap and poured a handful in my palm while she watched.

A puzzled look flashed on her face. "Is it scented?"

"Vanilla." I chuckled.

Her laugh cut off as I turned over my palm and let the oil drip from my fingers, drizzling onto her skin. Her eyes hooded when I put the bottle down and set my hands on her, streaking the oil across her chest until it was glossy.

I repeated the process slowly all over her body, warming the oil before dispensing it. *Pour. Drip. Slide.*

My hands had the same sheen as her skin, and I kneaded the muscles in her calves, one leg, then the other. Tara wobbled between pleasure and satisfaction. My massage turned her on, but it also relaxed. She became pliable in my hands as I worked upward.

I stroked her thighs, working loose the muscles.

I probably spent too much time on her breasts. I loved the way they looked as they slipped through my fingers. The only spot I didn't pay attention to was covered by her skimpy panties. Shit, they were sexy.

"I'm going to want this again," she whispered, "on Saturday night."

"About that . . ."

My palms slalomed over her curves, down her flat stomach, and to the tops of her thighs, only for me to slide them inward and ease her thighs apart. I turned my palm down and ran my hand between her legs, my knuckles brushing over the lace and her clit hidden beneath.

Her breathing picked up. "About that, what?"

I'd been standing beside her, but now I rounded the table, seized her ankles, and dragged her closer to the table's end. She gasped in surprise, but again, she didn't protest. Did she trust me not to hurt her? Her knees were up and together, and I put my hands on them, slowly pushing them apart as I spoke.

"I want to meet them."

I'd proven myself, but I was desperate for more. I wanted to see this side of Tara, because I wanted *all* of her.

I didn't give her a chance to respond. I threw my hands on either side of her hips, leaned down, and licked the crotch of her panties.

She jolted. "That's against the rules!"

"Is it?" I did it again, dampening the lace further. "You still have your underwear on."

When her legs tried to close, I put my palms on her knees and pinned them to the table. It was gentle enough she could easily overpower me if she wanted to stop, but firm enough to remind her she liked when I took control.

"Oh, *fuck*." She recoiled off the tabletop, her body bending upward as she bucked from the sensation. I traced the pattern of lace with the tip of my tongue. This walked the line of being wrong, but I didn't fucking care. If I'd been in competition with them, I'd clearly won. Maybe it was time they took some orders from me.

I sucked at her clit through her panties, drenching them. "Do you want me to stop?"

She couldn't answer with words, but as she shook her head, she curled a fist into her hair and closed her eyes. Dark victory burned through me. I'd wanted this for so long, it felt like years.

Once I had her underwear soaked, I hoped it would feel like no barrier between us at all. I placed my fingers over the crotch of her panties, stretching the lace tight against her skin until I could make out the swollen bulge of her clit, and went to work.

"Saturday night," I ordered, lashing her with my tongue.

Her moans were a melody of sex, and I brought on her crescendo when I added, "I want to watch you fuck them."

"Oh my God," she moaned. She squirmed against my mouth, reminding me of the first time I'd done this, only then I hadn't been hindered. I needed it. I wanted that for us.

I flicked over the lace, stoking the fire. "And then you're mine. They only get to fuck you when *I* say so."

She sounded panicked. "You're going to make me come."

"Because of what I'm doing? Or because you like the sound of that?"

"*Yes*," she cried, then gulped down an enormous swallow of air.

It wasn't clear if she was answering me or encouraging me to push her over the edge, but I assumed it was both. One last stroke of my tongue, and her thighs locked around my ears. She contracted and flinched, jamming a hand in my hair to hold on as the orgasm roared through her body.

Power rolled down my chest, flooding out to my limbs. Making her come was amazing. Perhaps it was good I hadn't done it that night at the club. I would have been as hopeless as I was now, halfway in love with her.

The only thing stopping me from falling all the way was my guilt over lying to her. It was another reason why I'd asked to meet them. I'd show her how comfortable I was, and when she came clean about the club, so would I. We could have it all. Sex and love, without shame or judgement. Pleasure and commitment, both kinky and vanilla.

I rested my head on her thigh, content just to listen to her soft sighs while she got her shivers under control.

Finally, she lifted her head and peered down at me over the slope of her body. "Give me another minute," she said, "and I'll text them."

chapter TWENTY-FOUR

GRANT

When Tara's alarm went off at four a.m., I was already awake. I didn't move, pretending to sleep as she rolled out of bed and quietly tiptoed across the dark room to her bathroom. The door shut, light glowed from beneath it, and a shower handle squeaked as it was turned. Water beat against the porcelain tub and gurgled down the drain.

I wasn't having second thoughts about this evening.

This couple, Silas and Regan, had invited us over for drinks at Regan's place, and I was looking forward to it . . . mostly. But I was anxious. Tara had said it would be casual because when you started planning specifics, that was when it became tricky and awkward. If things were supposed to happen, they would.

It didn't matter if Silas and Regan approved of me when it came to her. Tara reminded me of what she'd said before; if she didn't like a dom's rules, she'd find a new one. But I still wanted their approval. They had been a significant part of her life for almost a year.

So, while I was sure I wanted to go through with the meeting, this morning I was wishing I hadn't been so stupid and asked for it the same night as her audition. I'd added more stress to what would already be a stressful day.

Behind the bathroom door, the shower curtain slid

across the rod with a metallic jangle.

The longer I lay in her bed, with the sheets that smelled like her, the more my nerves gnawed at me. She said it didn't matter, but if Silas and Regan disapproved of me, wouldn't that give her pause? Our connection was strong, but what if theirs was stronger?

I needed to make a good first impression. That should be easy. I'd done it with Tara.

A dark corner of my mind whispered to me. *What about the first time?*

There was a black ledger in the drawer, less than a foot away from my head, which could answer that. All I had to do was page to the date and read it.

Doing that would be wrong. Looking in her journal was invasive, but the desire to know what she'd written about me was fierce. I was good at controlling her, but terrible at controlling myself. I reached over and tugged the drawer open. It was too dark in the room to make out what was inside, but my phone rested on the nightstand.

I grabbed it, sat up, and flipped on the flashlight app. It cast light across the leather cover of the journal, and I scowled. Part of me had hoped she'd moved it somewhere else, saving me from myself. But, no. It was right there.

The shower was still running, the door to the bathroom closed.

Don't do it.

I didn't listen. It was a shitty justification, but after everything we'd done together, she still hadn't told me about the blindfold club. We were both keeping secrets from each other. This was small. What was one more?

I grabbed the book, shut the drawer, and swung my legs over the side of the bed so my back was to the bathroom door. I juggled the phone in my hands as I searched for the right page.

Her script handwriting reminded me of the way she danced. It was delicate and feminine. It flowed across the pages, and I imagined her writing it with the same energy she had when she performed.

My heart thundered as I flipped through the pages, finally landing on the one I wanted.

It was three paragraphs long.

She'd written the negotiated price of fifteen hundred, and below that the deal had been canceled and I'd been escorted from the club. They hadn't told her who I was, but I assumed either this, or that she hadn't connected on my name.

To her, I'd come off as unsure in the beginning. Either shy or nervous, she couldn't tell. But then I'd been sweet, using the ice cube against her mosquito bite, which she'd liked. And what she'd *really* liked, was when the ice unexpectedly turned into sensory play, and I put my mouth on her.

As I'd suspected, I'd brought her to the edge of an orgasm. If I'd been pulled from the room just a minute later—

"Grant?"

Instinct forced me to drop the journal. It fell and landed noiselessly on top of my open overnight bag.

"Shower's ready." Tara's voice was curious. "What are you doing?"

I bent over and grabbed my toiletry kit out of the bag, covering the journal with a sweater. "Nothing, just getting my things together."

"You can turn on the lights, you know," she teased. There was a snap of a light switch and I blinked at the brightness.

"Right." I turned off the flashlight and stood to face her.

She wore the blue robe, her hair wrapped up turban-style in a gray towel. She looked at me expectantly, and when I didn't move, she glanced at the alarm clock. "Are you going to be ready to go in twenty minutes?"

This was her way of telling me to get my ass in the shower and not make her late. I nodded and grabbed my bag, trudging toward the bathroom.

I was fucking stupid. Now I'd have to find a way to get the journal back in the drawer while she wasn't nearby, and preferably before she noticed it was missing.

We ate a breakfast of Clif bars while we stood outside the Auditorium Theatre, and as she'd predicted, the line went on for blocks behind us. Before the sun had risen, I left her sitting on the chilly concrete beside my cello case and grabbed us coffee. It was cold outside, and when I returned from Starbucks, she'd pulled the blanket from her bag and wrapped it around herself to combat the wind.

She was nervous. Tara was normally cheerful, but this morning she was a thousand-watt lightbulb of energy. I probably should have gotten her decaf. While we spent the hours camped out and waiting for the doors to open, we talked about random things. Movies we liked. Favorite songs to perform. Places we wanted to visit on our bucket list.

"Do you miss it?" she asked. "South Africa? I bet it's beautiful."

"Parts of it, yes."

"Elephants and zebras and giraffes, just wandering around." She got a dreamy look in her eyes. "I can't even. I'd love to go someday."

I grinned. The South Africa she imagined was the tourist version, and very different from my time growing up. "The elephants and giraffes and *zebras*," I pronounced it the correct way, which was *zehbra*, "mostly wander around in the protected parks. Johannesburg isn't all that different than any other urban city."

"Zehbra," she repeated, tickled.

She made me teach her a few dirty phrases in Afrikaans, which had us both laughing by the end. Her accent was horrible, and I loved it.

Twenty minutes before the doors were set to open, she left me to hold her spot while she found a restroom in one of the open shops nearby. As she came back, a girl stepped out of line and waved. "Ms. Tara," she called.

Tara stopped and gave the girl a bright smile. "Kelsey. How are you?"

"Oh my God, I'm so nervous." Kelsey was cocooned in a puffy coat and stood beside an older couple. She was so young, they had to be her parents. In fact, most of the people in this line were either five years younger or fifteen years older than Tara. The girl shoved her hands in her coat pockets, and her tone was polite and friendly. "Who are you here for? I thought Ms. Elena said I was the only student going out for this."

Tara didn't falter, her smile held firm. "I'm here for me."

Confusion splashed through Kelsey's expression. "You're . . . auditioning?"

"Yup."

A range of emotions played out on the girl's face. Disbelief. Skepticism. Judgement. It was followed by the best emotion of all—worry. This girl was nervous about competing against Tara.

Good. You should be.

I thrived on competition. I was a fighter, but Tara was subtler, a silent warrior. She didn't have to tell people she was talented. All she needed to do to prove it was show up.

"Oh, wow," the girl mumbled. It was clear she didn't know what else to say.

"I'm sure you'll do great." Tara sounded heartfelt. "Good luck!"

"Yeah, you too," Kelsey chirped.

She came back to me, and if the interaction bothered her, it didn't show. I took her hand in mine as the doors opened and the line began to move.

It had been so cold outside, it felt muggy in the fancy lobby. There were tables of production assistants and some on headsets milling about as we came up the marble staircase and filed in. The room was full of gold accents and arches, and the lighting was warm, like artificial candlelight.

She handed over her packet of paperwork, answered some questions, and was given a number badge to pin on before her audition. Arriving early had paid off. Tara would be in the first group of ballet dancers, and the fourth group to perform overall. It meant she had to get ready almost immediately, so she could begin stretching.

It was a "hurry up and wait" schedule, very much like rugby matches could be, and I did my best to support her however I could. With her paperwork taken care of, we moved out of the way and down a corridor the wasn't as loud or crowded. She pointed to a spot by the wall, out of the way, and I set down my cello.

She began to shed her outer layers, stripping down to the same outfit she'd worn for the ChiComm performance, exposing her flat stomach and shapely legs. I tried not to get distracted as I took her jacket and pants and packed them away in her bag for her.

All around me were reminders of how out of my element I was.

Dads dispensed bobby pins while moms applied make-up to the faces of their daughters. The elegant, carpeted hallways of the theatre became rehearsal space. As Tara laced up her pointe shoes, I watched a guy across the room dance hip hop while wearing earbuds and a focused expression. A couple near us practiced what I assumed was the tango.

"How am I doing on time?" she asked, tucking the ribbon she'd just knotted into the inside of her ankle.

I checked my phone. "It's eight forty-six. Your group is at nine ten."

She used the selfie mode on her phone to check her makeup and seemed satisfied with the situation. Her hair was twisted back into the prerequisite ballet bun. Her costume was understated and all black . . . but her lips were a bold, vibrant red. I wanted to kiss her before she went but didn't want to risk messing them up.

"I'd better go," she said.

I wasn't sure if she wanted a pep talk or not, but she was getting one regardless. I grabbed her hips and pulled her close. Her eyes were wild and unfocused until I captured her face in my hands. "Good luck, even though you don't need it. I know you're going to be amazing."

She looked at me with so much feeling, I wondered for a moment if it was love.

chapter TWENTY-FIVE

GRANT

Tara's blue eyes deepened as she sucked in a breath. "Thank you."

Her kiss was chaste and quick, and I was sure it was a fraction of what she wanted to give me. She pulled away, lingering for another moment, before turning and hurrying to join the other people headed toward the warmup area.

Was it possible I was more nervous than she was for herself? I wanted this so badly for her. I picked up my cello, slinging her bag and my own over my shoulder, and made my way into the theatre.

The main floor was sprawling, a sea of gold colored seats, and parents and friends were sprinkled about them, respectfully watching the audition happening on stage. An angsty melody flowed from the theatre's sound system, and the large, black stage was full of people moving and leaping, each dancing their own choreography to the song. From the back of the room, it looked like madness at the front, but it didn't take long to focus in on the dancers who were a cut above the rest.

A woman in an official looking *Dance Dreams* t-shirt weaved her way through the group, watching and studying, and then whispered into the microphone of her headset.

"Numbers twenty-seven and twenty-nine," a male voice

announced over the music still playing through the speakers, "thank you."

Two dancers, a man and a girl, slowed to a stop while everyone around them kept going. They trudged to the left side of the stage, and as the girl came down the steps onto the floor, tears flowed down her crumbling face. Her mother hurried down the aisle to console her and pull her away.

I had to look elsewhere, not wanting the girl to feel like she was on display at the moment her dream was being crushed. I picked an empty row off the center aisle, just in front of a balcony column so I had an unobstructed view, and quietly got settled to watch.

More numbers were called out, more dancers dismissed, until the herd was thinned to five. It had been crowded with so many people at first, but now I stared at the stage and saw how impressive it was. A series of golden lights arched over it, and although the curtain was up, a few feet of the rich fabric were still visible at the top.

The theatre was old and ornate, and very beautiful, but looking around made my anxiety worse. If the judges weren't frightening enough, surely this stage would be. I swallowed the hard knot in my throat. If Tara made it to the solo round, I wouldn't allow myself to be intimidated.

The music faded out, and the five dancers stopped, all turning their focus to the judge they shared the stage with.

"We're going to ask you to perform a second time," she said, her voice raised so they could hear her. "The music will begin in thirty seconds." Then she turned around, gave a thumbs-up signal to the announcer in the lighting booth, and exited the stage.

While they waited for the music to start back up, the dancers eyed each other, sizing up the competition. Like runners waiting to get to the line and set, they shook out their muscles, staying loose.

This round only lasted a minute. For the dancers on stage, maybe it felt longer, but whoever was judging in the booth didn't need more time. The song cut off abruptly and left the group on stage dancing in silence for a moment.

"Number fourteen, please go stage right to get your blue pass. The rest of you, thank you for coming."

Fuck me. Out of thirty dancers, they'd only taken one to move on to the interview round. *One.*

On the second round, which was ballroom, they took two. Both women, whose partners weren't strong enough, and I couldn't help but wonder how that was going to affect their dynamic in the future.

The third round was hip hop, and I cringed watching one guy who had no business auditioning. Had he had too much to drink last night and his friends convinced him to come? He looked like a guy at a wedding reception with hubris about his dance skills—the one who usually ended up getting injured while trying a stupid stunt he'd never done before.

They weeded him out in less than twenty seconds.

I couldn't sit still in my seat as the performers were whittled down. Tara's group was up next, and I hadn't prepared myself for any other outcome than the one we wanted. What if she was cut? All her hard work, and no one would see it. My stomach turned sour.

My pulse went into double-time as the hip hop round concluded and the next group took the stage. There was jostling as the dancers rushed to secure a spot in the front, wanting to make sure they were seen.

It was easy to find her, even though she was near the back—Tara was taller than almost everyone else, and her blood red lips stood out against the crowd of black leotards and men in leggings with white shirts. I was obviously biased, but all the rest of them looked generic. Easily replaceable.

All except her.

The female judge on the stage gave the same announcement I'd heard twice before, reminding them not to travel too much and be aware of the space around them to avoid collisions. But she added something new at the end.

"Ladies who will be dancing en pointe, please move to the right side of the stage."

The shuffle allowed Tara to move closer to the front, and although I believed it didn't matter, I was glad she was being aggressive.

"You'll get a tone, and then the music will start," the woman announced. "Everyone set?" Heads nodded, a few dancers responded with an eager *yes*. "Good luck," she added, and signaled her thumbs-up.

The pleasant tone rang out at the start of the song, but it was like a gunshot to me. I stopped breathing. The song was a classical piece. *Clair De Lune?* I'd performed it once years ago, and the melody was familiar.

Tara moved with grace, and even though I was halfway back in the theatre, I could see the smile in her eyes. She fluttered, bounded in place, and lifted her leg to the rafters as if none of it required any effort. Where the other dancers around her had determined, sometimes pained looks,

Tara had joy.

The announcer's voice blared from the speakers. "Numbers ninety-four and one-sixteen, thank you."

Fuck, what was her number? One hundred twelve . . . or one hundred twenty-two? It was on the paperwork she'd given me, but I wasn't about to stop watching and hunt for the paper in her bag.

Three more numbers were called out. As one of the dancers on the front line left, Tara seamlessly moved in to fill the spot, and I smiled. Her badge was pinned to her hip, and I could read it as she posed, the full weight of her body resting on her pointed toe.

The best dancer on the stage was number one hundred twenty-two, and she was currently schooling the rest of the kids.

She balanced perfectly while the girl beside her in a similar pose wobbled and fought to keep her balance. Tara's arms swayed beautifully in time to the music, gliding like water. She moved like wind through a tall, grassy field. The way she danced was arresting.

More numbers were called out, and my jaw ached from how hard I had it tensed. *Please don't call her number. Do not say number one-twenty-two.* It was the longest two minutes of my life and . . . was it possible to develop an ulcer that quickly?

It was down to six performers when the music stopped, and I finally caught my breath. She'd made it past the first hurdle. There was only one other girl in the group I thought was a threat. The girl was gaunt and bony, but there was muscle hidden in there somewhere. She'd been spinning like a top, reminding me of an ice skater.

"Please reset," the judge with the headset said. "You can spread out and use more of the stage now. The music's coming back on in thirty seconds."

Spinner Girl glanced down the line of dancers, and her mouth fell open when she saw Tara had survived initial cuts. Everyone was dressed for traditional ballet, their bodies covered in utilitarian outfits, but Tara's bare midriff and sultry makeup only emphasized her sex appeal. Spinner Girl looked barely eighteen, and it was obvious she felt Tara didn't belong. She wasn't even subtle when her eyes narrowed.

Fire burned inside me, but then the music resumed, and I immediately forgot all about it. I stopped thinking about anything else.

Because with her newfound freedom, Tara now had room to let loose. She floated, leaped, and soared. She fucking flew across the stage, gliding on her tiptoes as the top half of her was still as a statue. My pulse picked up, matching the rapid set of jumps and turns she executed. Tara threw everything she had into the audition—no matter what happened, at least she knew she'd put it all out on the stage.

The first two minutes had been nerve-wracking, but not this time. I forgot she was competing and simply enjoyed the show. When the music stopped, I jerked back to the moment, the smile frozen on my face.

Every muscle in me twisted and corded.

"Number one-twenty-two," the announcer said, "please see Michelle at stage right for a blue pass." Perhaps he thanked the rest of the performers, but I didn't hear it. My brain emptied at Tara's brilliant smile.

She'd done it.

chapter TWENTY-SIX

TARA

Physically, the blue pass wasn't anything special. It was a printout on teal paper with my number written in a box, instructions about my pending interview, and a signature from a producer. But it might as well have been printed on gold. I held it gingerly as I left the stage, moving swiftly down the steps and up the center aisle.

I still hadn't caught my breath from performing, and I heaved air into my lungs, walking in a daze.

"Congrats," a woman in the seats whispered as I walked by.

"Thank you," I breathed. I didn't know her, but the genuine gesture made reality feel further away. Had that just happened? Had I really passed the first round?

Grant stood from his seat and stepped out into the aisle. I wanted to scream, run, and throw my arms around him, but another set of auditions was about to start, and I needed to be respectful to those dancers.

His smile was dazzling. I didn't think I could be any happier until I looked at him. His eyes glittered as if he were fighting back emotions. He was thrilled for me, and . . . *proud.* I had to tear my gaze away for a moment to hold it together.

I probably looked like a diva as we silently made our way to the doors at the back of the theatre. He was carrying both of our bags and his large cello case, when all I had was a single slip of paper.

But it was blue.

And it was proof I'd made the right decision on not giving up on my dream.

We made it twenty feet out the door and down the empty hallway before he set down his case, dropped our bags, and swept me up in his arms. I gasped and laughed, but then his mouth was on mine, and the world stopped.

The kiss was over too soon. His forehead pressed to mine, his eyes closed. "You did it."

"I was so fucking nervous." The advantage to going early meant I didn't have all day to psych myself out about the audition. Of course, the clock had been reset. As long as I didn't fail the interview, who knew how long I'd have to wait to perform my solo?

"Why?" He opened his eyes and grinned. "I told you that you were going to be amazing."

I used my thumb to smear away the red stain of my lipstick from his lips. He relaxed his hold, and I slid down his body until my feet were back on the carpet.

"What happens next?"

I looked at the paper. "I have to report to interview taping."

"When? Now?"

I nodded.

He grabbed our things without hesitation. "Lead the way."

Grant was sitting on the lobby floor, his back against a wall and his focus on the screen of his phone, when I came out of Ganz Hall. It was a much smaller theater that was part of the Auditorium, and the *Dance Dreams* production team had inhabited every space of the sprawling, historic building. There were rolling carts and spare lighting rigs tucked in hallways, equipment stacked out of the way, making the show's presence undeniable.

Grant looked up as I came through the door, and as soon as he saw me, he was on his feet.

I flashed a smile, but it was strained, trying to convey the interview had gone well, but I wasn't out of the woods.

The staff member manning the exit door was a guy not much younger than I was, and he wore a bored expression. Like he'd been seated behind the laptop computer at his folding table for a century.

"Number?" he asked, not even looking at me.

"One twenty-two."

"Music?"

Grant dug out the CD I'd burned and passed it to the guy.

The man opened the jewel case, popped the CD into the computer's DVD drive, and grabbed a set of headphones. "Track one?"

"The piano part of it, yeah," I said.

He paused, the headphones on, but he obviously hadn't started the song yet. His eyes finally connected with mine. "What?"

Grant and I exchanged a look. Moment of truth. My tone was nonchalant. "I'm going to perform with live cello music too."

The guy's face contorted as he removed his headphones. "What?" he repeated. "Someone's going to be playing the cello at your audition?"

"Yes. Me," Grant said.

When the man evaluated Grant, his confusion cranked up to level ten. Then he frowned. "No, the music needs to be pre-approved."

My pulse stumbled, but Grant put his hand on my shoulder, and the simple connection helped keep me calm.

"All right," Grant's tone was straightforward. "I'll play it for you." He strode to his cello case, laid it down, and unsnapped the clasps with practiced efficiency.

Unease flooded the man's face as he stood from the table, and I caught his name on his badge. Andrew wasn't sure what to do when faced with something new. "No," he said, "it needs to be a recording."

"That's not in the rules." My throat was tight, pinching the words. "Tap auditions don't use music at all." When he scowled, I softened my voice. I needed to be charming, not confrontational. "I know it's a little unusual. Is there someone else we can get additional approval from?"

To him, I was a problem, and I'd just given him an out so someone else could handle me. Andrew took the bait. He got on his phone and called a production head over to his station, all while Grant continued to set up his cello.

When the woman arrived, her expression was already irritated. Tina, her name badge read. "What's going on?" she demanded.

"This contestant," Andrew gestured to me, "wants to audition with live music."

Her eyes narrowed. "What kind of music?"

Had she missed the enormous man with the enormous cello, standing only ten feet away? I plastered on a friendly smile, wanting to win Tina over with kindness. "Cello."

"No," she said instantly. "It's an unfair advantage over the other contestants."

I pulled my shoulders back. "How do you figure that?"

She didn't have an answer for me. Instead she folded her arms across her chest and looked pressed for time.

"What about the contestants," I continued, "who hire a professional choreographer for their solos? I'd argue that's an unfair advantage over the people who can't afford one, but it's not against the rules. Just like performing with live music isn't."

She considered my argument critically. I saw my opening.

"Any contestant can use live music," I added. "They've just made the choice not to."

"All right." Her sigh sounded very much like a 'fuck it.' "But off stage, so it's not a distraction."

Alarm tore through me like fire. "No, please. He needs to be on stage with me."

"Absolutely not." Tina's expression was plain. "Sorry, honey. Only contestants are allowed in front of the judging panel." Decision made, Tina turned to leave, eager to get to the next fire she had to put out.

My heart hammered, but I'd prepared for this. "That's not true. Ballroom dancers get to audition with their partners, even if they don't make the next round."

Her back was to us as she pulled to a stop. "Yeah, but they can't perform without them."

I swallowed a huge breath. "He's part of the routine."

She gave me side-eye, skeptical. "Are you saying you can't perform without him?"

My mouth went dry. If I said yes and she allowed this, what if my solo was scheduled during his rugby match? He told me he'd never missed a game in his entire life. I'd asked so much of him the last month—

"Yes," Grant said automatically. "If you put me off stage, her choreography won't make sense."

Tina's sigh was bigger and more dramatic. Her eyes drifted from us, and I could hear the faint sound of chatter in her earpiece. What I was asking for wasn't difficult. It probably seemed like nothing in the face of the bigger problem she was listening to.

"I don't have time for this. Fine." She gave her approval to Andrew, then focused in on me. "Word of advice. I don't know how the judges are going to react, so have a backup plan. Be prepared for them to ask him to leave the stage."

"Yes," I nodded, "thank you."

She waved the comment away as she abandoned us, moving down the hall at a fast clip.

Andrew didn't make Grant play for him. He listened to the piano part, finished filling in the form on his laptop about the music, and handed me an orange card. My throat closed as I read it.

I was to be standing by to perform my solo at three-forty p.m.

"Uh . . ." I started.

As Grant read the card over my shoulder, Andrew's gaze burned into me. He looked up at us like he wondered what the fuck I was still doing here.

"Thank you." Grant grabbed my wrist and gently pulled me away, guiding me toward our pile of stuff. His voice was hushed. "It's all right, Tara."

"But your game."

His warm smile made his blue eyes more vibrant. "I already called my coach and told him I couldn't make it."

"What? When?"

"As soon as you went for your interview."

Oh my God, this man made me go boneless. He'd just put my desires above his own, and I struggled to remember a time in my life when anyone else had ever done that for me. Before him, I'd felt invisible. Maybe that wasn't the right word. Indistinguishable was a better one.

Yet Grant *saw* me.

Tonight, I'd tell him everything. I'd lay it all on the line, and if he wanted me to leave the blindfold club and never see Silas and Regan again, I'd easily put his desires above my own. And it had nothing to do with me being a submissive.

It was because I was falling for him, and falling hard.

"I'm running out of ways to say thank you," I said, blinking back tears. It'd been an emotional day, and we weren't even halfway through it. "But, *thank you.*"

"Of course." He smiled. "Besides, Milwaukee is terrible. The guys can win without me."

A short laugh burst from me, and it felt good. I needed the stress relief.

"The interview went well?" he asked.

"Yeah." Of all the steps today, this was the one I hadn't been nervous about. I talked to strangers all the time—and usually I was naked when I did it. "It was easy."

He glanced at the screen of his phone. "We've got a few hours. Should we get lunch?"

I was too nervous to eat, but it would keep me occupied. "Yeah, and I'm buying."

The Auditorium Building was attached to Roosevelt University, and at the student commons, there was a pizza place. We sat in the cafeteria area, and Grant ate voraciously while I nibbled. I didn't want the pizza to make a return trip. I'd never thrown up before a performance, but then again, I'd never had one quite like this.

As he inhaled his food and I watched, I told him about the interview. The theatre had been dark, but huge lights were erected on the stage, shining out onto the seats where I'd been instructed to sit. There were cameras and a man in a *Dance Dreams* shirt sitting on the end of the stage, who'd asked about my background, why I was auditioning, and what it would mean if I won.

Grant wiped his face with a napkin, balled it up, and tossed it in the nearby trash can. His focus landed on the single slice of pizza in front of me. "You don't like it?"

"I'm not hungry."

His brow furrowed, and Jesus, his concern was sexy. "You need to eat. You'll want the energy later."

I twisted my hands together, not sure what else to do. My stomach churned, and I worried I was going to rattle apart. "I don't think I can."

He blinked slowly, considering something. Then, as he sat back in his chair, he crossed his arms, putting his thick biceps and gorgeous forearms on display. "What if I told you to do it?"

My breath hitched. "Like, an order?"

He nodded cautiously. He hadn't attempted to dominate me outside of the bedroom, at least not this outright.

"Well, then," I dropped my voice to a hush, "I'd do it."

His eyes flared with power, intense and sexual. "Eat."

So, I did. I didn't taste the food as I chewed and swallowed, and it didn't satisfy the hunger growling inside me. He watched me attentively and pleased, not speaking until even the crust was gone.

The food seemed to settle my stomach, or perhaps it was the distraction of him, but when we were done and headed back to the main lobby, the nerves stole back into my system.

"I'm going to get changed," I announced. "You want to find a quiet place for us to practice?" He'd need to find a space where his music wouldn't disrupt anyone else.

"Are you sure?" There was a clock in the lobby, and he checked the time. "We've still got two hours before standby."

Like a gazelle fleeing a lion, I wanted to bolt from the threat of anxiety. Escaping to a restroom was better than nothing. And once I was dressed in my soloist costume, I could focus on practicing. "I . . . the waiting is killing me."

He understood. "All right. If I'm not back before you're ready, just hang out here."

The ladies room had a sitting area in the front, and after I'd wiggled into my costume in a handicap stall, I checked myself out in the full-length mirror. The costume was white and two pieces, and the halter top was accented with rhinestones and beads crawling along the left strap.

I'd had them added after changing my music. How could

I dance to a song called "Chandelier" and not have some sparkle? Otherwise, the costume was rather simple and flattering. The top flattened me down for support, but also had padding so I kept a nice shape.

Once again, I went with a bold, deep red lip color and muted makeup elsewhere.

Grant was waiting for me when I was finished, and his appreciative gaze swept down. "You look beautiful."

I smiled nervously. The pangs were back in my stomach.

He'd changed too, although all it required was putting on a black button-down dress shirt. He'd kept it untucked from his jeans and rolled the sleeves back, leaving the top two buttons undone. He looked casual and cool. He'd offered to dress up, but I nixed it. He was an extension of me in the performance, so I didn't want either of us to look stuffy.

"Did you find us a spot?" I asked. He must have. He didn't have his case with him.

"Yes. I even stole a folding chair." The corner of his mouth tweaked up into a smile.

We took the tiny, ancient service elevator up to the top balcony floor, and I'd swear we walked a mile to the end of the hall. The thick carpet swallowed up our footsteps, and the softly lit hallway was empty. Well, except for the large, rolling equipment case with the production company's logo on its front.

"It's not much space," Grant said, disappearing behind the huge box, "but it's quiet." He reappeared, his cello, bow, and something metal in his hand. "I can use my mute, which works pretty well at keeping it quiet. At least, my neighbors haven't complained about my late-night practices yet."

Why the hell would they complain? I could listen to him play for a hundred years and never get tired of it.

"This is great," I said. The hallway was narrow, but it was long and the ceiling high. I saw the folding chair he'd borrowed and set it in the center for him.

"The mute fucks with my strings, so I'll need to retune before we go on stage."

"Oh," I said.

His comment reminded me of what was going to happen and sent me into a spiral. I would be fine once we reported in for the solo, because then it would feel too late to back out. I could only focus forward at that point. But currently the panicked side of my brain was coming up with ways to abort the whole thing.

Even though I wanted it so badly, I was terrified.

Abruptly I was right back in the Chicago Ballet Company's rehearsal studio from three years ago, and all I could see was the director and his disapproving face as I stumbled out of a series of *Fouetté* turns. That stumble had been the moment I knew it was over.

"Tara." Grant's voice was sharp.

I blinked, disoriented. His cello was lying on the ground and his arms were around me. "What?"

"Look at me," he commanded. I did, and his eyes teemed with worry. He held me tighter as I struggled to step back. "No. Breathe."

Because I was so out of breath, I was verging on hyperventilating.

chapter
TWENTY-SEVEN

TARA

When I couldn't escape, I went the opposite direction and clung to Grant for dear life. He was solid and firm, keeping me steady, and as I sipped air into my body, I regained control.

"You're all right," he reassured. "I'm here. You're fine. Everything's fine."

"This is so stupid," I whispered to him. "I want this. Fuck, I want it so much, and once I get on that stage, I know I'll be okay. So, I don't know why I'm acting like this."

He stroked a hand down the back of my neck, tickling the tendrils of hair that wouldn't be tamed into my bun. "It's all right. If you can recognize it's just anxiety, it can help you work through it." His voice was soothing. "I looked up some stress relief ideas earlier—"

"Have I been this bad all day?" I drew back just enough so I could look at him.

He looked sheepish. "No. I, uh, looked them up for me."

Grant was nervous too? It made me feel so much better. "Oh my God," unexpected laughter burst from me, "I love you."

We both froze. I'd meant to say, "I love *that*," but the anxiety had fried my brain. My eyes went so wide, I wondered if they'd fall out.

"Um," I blurted, "that came out wrong. Pretend I didn't say it. I have no idea what I'm doing right now."

What was that flicker in his eyes? Had he . . . liked hearing that I loved him? Because surely he thought it was too soon, and it'd make him want to put distance between us.

Great. This fuck-up gave me something else to worry about. "Okay," I added, "what are some other ways to fight our anxiety?"

A shift went through him. I didn't believe he was nervous, because the man in front of me looked like he had plenty of confidence. His tone was heavy, right on the edge of seduction. "I can think of one."

Oh.

There was so much adrenaline in my body, the need instantly became overwhelming. Crushing. I didn't resist as he took me by the hand and pulled us behind the equipment cart. He put his foot on the side of his open cello case and pushed it out of the way. As it slid across the carpet, the lid slammed shut with a thud.

Grant didn't pay any attention to it. His gaze was locked onto me.

The cart wasn't very tall—it came up to my natural waist—but it was long, and we were easily hidden behind it when he lifted me off my feet and laid me down on my back. The carpet was rough against my skin, but I ignored it, wrapping my legs around his hips as he hovered over me.

Was he going to kiss me? I reached up, grasped his chin, and pulled him close, but his mouth veered to the side at the last moment. "Your lipstick," he murmured against my cheek, "looks better on you than me."

I grinned and closed my eyes. His lips against the tender spot on my neck lit me up like fireworks.

A sigh seeped from me as he coursed a hand between my legs, rubbing me through the lined shorts I was wearing. He was skipping over the other foreplay we usually did first and went right for the kill.

And when he eased his fingertips beneath the top of my shorts, I nearly broke apart. He was taking too long. I needed him to touch me *now*, and jammed my hand into the waistband, working the stretchy material down.

He gazed at me in surprise. He rose onto his knees and peered over the top of the rolling cart to make sure we were still alone, and when he confirmed we were, his gaze returned to me. It sucked all the air clean from my body. Grant's expression dripped with lust. It was wicked. Carnal. He grabbed the shorts I was still struggling out of and jerked them down until I had one leg free.

"You're not wearing underwear." He said it like it was a secret he wasn't supposed to know.

"I don't need panty lines, thank you. Is this a problem?" I teased.

His face was intensely serious. He knelt between my legs, planted his palms on the carpet on either side of my hips, and dropped a line of kisses down my trembling stomach. His voice rasped, thick with desire. "Just that I'm going to break a rule."

It came from him as a challenge. A threat. If I didn't want him to do it, I had to speak up now. Instead, I spread my legs wider and moved my hips, bringing his lips closer to where I wanted them. The tip of his tongue traced a line dangerously close to my clit.

"We've waited long enough for this, don't you think?" His

voice was sinful and echoed the wicked one inside my head.

"Yes," I whispered. It was all the permission he needed.

He let out a tight, sharp breath, and leaned in.

The first stroke of his tongue made me flinch, the pleasure was that acute. I made a fist and bit down on my index finger to keep myself from moaning too loudly. He swirled his tongue against my clit, and I lifted my head to look down and watch.

He shifted on his knees, finding a better position, and pressed one of his wide hands against my stomach, keeping me pinned to the carpet and under his command. Heat spiraled and grew with each flutter he delivered. I moved as best I could, riding his face as he fucked me right back. It was insane and fantastic.

It felt like we'd waited a lifetime for this, and once one rule was broken, I was ready to throw them all aside. "I want your fingers inside me," I begged.

"Do you?" He sucked and teased, extracting whimpers from my lips.

"Please," I amended.

He granted my wish, plunging one long finger deep inside. The sensation caused me to buck and groan. That finger, working in tandem with his tongue, was going to annihilate me.

I bit down so hard on my knuckle, I left bite marks, but it didn't matter. I needed this. Release, or him, or all of it. I was crazy, out of my mind desperate.

"Tonight, I'm going to put my cock," he eased a second finger inside, "right *here*."

An earthquake shook my body.

Bliss ruptured in my core, shooting sparks across every nerve ending, heightened by the chemicals my emotions had created. I seized, contracting in waves, but he kept licking, and I had to shove his head away before I screamed.

Gasps poured from me. The fire of the orgasm was fierce and consuming. It burned until there was nothing left but me and him.

"Holy Mother of God," I whispered, struggling to catch my breath. "That was amazing."

Rather than seem pleased, his eyes were intense and determined, and he asked it like I needed to be scolded. "Do you think I'm done? I've wanted this pussy for so long, you're not going to rush me."

I stared at him, stunned. The more intense the session, the more I brought out the alpha in him. It kind of made sense. His music brought out the best in me when I danced.

He nuzzled in between my thighs, and as soon as I got over the hypersensitivity, I started the climb once more. Sweat dotted my forehead and temples. I was going to have to redo my makeup, but . . . worth it. So fucking worth it.

My second orgasm took longer to achieve, but Grant never showed signs of fatigue. He was quite at home, one wide hand sprawled on the inside of my thigh, and the other pumping his fingers in and out of me. When I came, it wasn't as strong as the first, but it lasted twice as long, and when it was over, I felt relaxed.

I was myself again.

I closed my eyes and put my hand on my forehead. The absence of the panic made me feel like I could do anything, even walk out on that big stage in front of a panel of judges and cameras, and perform my fucking heart out. And he'd be with me no matter what.

When I sat up, it forced him back on his knees. I reached for his shirt, lifting it out of the way so I could get at his belt, but he grabbed my hands. "Wait." He looked strange. Like he was full of guilt. "We broke two already."

"I don't care about their rules right now."

He looked pained. "I can't believe I'm saying this, but I do. I wanted to make a good impression on them." Grant settled back on his haunches and raked a hand through his hair, putting it back in place. "It's better this way. Next time, no restrictions, no time limits, no worrying if someone's going to catch us and throw us out."

He made excellent points.

I was still naked from the waist down. I grabbed my shorts and hurried to pull them back on.

"Okay," I said reluctantly. "But what about you?" He'd given me two amazing releases and hadn't gotten any in return.

His smile was dry. "Don't worry about me. Do you feel better?"

"Much."

"Good." He helped me to my feet, kissing my neck as I stood. "Then I do too."

chapter TWENTY-EIGHT

TARA

Grant held his bow in one hand and the cello in the other while I grasped the folding chair, fidgeting nervously behind the curtain in the wings of the theatre.

Our plan had been approved by Tina, the production head, yet the staff fought us at every step along the way. They argued Grant hadn't signed a release to be filmed, like this was a problem that couldn't be easily solved. Then they told him we couldn't bring on the folding chair, saying "props" weren't allowed. It was another bullshit excuse to try to get me to toe the line.

Earlier this afternoon, they'd let a girl go up with a ribbon swivel stick. It had been one of those 'fail' routines, a total train wreck, which I always thought were mean spirited. But the idea the chair Grant would sit on while he played was considered a *prop* was ridiculous, and they couldn't arbitrarily make up rules if they weren't going to follow them, anyway.

As Grant had suspected, filming was behind schedule. They were supposed to begin solos after lunch, but we'd heard setup had taken longer than anticipated, and they'd started late. Nearly every contestant ran over their allotted time, but it wasn't their fault.

"The judges are awfully chatty today," the assistant standing beside me remarked. She was the one who'd give us the green light on when we could go on.

From where we stood behind the curtain, we could see the right side of the house of the theatre, including half the panel of judges. A platform had been erected in the orchestra pit so the judges were level with the front of the stage, and I watched Hugh Freeman's discerning gaze zero in on the feet of the tap dancer who was currently performing.

There were four judges. Hugh, Rita, and Shonda were the core three—the ones at every audition and show. The fourth was a guest judge I couldn't see or recognize by voice. He didn't speak much either, so that was no help.

Beyond them, I could see lots of people in the seats, more in the balconies. It was friends of soloists, or people who hadn't made the next round and wanted to watch.

"I don't want to freak you out," Grant whispered, "but the stage is fucking huge." Had he forgotten I'd already performed on it once? He looked clammy. "It looks even bigger down here."

The response was automatic from me. "That's what she said."

My juvenile comment earned me half a smile from him.

I cast my gaze across the theatre and was flooded with feelings. This was where the Chicago Ballet Company performed. Fate worked in funny ways, right?

If I'd been accepted into the CBC, I would have danced on this stage, but I would have always shared it with at least a dozen other members of the corps. Today, I would be the principal dancer. I wouldn't have to blend. I wouldn't be staged near the back or side.

For two minutes, and hopefully not less, I would be seen.

The dancer concluded his solo, and his taps clicked as he walked to the microphone at the front.

"Okay," the assistant whispered to us, "stand by. When the interview is over, you two are up."

I pressed my feet into the toe box of my shoes and rolled up into *relevé*, a superstitious tick I always did before performing en pointe. If the shank was going to break or a ribbon come untucked, now was the time to find that out.

Grant's clamminess graduated into a full-on sweat. I grabbed a tissue from a dispenser nearby and dabbed at his forehead. "Hey," I said, hushed and only for him. "We've got this. I'd say you're going to be amazing, but . . . you already are."

There was applause as the tap dancer left the stage, drowning out whatever Grant wanted to say. But his eyes spoke loudly. They said he believed me.

"You're on," the assistant announced. "Good luck!"

Oh, Jesus. I grabbed the metal folding chair, my palms slippery with nervous sweat, and glanced at Grant. He looked surprising calm and ready, and gestured with his bow, wordlessly saying, "After you."

I compartmentalized everything into tasks, so I could tackle them one at a time.

First, I strode to the center of the stage and placed the "prop" chair where I wanted Grant to sit. He took his seat, and our gazes connected for a second, just long enough to smile and mouth, "Good luck."

Second, I walked to my mark, front and center, and took in the view. The house was full other than the front seats, where the judges' panel on the platform obstructed the view. My gaze moved to Hugh, who wore his signature black-framed glasses and a colorful pocket square peeked out of his suit coat pocket. Then I drifted on to Rita, the ballroom dance specialist. She had on a bright red dress, heavy eye makeup, and a huge smile. She was considerably older than I was, but she still had it going on.

Shonda was a Tony and Emmy winning choreographer. Direct, but fair, she was the one I was most excited to hear feedback from. She wore her hair in long braids, which was a change from last season, and it looked beautiful on her.

The final judge—

Oh, no.

I swallowed hard, and my knees threatened to knock together as a tremble roared up my legs.

"Hello, darling," Hugh said in his posh British accent. "What's your name?"

I channeled all my fear into a bright smile. "Tara Vannett."

"May I ask what's happening here?" He pointed to Grant.

"He'll be playing my audition music."

Rita straightened in her seat and flashed a saucy smile. "Oh, getting some live music, are we?"

She gazed longingly at Grant. Rita was a dirty old woman, always making provocative comments, and I adored that about her. Her question seemed to be rhetorical, and everyone turned their attention back to Hugh, the showrunner. This was his call, and they wanted to know if he was going to allow it.

He didn't seem to mind. "All right, dear. Where are you from, and what style will you be performing for us today?"

"I'm from Chicago, and I'll be dancing contemporary ballet."

"Oh?" He glanced down the panel of judges. "Then you probably know Michael Carlisle, the director of the Chicago Ballet Company."

Emotion swirled inside me, but I hoped none of it showed. I kept my tone upbeat and light. "Yes, I've auditioned for him a few times."

There was no point not addressing it. Rita picked up what this meant right away. "Ruh roh," she said under her breath.

Hugh was just as quick, and I could see the wheels turning in his head. I'd auditioned several times and not been accepted into the CBC, so he was skeptical about how good I could be.

My heart sank. It looked like the interview was over, and I'd already been written off.

"Well, let's get to it, then, shall we?" He gave a cursory, hollow smile. "Off you go."

I nodded and hurried to my place behind Grant. Could he feel the tremors in my hands as I placed them on his shoulders? Was his heart a war drum in his chest like mine? I rode the heavy rise and fall of his deep breath, and with the connection to him, something in me snapped.

Maybe the judges had already written me off, but *fuck that*. I didn't come here to get rejected. I came to win the whole goddamn thing, and the fact that Michael Carlisle was a judge? It was icing on the cake. I'd show him how wrong he'd been about me.

"And . . . cue music," Hugh announced into his microphone.

The piano intro drifted from the speakers, and Grant's shoulder tensed, the muscle in his arm flexing to draw his bow across the strings. He was a flurry of activity, and I took off, matching his intensity.

I'd incorporated him into the routine, often mimicking the long, elastic slide of his bow, or the short bursts of staccato notes. I danced with a fire inside me, letting it pour from my limbs. It lengthened my lines, helped me reach new height on my leaps, and made my turns tight and perfectly balanced.

I prayed at least a fraction of the passion I felt showed through in my expression. The lyrics weren't heard in this version, but I spoke them with my body. Today, I'd live like tomorrow didn't exist, and danced as if it were my last time—

Because it could be.

There was a tricky combo I'd put in. A roll to the floor where I gathered momentum and then burst up into a huge split leap, and as I exploded off the floor, I heard cheers from the audience. It only made me soar higher on my next jump.

Grant's cello wasn't on a mic, but the music was so powerful it filled the house and demanded the audience's attention. They watched as I traveled the stage, whirling around to give the impression of swinging on a chandelier.

The lights were hot and blinding, and I couldn't see beyond the judges, who I only got flashes of, anyway. My choreography made use of the large stage. A bead of sweat rolled down the back of my neck, but as we approached the two-minute mark, my energy grew. It had to be the same for Grant. I could feel the excitement leaping off his strings. It vibrated in my bones like a struck tuning fork.

I'd saved a complicated series of pirouettes for the end, hoping by that point the judges had seen enough to green light me to New York and I wouldn't have to perform them, but now I was glad. I planted my standing leg, prepared, and then lifted into the rotation.

It was the greatest set of pirouettes I'd ever executed. I whipped my head around while spotting my turns, and as I opened out into à la *seconde*, my working leg was perfectly parallel to the floor.

Turns with an extended leg were much harder, but my center of balance never wavered. The crowd's appreciative murmur swelled into a roar as I continued to turn.

And turn.

And turn.

I finished into fourth position, and only rested for a single breath before moving on to the final sequence. My toes beat so softly against the floor, I wanted it to look like I was floating across the stage. My thighs and calves burned from the exertion, but I pushed through. And when I arrived beside Grant, I softened and slid down to my knees, lowering the intensity of my movements.

The song was winding down, and his cello went from bright to mournful in one measure. I'd given everything to the routine, and it had taken all of it. Blood rushed so loudly in my ears, I could hardly hear anything else while I finished.

I ended the routine with my body wrapped around Grant's leg, clinging to him for life as his bow slid across the final, long note.

On the balcony, people were on their feet. There were whistles and shouts punctuating the steady sound of applause, and I stared at the audience, awestruck. I couldn't believe what I was seeing and looked to Grant for confirmation. His stunned expression had to mirror mine.

The judges had remained in their seats, but Hugh waved a hand, signaling for me to come up to the front. As a staffer brought out the microphone stand and placed it before the panel, Grant stood and offered a hand, helping me up onto my shaky legs. I wasn't just tired, I was overwhelmed. I wanted to remember this moment for the rest of my life, standing on stage, my hand in his, as the audience cheered for us.

But I couldn't stay there forever. Grant nudged me forward, a brilliant smile spread wide on his face.

"Holy Toledo," Rita said before Hugh could get a word in. She used a piece of paper to fan herself. "You were on fire. I mean—Lordy, that was something."

"It was something." Hugh echoed her. "And that *something* was . . . 'wow.' It was just fabulous to watch."

I hadn't caught my breath, and how the hell was I going to now? I gasped it out, pressing a hand to my chest, like I could somehow stop it from heaving. "Thank you."

"Stunning," Rita said, nodding. "It was thrilling, and I enjoyed the hell out of it. Everything from that insane first jump you did, to this hot cello guy you got to put your hands all over. I mean, I can't blame you."

The crowd giggled and gave me another moment to breathe.

Shonda leaned toward her microphone. "Who choreographed the piece?"

Her expression was unreadable. It wasn't clear if she liked it or hated it. I swallowed hard. "I did."

"The way you moved and transitioned, it was so unexpected." She stared at me, her eyes intense, but excited. "I adored it. The concept and the execution. Was it your idea to stage him in the center?" When I nodded, she added, "Smart. You used him to your advantage. I don't think I would have had such the positive reaction I did if he'd been off to the side."

Hugh glanced down to the other end of the panel. "Michael, what did you think?"

He might as well have asked Michael how he liked them apples, because his expression was that smug.

Michael gave a soft smile. "I will be honest, I don't remember you auditioning for me before. But, after today, I absolutely will. You danced with such passion, and your leg work was outstanding. Bravo." He turned his attention to Hugh. "To answer your question, I thought this was something truly special."

"Well, then," Hugh said, "should we go ahead and—"

Rita grabbed his arm. "Hugh, just wait a minute. I want to know more about this cellist."

"Like, if he's dating anyone," Shonda teased.

I laughed, pressed my hand to my heart, and lifted an eyebrow. "Sorry. He's taken."

"Oh, girl . . ." Rita grinned wickedly. "I figured. He couldn't take his eyes off you."

"Of course, he couldn't," Hugh said. "She's got legs for decades." He shuffled the papers on the table in front of him. "That's enough out of you, Rita. Stop holding up this girl when she's got to come here and get her ticket to New York."

The crowd cheered.

My eyes welled with tears and my legs threatened to give out, but somehow, I made my way down the stairs and up the steps onto the judges' platform. The ticket was a fake airplane one, the airline listed as *Dance Dreams*, and it was surreal to hold it in my hand. I blubbered out 'thank you' at least a dozen times to the judges as I accepted both the ticket and a few additional compliments spoken only to me.

Grant was waiting at the bottom of the steps. I wiped under my eyes with my thumb and reached out to help him with the folding chair. Oh, shit, I'd left him on stage with it and his cello.

"Oh, I'm sorry, I . . ." My voice wavered with emotion.

He laughed like I was being silly. "No, I've got it." Seeing me with unshed tears in my eyes had a powerful effect on him. "Congratulations, Tara. You did it."

"No, we did. I couldn't have done this without you." I didn't care that we were standing beside the judges and in front of an enormous audience, or that his hands were full and he couldn't stop me. I lifted on my toes and put my mouth on his, sinking all that I had into the kiss.

"Get a room," Rita teased lightheartedly.

I wanted to tell her she'd better believe that was going to happen, but instead I finished the kiss, clutching my ticket in one hand, and the most important person in my life in the other.

TWENTY-NINE

GRANT

It was nearly eight o'clock by the time we left the Auditorium Theatre. Tara had disappeared into a room with the legal department to go over paperwork, and while she was gone, I texted Ruby to tell her the good news. My girlfriend would be a contestant on the selection show of *Dance Dreams*, and if she danced well enough there, a choreographer would pick her from the other sixty hopefuls to join their team.

We were physically tired but also wired during the cab ride back to my place, and as she burrowed in under my arm, she texted her friends the news, starting with Elena.

"Are you going to tell your sisters? Your parents?" I asked.

"Not tonight." She shrugged. "I don't think they'll get it, and I don't want the buzzkill."

I understood. I didn't want anything to ruin this night for her either.

She tapped out a new message, and from the way she held her phone out where I could easily see, it felt like she wanted me to read it.

> Tara: Good news, bad news.
>
> Tara: Got my ticket to New York, yay! But Grant and I broke some rules.
>
> Regan: CONGRATS! We're so excited for you!

> Regan: Which rules did you break?

> Tara: Not the big one. He went down on me and
> used his fingers.

After she sent it, she stiffened, like the thought had just occurred to her. Her voice was nervous. "Uh, is it okay I said what we did? I don't keep secrets from them."

Just me, I guess.

I wanted to scowl at the thought. It wasn't fucking fair, because I was keeping secrets from her too. Not just that I knew she worked at the club, or the first night we'd met, but how I was fairly certain I was in love with her. Her slip-up earlier today still buzzed in my ears. I wanted her to say it again, and this time, not retract it seconds later.

"Yeah, it's all right," I said. "Honesty is important."

She made a face like she was going to be ill, but was distracted as a new message popped up.

> Regan: I'm disappointed you couldn't obey, but
> respect you telling us.

> Regan: Your punishment is he spanks you hard
> enough I can make out the fingers. We expect a
> picture shortly.

It was strange to take orders from someone else, but not . . . unpleasant. Her demand made me hot. Perhaps I would be less receptive to the idea if I wasn't so intrigued to follow it. The concept of taking Tara over my knee and then sending the picture proof to her doms was sexy.

Tara's eyes glittered with desire in the dark of the back seat. "Do you want to do that?"

She was asking me if I was comfortable with this. Spanking her. Following the command. The word was thick with lust. "Yes."

I put my cello case down in the corner and dropped my bag in my room, then focused my attention on her. Tara stood patiently in my living room, waiting. I was her de facto Dominant and she was my submissive, and when I sat in the wooden chair I used for practice, she moved to stand by my side. I liked how she was so attentive. Always attune to what I was thinking.

"Are you ready?" she asked.

I gave her a skeptical look. "Are you?"

She'd changed before we left the theatre, slipping into glossy black leggings, a gray t-shirt, and a maroon biker jacket. As usual, she was a total smoke show. She'd shed her boots and jacket when we'd come into my apartment, and now she wiggled down the top of her pants until they were below her ass.

I stared at her nakedness and began to grow hard. Did it make her uncomfortable to lie over my lap, my swelling erection digging into her stomach? She said nothing. Instead, she put her arms behind her back and grasped her elbows with the opposite hand.

The pose punched a sound of satisfaction from me. I caressed a palm over the smooth globe of her ass and enjoyed her gentle sigh. "This doesn't feel like punishment," I whispered.

She sounded amused. "Probably because you haven't done it yet."

I took in a preparing breath and reared my hand back. I wasn't sure if I was asking her a second time, or myself. "Ready?"

"Yes."

I didn't want to hurt her, but I also wanted to obey the rules, and figured she could handle it. She worked for years at a BDSM club, after all. I brought my hand down, and the sharp slap was followed by her gasp.

I was nervous until she turned over her shoulder and looked at me with a surprised grin. "You went for it. I thought you might not do it hard enough."

"I was supposed to leave a mark, yeah?" When she shifted, it felt good and uncomfortable on my cock at the same time. "Give me your phone."

She did, and I took the shot then passed it back to her. A smile teased her lips as she viewed the image. There was a perfectly pink handprint across her pale skin. "Nice work."

"Anytime," I said. And I meant it. I wasn't experienced in this area, but like everything new, I was curious and excited to learn.

She rose off me, sent the image, and Regan's reply came as Tara pulled up her pants.

> Regan: I'll give you one on the other side tonight. So you have a matching set.

She typed back a response, and since she didn't have pockets, she nestled her phone in her bra. "I'm hungry, but also sleepy, and I can't decide which I want first. Dinner, or a nap."

"I wasn't tired until you said the word *nap*, and now it's all I can think about."

We shuffled along into my dark bedroom, put our phones on the nightstands, and collapsed on the unmade bed. We were still in our clothes, but neither cared as we snuggled together under the covers. She fit so perfectly in my arms and in my bed. Did she feel the same? Was I enough for her?

"What are they like?" It was stupid to ask now since we'd meet them in a few hours, but I was curious about how she saw them.

"Silas and Regan?" She laced our fingers together. "They're an interesting pair. She's an accountant, and he's an artist. Practical meets creative. Actually, he's the one who did my tattoo."

For a moment, I hated him. He'd literally put his mark on her, and it was permanent.

But his artwork was also undeniably beautiful, and if he hadn't . . . I never would have recognized her.

"It's very pretty. Does it have meaning?"

"Yeah. When I was six years old, I wanted to wear this crazy leotard to my first day of ballet class. It was pink and purple and had this pattern on it, the one that's my tattoo. My mother told me I had to wear black, so I'd match the other girls, but I didn't care. I thought it was pretty, and I didn't want to look like everyone else."

She curled in closer, putting her leg in between mine.

"We fought all week about it, until my mom finally told me if I wasn't going to wear the approved attire, I couldn't go." It was dark enough I couldn't make out her expression, but I could hear the smile in her voice. "I wore the leotard I wanted to, and the black one over it."

I chuckled, and her story made me appreciate the tattoo even more. A sign of her defiance, her desire to be unique. "You can cover it up, Tara, but don't worry. There's no one else like you."

Lying together in the warmth of my bed, it didn't take long for us to drift to sleep.

When I woke, the bed was empty. My bedroom door was open, and light streamed in from the kitchen. A timer beeped and was shut off, followed by the sound of my oven door opening.

Was she cooking? I glanced at my phone. Was she cooking . . . at eleven-thirty at night? I climbed out of bed and went to see what was going on, only to have the smell of pizza slam into me. My stomach growled.

Tara set the cooked pizza on top of the oven, grabbed the glass of wine she'd poured for herself, and glanced at me. "Oh, hi. I was just about to wake you."

"Pizza again?" I asked. She'd found my stash in the freezer, judging by the label and plastic wrap sitting on top of the trash can.

"I thought you said you could eat it for every meal."

"I can. I'm just surprised you're all right with eating it again."

"I'm hungry, and this was fast. We're supposed to head over to Regan's soon."

She poured a glass of wine for me, and we ate quickly. My excitement mixed with my unease about not telling her the truth, and as we finished, I couldn't help but think she felt the same way.

We took an Uber and arrived a little after midnight, which added to the atmosphere of the evening. As if what we were doing wasn't suitable for normal hours. Silas was on a deadline for a project, and his most creative time was at night, I'd been told. We hadn't known how long the audition was going to run either, so had scheduled our late-night get-together very late.

After we were buzzed into the apartment building, I followed Tara up the steps, carrying a bottle of red wine. My hold on it might have been too strong. I was tight with anticipation, like a string on my cello that had been keyed too tight and could snap at any moment. My pulse leaped as she turned and knocked on an apartment door. What if I didn't like them? What if our personalities didn't match, or they only listened to country music? Anxious questions spun through my mind, but it was too late.

The door swung open.

Despite everything else, my first thought was I needed to know if Silas was any good at sports, because he was built for the front row of rugby, and we needed fresh blood on the Lions.

He took up most of the doorway, and when he saw me by Tara's side, he immediately began to size me up. I did the same. There were tattoos sprawled across his meaty forearms, and the ink disappeared beneath the sleeves of his shirt. I wasn't attracted to men, but I was open enough to begrudgingly admit he was good looking.

Maybe better looking than I was, and the primal male

instinct of competition didn't like that. As his blue eyes scanned me, they shuttered. It looked a hell of a lot like he was thinking the same thing about me.

"Silas," Tara said, "this is Grant."

"Hey, man." He extended a hand, which I took, and the handshake was aggressive from both sides.

"Nice to meet you," I said.

When he released his grip, he stepped back and gestured to the apartment. "Come on in."

The place was nice and open concept. The artwork on the walls—no doubt his—was eye-catching. Full of patterns. The couple had obviously set the mood. The lighting was soft, a few candles flickered, and the music that tinkered from the kitchen sounded like Sigur Rós.

But something was missing.

"Where's Regan?" Tara asked.

"She should be here any minute. She left the club a while ago." He motioned toward the bottle of wine in my hand. "Want me to take that?"

I didn't move. Tara had said Regan was an accountant. That she'd met them at a wedding. I tried to keep dread from my voice. "Club?"

"Oh." Tara's expression was vacant, masking her thoughts. "Regan . . . uh, she sells wine at the club too."

Silas looked confused on multiple fronts. I still hadn't handed over the bottle that was clearly a gift, and he also didn't like Tara's statement. "She doesn't sell," he gave her a pointed look, "she just negotiates."

"Right." She looked stricken but tried to play it off, and grabbed the bottle from me, passing it to Silas. "This is for you."

"Thanks."

As he deposited it in the kitchen, hairs tingled on the back of my neck, and I turned my head to alleviate the strange sensation. It must have been my subconscious trying to warn me, because my gaze caught a bright swath of red. It was a framed photograph of Silas, resting on a bookshelf.

His arm was around the redhead from the blindfold club.

My heart jerked to a stop.

I had to get Tara out of here before Regan came home and recognized me. Bloody *fucking* hell. Why hadn't I just told her the truth? Why didn't she trust me enough to tell me, so I could have come clean? Panic swamped my head.

I must have looked terrible, because Tara grabbed my hand, her face full of concern. "Are you okay?"

"No," I said. "I'm sorry, but we need to leave."

I'd let her believe whatever she wanted right now. That I was deathly ill. That I was having massive second thoughts about meeting them. Anything would work, as long as I could get her out of this apartment and into the back of a cab, where I could explain the whole thing on my terms. Like I should have fucking done from the start.

Her concern escalated. "Of course." Her focus left me only for a moment to speak to Silas. "I'm sorry, we—"

The front door swung open behind us, and I was doomed.

"Sorry I'm late," Regan sounded short of breath, as if she'd hurried up the steps. "The train was delayed for some stupid reason."

"They have to leave," Silas said.

Tara didn't know the reason, but she covered for me

regardless. "Grant's not feeling well."

The competitor in me wanted to turn and face Regan head-to-head. She was going to take away my chance to tell Tara everything, and I selfishly wanted to keep it in my possession. But I couldn't see any way out of the mess I'd created, so I simply stood there as she strode over to Silas and stepped into view.

She looked like I'd remembered her. Professional, yet sexy, wearing a black, tailored suit over a corset and her vibrant red hair up in a high ponytail. I must have looked the same to her, or at least similar enough, because she went ramrod straight and dark storms filled her eyes.

"What the fuck are you doing here?"

chapter THIRTY

GRANT

Tara's gasp was sharp, slicing deep. "You know each other?"

"Yeah," Regan's eyes narrowed to slits as she focused on me. "Julius told you to stay the fuck away from the club."

This time, there was no sound at all from Tara, and it was somehow worse. She dropped my hand like it was an anchor she couldn't be attached to and stepped back. The way she looked at me . . . it was bloody awful. Her expression was surprise and hurt and distrust, all mixed together.

She stared at me like I was a stranger.

Her attention darted to Regan for a moment, and she whispered it as if she didn't want to know the answer. "He's a member?"

"No—" I started.

Regan cut me off. "He tried to become one."

Tara pressed her fingers to her lips, possibly to hold in the sound of shock she wanted to make. "You *knew*?" Her eyes were oceans of hurt and betrayal. "When?"

The only thing I could control at this point was my ability to tell the truth. "From the beginning."

It was impossible to organize my thoughts and find the right words, and before I could, her shock began to morph to anger. Her glare was so heavy it was hard to stand beneath it, but she directed the question at Regan. "You said he tried to become a member. What happened?"

"He lied about who he was. He'd come to the club to get a story, but I pulled him out of your room and Julius threw him out."

I'd wished it could have been said differently, but I couldn't argue with the truth. I was wishing for a lot of things right now. Mostly that I could go back in time, do it right, and wouldn't have to watch Tara's face as even more dismay washed through it.

"That was you?" she cried. "But it couldn't be. That guy didn't have an accent."

I needed to take charge of this conversation. "If I concentrate, I can speak without one. While it's true I went to the club looking for a story, that's over. That was before we got together."

When I tried to advance, Regan stepped protectively between us. I remembered how she'd acted that night in the club, and it made more sense now. Beyond Regan, I could see that every inch of Tara's body language was screaming she didn't believe me.

"I didn't know you worked there when we met," I said. "Think about it. You fell, and I caught you. I didn't seek you out, and I didn't know until the next night when I saw your tattoo. I was supposed to stay away, but I'd already agreed to help with your audition."

Fire burned on her face. "Okay, but then why the fuck didn't you tell me?"

"Julius made it real fucking clear to leave his business alone, and honestly, Tara," I said, letting the hurt seep into my voice, "I was hoping you'd tell me."

"I was going to," she said. "I wasn't sure if I could before. You told me you were looking for a story."

"I'm not. I mean, I was, but not anymore."

Regan lifted an eyebrow in displeasure. "Why should she believe you, if you've been lying to her from the beginning?"

Irritation simmered in my core. This conversation was supposed to be between Tara and me. "I've known about the blindfold club for a while now, and have any stories come out about it?"

Silas hadn't participated until now. He frowned. "That doesn't mean anything. Her bosses would squash that story, just like they did with—"

"*Silas*," Regan hissed.

Tension was already high, but her single word took it to a new height. The silence between us was taut.

Tara's focus swung from me to the couple. "What does that mean?"

"He meant that Julius would handle it," Regan answered quickly.

"I know what I heard. He said *bosses*—as in—plural."

Regan's breathing picked up, but otherwise, it was hard to tell if she was nervous. "We can talk about it," her gaze flicked to me, "in private."

"No, I'm done with secrets." Tara crossed her arms over her chest and looked dubious. "Julius runs the club by himself, so explain how you have more than one boss."

"What if," I said quietly, "she works for someone else?"

The mob? No, that didn't make sense. They had a lot of power, but not enough to kill a story. Who had that kind of authority?

Bloody hell.

I couldn't make sense of it. "Do you work for the government?"

"No," Regan snapped.

It was a lie, and we all knew it from the way Silas reacted. He'd turned away, unable to look at any of us, trying to hide his expression.

"Oh my God," Tara gasped. "You're . . . a cop?"

Regan lifted her reluctant gaze to the ceiling. "Not exactly." She let out a deep sigh. "Goddamnit, Silas."

"I'm sorry," he said, but as he continued talking, he built steam. "Look, I didn't mean to 'out' you, but . . . you know what? I'm with Tara on this one. I'm fucking over it with all the lies."

Fury rolled into Regan's expression. "Holy fuck. Did you do it on purpose?"

"What? No." He looked seriously pissed at her accusation. "Yeah, I won't be sad if you don't have to work there anymore, but Jesus. It was an honest mistake."

"I'm still struggling," Tara said, "with what 'not exactly a cop' means."

Regan didn't like being caught and wanted someone to blame, and I was an easy target. She gave me a hard look. "I know you probably think you've hit the jackpot here, but your story will never get off the ground. The FBI will kill it, make you look bad in the process, and the only thing you'll end up doing is getting me reassigned." Her expression shifted and took an edge of desperation. "I won't be able to protect the people I care about."

Tara didn't seem to hear the last part. She balled a hand

into a fist and held it against her stomach. "You're FBI." It was impossible to tell if it was a question or a statement from her shell-shocked voice. "I can't . . ." She put her hands on her temples and stared at the ground, completely overwhelmed. "I can't do this right now. It's too much."

When she moved for the door, we all went to stop her.

"Wait," the couple said.

I ignored them. "Let me take you home."

"No." She threw open the door, and I followed her out into the hallway, which she rushed down. "I need some time."

Down the stairs she went, her leggings glinting in the light as she moved at a fast clip. I was bigger, but it was surprisingly difficult to keep up.

"I know you're dealing with a lot, but can I explain?"

She flung open the apartment building's main door, not checking to see if I was still following. She knew I was. "What part of 'I need some time' do you not understand?" She whirled around to face me, and she was both angry and scared. Like a wounded animal trying to survive a threat. "I just found out that *everyone* I care about has been lying to me. And, yeah, I'm aware I'm not innocent in this either, but you're going to give me one night to work through this shit."

It hurt to see her like this, especially since I was the cause. "Can I please just take you home?"

A cab with its sign lit turned the corner, and she waved before turning a cold stare my direction. "I already told you no, and you need to respect that."

It wasn't a battle I could, or should, win. "You're right. I'm sorry, and I'm sorry I didn't tell you. But Tara? I don't care about the club or what you do there. I'm with you. That's all that matters to me."

I should have left it alone, instead all I did was add to her confusion. She said nothing as she climbed into the back of the cab and murmured her address to the driver. Then she yanked the door closed with a slam, and the car pulled away. Her head never turned. She didn't look back to see me standing there, feeling like I'd just lost everything.

I came home directly after. Maybe it was rude not to say goodbye to Silas and Regan, but that would have been fucking awkward, and I just wanted to be alone. Well, that wasn't true. I wanted to be with Tara right now. For selfish reasons, but also to comfort her.

She'd trusted Silas and Regan and been honest with them about everything. Their betrayal had to sting, and worse—was she in legal jeopardy? Regan insinuated she was protecting her.

Did Julius know she was FBI?

For once in my life, I wasn't curious. All I could think about was how I'd ruined what was supposed to be one of the best days of Tara's life. Hopefully, she'd get a decent night's sleep, and in the morning, she'd see that our lies canceled each other's out. We could talk about everything openly and figure out how we'd move forward.

I stared at the used wine glasses beside my sink, Tara's lipstick faintly kissing one edge.

It felt like I'd just played two rugby matches back to back, and they'd been blowout losses. I locked my front door, turned off the lights in the living room, and made my way to the bedroom. My overnight bag was in the corner, and I went to unpack it, only to be crushed for the second time this evening.

Her ledger.

I still had it.

My knees softened, and I sat on the edge of the bed we'd slept in only a few hours ago, my hands gripping the black book. She'd asked for one night of space, and I was going to give it to her, but first thing tomorrow, I'd tell her what I'd done. It was too much to ask her to deal with tonight.

I was exhausted, emotionally and physically. Weak. It was why I opened to my page in her journal and read it again, running my fingers over the ink she'd spilled about me. It was black and the pages thin, and I could make out words from the page behind mine. Words like *Mr. Gold* and *humiliated* and *scared*.

She'd stopped working recently because a client had gotten too attached, she'd said. I turned the page, unable to quench the thirst to know what had happened. I needed to know she was safe. It was the last page of handwriting in the journal.

I shouldn't have read any of it. I knew nothing good could come from it, but I couldn't stop myself. I read about the vile shit he'd said to her and how she'd told him they were finished. She was worried he wouldn't handle it well. He was powerful and rich, and one of the best clients at the clubs.

It seemed like he'd been a regular, and I wanted to know

more about him. Had he always been this horrible little man? How often had she seen him? Did she know his name?

Paging through her journal, I lost all track of time and any fucking sense.

I read it cover to cover, nearly three years of entries. It was scintillating. Erotic. And utterly fascinating. Every part of Tara was revealed in these pages, and I fell even more hopelessly in love with her. She was kind, and funny, and unapologetic about the way she lived her life.

When I finished, I placed the journal on the empty pillow beside me in bed, where she'd slept earlier this evening and it still smelled like her, and hoped she could forgive me.

I fell asleep for the second time with my clothes still on, but it was restless. I wondered if it was because she wasn't here, but as my phone vibrated a second time on the nightstand, I realized what was happening. Pale light came from the screen. Someone was texting me at four a.m.

> Tara: Did I meaning anything to you?

> Tara: Or was I just a story?

I bolted upright in my bed and thumbed out my response, my heart pounding ferociously.

> Grant: You mean everything to me. It was never about a story.

The bubbles flashed on the screen, indicating she was typing, and when the message came through, my heart plummeted in my chest. *Fuck.*

> Tara: THEN WHY DID YOU TAKE MY JOURNAL???

chapter THIRTY-ONE

TARA

I didn't sleep much, even though my body wanted it. My mind was too loud and too angry, and my heart was too hurt. It was an invisible wound, bleeding in my chest where no one could see, but I felt it with every painful breath.

Everyone had lied, which was hard to handle, but I wasn't sure I'd survive Grant's latest betrayal. He hadn't just lied, he'd deceived. He'd stolen from me. Taken something I didn't want shared with anyone else. Had he learned nothing from what his ex-girlfriend had done to him? This was a million times worse.

On top of all that, he'd let me squirm on a hook of guilt for more than a month as I wrestled with revealing what I did for a living. I'd had massive angst it was going to drive him away. But he already knew, and had just played along, making me a total fool.

All so he could get his precious story.

As I stood in front of the apartment door, a cardboard tray of Starbucks coffee in one hand and a paper bag of blueberry scones in the other, I fractured. I didn't want to be here. I didn't want to have to do this.

Suck it up and get it over with.

I knocked on the door, and a moment later, footsteps approached.

262 | NIKKI SLOANE

When it swung open, Hector stood there, wearing a white t-shirt, plaid patterned pants, and his hair was askew. I knew they'd been awake for a few hours, but it was a lazy Sunday for them. He was in his late forties, patches of gray in his short beard, and in great shape. I'd passed him plenty of times as he was leaving or coming back from a morning run.

"Hi," I said, mustering a bright tone when I was all darkness inside. "We haven't officially met, but I'm Tara. I live downstairs."

"Hey, there." He didn't seem put out by my intrusion, just confused. "I'm Hector. Is Brad being too loud? I know he's a heavy walker."

Between the two of them, I was sure Hector was worse, but I said nothing. I was barely holding it together. "These are for you." I shoved the tray and the bag at him. "Coffee and scones."

His confusion shifted into worry as he cautiously took them from me. "Um, thank you. Is everything okay?"

I pressed my lips together and tried to nod but couldn't. My eyes watered. "I was wondering if I could ask you and Brad," I sucked in a calming breath, "for a really big favor?"

Hector shifted the contents in his hands. Was he nervous I was going to ask for money? Or worse . . . a ride to O'Hare?

Brad appeared over Hector's shoulder. He was younger than his partner by a few years. He was handsome, but when he smiled, the dimples came out and made him seriously cute. "Hi, neighbor," he said casually, but picked up on Hector's mood right after and turned serious. "What's up?"

"I'm sorry to bother you, but my," I stumbled with the right word, "ex-boyfriend is coming over soon to return something, and I was hoping you guys wouldn't mind hanging out with me while that happens."

Both men's eyes went wide.

"Did he threaten you?" Hector asked. "If you don't feel safe, you should call the police."

"No, no, it's not like that." God, this was embarrassing. "It's just, he's going to want to talk to me, and I don't want to hear it. He needs to drop off my book and leave, and I don't want to . . . cave."

Brad's mouth rounded into an 'oh.' "You need to stay strong about kicking his ass to the curb."

"Yes. If you guys are with me, he won't push as hard for a conversation." Because Grant wouldn't talk about the contents of my journal or the blindfold club in front of strangers, would he? "I'm sorry to spring this on you, but he's going to be here soon, and my friend isn't available."

Elena was with her mother, whose church was across town. I didn't see the point in her coming all the way here for something that would hopefully take two minutes.

Brad hung his arm around Hector's neck, who responded by putting his hand on top of his partner. It was a loving gesture, wordlessly communicating they were a united front.

Hector's voice was full of understanding. "Of course."

The silver lining to the whole terrible situation was I got to know my neighbors while we waited for Grant's arrival, and they were the nicest guys. They didn't pry for details, but also didn't shy away when I got emotional. We were strangers to each other, but it didn't feel that way.

Maybe it was because we'd all heard each other's orgasms.

"What are you doing tonight?" Brad asked, sipping the coffee I'd brought him. He was lounging on my couch while Hector perused the titles on my bookshelf. "We're going over to our friend's place to watch the Bears game. You should come."

"Oh, thank you, but I'm not a football fan." American football wasn't rugby, but it was close, and I didn't want the reminder.

"I don't watch the 'sports ball' either," he said with a grin. "I usually end up playing Beerio Kart with the other people who got dragged there by their partners."

I gave a dubious look. "Beerio Kart?"

"Mario Kart with beer," Hector said, reading the dust jacket of one of the books.

Brad shrugged off his partner's flat tone. "Everyone has a can of beer, and you have to be done with it before you cross the finish line. But drinking and driving is illegal, so you can't race while you're drinking."

"Yes," Hector said, "he's in his forties and still plays drinking games."

Brad scoffed. "Whatever. He's just mad because I always beat him."

Hanging out with Hector and Brad's friends was better than being alone. "That sounds fun," I said. "You've convinced me."

"Awesome. I'll text Shawn and let him—"

The knock on my front door sucked the warmth from the room.

I was standing near the dining table, and as Brad got up to answer the door, Hector moved beside me. I couldn't tell if it was protective, or supportive, or both. I curled my hands around the back of a chair, using it to keep me steady.

Grant looked like hell.

There were dark circles beneath his eyes, announcing he'd probably gotten as much sleep as I had. He hadn't shaved. He'd showered and changed clothes, but he couldn't wash off what he'd done. He was coated in guilt and misery.

He'd been expecting me to answer the door, and when he came face to face with Brad, the first thing he did was check the number on my apartment. Slow realization dawned in him as he understood I didn't want to be alone with him.

It hurt to see him looking so distraught, but then there was my journal in his hands, and that made *everything* hurt. Needles stabbed at my eyes, filling them with tears. A hive of angry bees swarmed in my stomach. I couldn't stand to look at him and turned my head away.

"Tara." Hearing my name in his broken, defeated voice was a punch to my gut.

Brad's tone was firm. "You have something for her? I'll take it, and you can go."

"What? No, I'm not giving this to you." He sounded horrified. "I need to talk to her."

"No, man. That's not going to happen."

"*Tara*," Grant pleaded. "Please. Look at me."

I squeezed the chairback so hard, my hands ached. *Don't do it. Do not look at him.*

His eyes were wild. He was a mess, and while the angry part of me took pleasure in that, the rest of me suffered along with him.

"It was an accident," he said. "I didn't mean to take it. If we could just talk, I can explain."

I went down to the place inside myself where I was safe from emotion. Cut off completely from feeling anything. It wasn't subspace—the euphoric place I could reach sometimes while doing a scene—but a disconnected void.

I didn't recognize my own voice. "Did you read it?"

Shame was a terrible, heavy burden, and he put a hand on the doorframe to support himself. "Yes."

The bees in my stomach got angrier, threatening to come out. I swallowed a shallow breath. "All of it?"

"Yes," he whispered.

Which meant he knew all my sins. Every dark detail I'd put down on paper, which had only been meant for me. I wasn't going to buy any excuse or explanation on how he'd "accidentally" read the entire thing. No one had forced him to, or to steal it in the first place. Those were choices he'd made, and now we were both going to have to live with them.

"We have nothing to talk about." My skin was cold and unfeeling. "Give me my journal and get the fuck out. I don't ever want to see you again."

chapter THIRTY-TWO

GRANT

As soon as I handed over Tara's journal, the guy slammed her door in my face.

I stood in the hallway, shouting my apologies through the door, until he yelled back that if I didn't leave, he'd call the police.

My head was a jumble of terrible Afrikaans words, all ones I'd use to describe myself. I'd fucked this up on so many levels, I didn't know how I was going to undo any of it. How I was going to make it right. Was that even possible?

I texted Ruby from the steps outside Tara's apartment building and told her I needed to see her immediately.

> Ruby: I'm at Kyle's.

> Ruby: I mean my place. Come over, you can help us unpack boxes.

My jaw set. I'd forgotten she moved in with him yesterday, and in my foul mood, I didn't want to deal with McAsshole. But I didn't have a choice. I was desperate for her advice, and they were a package deal now. Maybe he'd be able to help.

I'd never been to his apartment before, and when I arrived, my irritation escalated. Not only was Ruby on the far side of town from me now, but she lived in a penthouse. The end unit was all windows and spectacular views of the

Chicago River.

"You look like shit," she said. We stood in the kitchen area beside the marble-topped island. Kyle was nearby, pounding nails into the wall to hang her series of pictures. He looked weird being handy. He was one of those guys who was always put together and polished. Like he'd just finished doing an Instagram photoshoot. He seemed more likely to know how to use a hair dryer than a hammer.

I scrubbed my hand over my face. "Rube, I fucked up."

She looked alarmed. "What'd you do?"

I set my hands on the countertop and hung my head. It was embarrassing to admit it, especially with him hanging around, but at the same time, I deserved it. I was a glutton for punishment right now.

"Tara keeps a journal. It's a long story, and I can't really get into the 'why,' other than I'm a curious motherfucker and a bloody idiot, but . . . I took it." I sighed. "And I read it."

Kyle's hammer stopped mid-swing so he could raise an eyebrow. "You read her diary?"

"Are you insane? What's wrong with you?" Ruby demanded.

"I just told you, I'm a fucking idiot."

She put her hands on her hips and scowled. "Does she know?"

"Oh, she's quite aware."

Ruby rounded the island and put her hands on my arm, shoving me toward the door. "What the fuck are you doing here? Go apologize."

I was nearly twice the size of her and locked my knees, which made me immovable. "You don't think I've done that? I just came from her place. She won't talk to me." I stared at my best friend, hoping she'd have the answers. "What the fuck do I do?"

Her eyes were compassionate and her voice gentle. "Do you love her?"

I hadn't said it out loud, but it was easy. It came without hesitation. "Yes."

"Then you don't give up." She exchanged a look with Kyle. "You keep trying until you find a way to get through to her."

All I wanted was to talk to her. Five minutes to tell her the truth about everything. But I wasn't a fool. I'd hurt her, and she was smart. She wasn't going to let her guard down or let me get near her.

She can't see you if she's blindfolded, and can't avoid you if she's restrained to a table.

Well, that wasn't going to work either. Julius wouldn't let me near her or his club.

My gaze settled on Kyle.

Last year, Ruby had slipped up and mentioned the blind-fold club. It was the first I'd heard of it. She'd been the one to plant the seed in my head and set me in search of the place, even when she said she knew nothing about it and to leave it alone. It had only been a misunderstanding with Kyle, she claimed. So, I knew he was somehow involved, but she had locked up any discussion. It was all attorney-client privilege, according to her.

He was an attorney as well. Would he be able to talk? It was worth a shot.

"Rube," I said, "do you mind giving Kyle and me a minute alone?"

He went wooden. It might have been the first time I'd

used his real name to address him. At least, that was the way they both were acting.

She hesitated, unsure. "Uh, are you going to be nice?"

I eked out half of a smile. "Yes."

She gave me the evil eye. "Okay . . . I guess." She went to him. "What about you? Are you going to be good?"

His tone was loaded with innuendo. "Me? I'm always good."

Her smile was coy as she went into the bedroom and shut the door.

As soon as she was gone, his smile faded, and he looked at me, wary of whatever I was going to say.

"There's a club here in town," I said. "A brothel where the girls are blindfolded."

Kyle's posture went stiff again. "If you say so."

"I went there," I announced. "I wanted to break the story on that place."

The hammer he was holding was thrown down on the counter with a loud clatter. He looked nervous, but also . . . adversarial? "Don't say anything else."

"I lied to get in," I continued, "and negotiated a deal."

He glared at me, his eyes full of fire. "Did you not hear what I just said? Why are you telling me this?"

"Because you're going to get me in there again."

His expression was pure surprise. "What? No. Why?"

I wasn't going to give away Tara's secret any more than I already had. "I can't tell you that."

"No," Kyle snapped a second time. "You're out of your goddamn mind if you think I'm going to help you. I couldn't even if I wanted to—which I don't."

"Why? You have a client who works there?"

His eyes were dark. "I have people in my life, who I care very much about, who are linked to that place."

If I wasn't so desperate, my curious mind would have wanted me to investigate that statement. Instead, my words were weighted. "I do too."

He considered my admission, and a jolt of surprise went through him. His voice was low. "Fuck. Tara's last name is Vannett, isn't it?"

My pulse leaped forward. "You know her?"

"No." He gave a hard, evaluating look. "But if I help you, you have to promise you drop the story."

"Easy. Already done."

He dug his phone out of his pocket and began typing.

"What are you doing?"

"Checking with a friend," he said. "He used to run the club, so he might have some advice."

Now my pulse kicked into overdrive. I'd read her journal, which meant I had a good idea who Kyle was texting. My mind raced as I tried to come up with a plan.

"If that's Joseph," I said, "I need you to introduce us."

Joseph Monsato met me for dinner at one of the restaurants he owned.

He was ten years older than I was, a precise man with dark hair and sharp eyes. As he stared at me, they cut deep and peeled back my layers. After introductions, it didn't take me long to confess everything. What parts I left out, the secrets that weren't mine to tell, he filled in. He already knew Regan was FBI.

I told the truth, no matter how terrible it made me look, and threw myself at his mercy.

He'd started the blindfold club and been Tara's first Dominant. He knew her better than most people and was the best judge on whether I had a chance at winning her back.

"I need some time to think about this," he said, "and what's best for her." He picked up his wine glass but paused before taking a sip. "What will you do if I say I don't think she should trust you again, and it's better if you walk away?"

My heart was a heavy stone in my chest, leaving hardly any room for hope. "If you convince me that's what she needs, I would do it."

He looked pleased. "That was the right answer. I may have an idea."

After dinner, I went home, and like any intelligent, high-functioning adult, I handled my situation irresponsibly.

I got drunk.

The first thing I did was draft a resignation letter. I hated my job, and life was too short to spend it doing something I despised. Morgan could become someone else's problem. I had an education, experience, and a great work ethic. I'd saved enough money that I could survive for a while as I searched for new employment. When I sobered up in the morning, I'd see how I felt about it. If I still thought it was the right decision, I'd turn the letter in.

And the second thing I did, since I was already sitting at

my laptop and had my word processing program open, was start a new document and begin typing. It would be my journal, only my handwriting was shit. So, whatever I was feeling or thinking, I put it down on the page.

It was supposed to be about me, but all I could think about was Tara. She lived how I wanted to live. She knew who she was and what she wanted, and fuck, it was inspiring. I typed, and typed, until my eyes were blurry, and the red squiggly mark underlined every third word. I closed the computer, crawled into my bed, and sent her a text message.

Grant: I'm sorry. I wish I could take it back.

Tara: Don't text me again. I'm blocking this number.

Joseph had told me to give her time, but I should have known better. When it came to her, I had no self-control.

chapter THIRTY-THREE

TARA

Monday morning, I had the worst hangover of my life. I'd committed the cardinal sin of "beer before liquor" and therefore, had never been sicker. I spent a good portion of the morning in bed, and the remainder of the day I continued to wallow.

It was strange how fast Grant had become a fixture in my life, and then disappeared. I'd cut him off just as quickly as I'd let him in.

On Tuesday, there was coupon in my mailbox for the pizza place he liked, and I went to hang it on my fridge, only to remember I didn't like it enough to order a large pizza for myself.

Wednesday, flowers arrived. Classic red roses with baby's breath and greenery, in a tall square vase. The card simply said, *I'm sorry.* I was still angry enough with him that I considered tossing all of it in the garbage, but it had been forever since I'd had fresh flowers in my place, and the arrangement was gorgeous.

I didn't want to admit to myself the real reason I kept them. I was a sucker for a romantic gesture. *Come on, Tara.* Apology flowers from boys were cliché, and I was a twenty-eight-year-old woman. Hadn't I outgrown that shit by now?

I sipped my coffee as I stared at the velvety red roses.

Apparently not.

A package was delivered on Thursday from the Law Offices of Sterns and Clifford. More paperwork from *Dance Dreams*? I'd already signed my life away, what was left to do? It was odd, though, that the address was on Wacker Drive here in Chicago, and not from New York. I tore open the end of the thick mailer and dumped the contents on my coffee table.

It was a cover sheet and a thin book, covered in black cardstock and bound with brass brads. There wasn't a title on it. I picked up the sheet and read.

> *I know you don't want to hear from me. I will do my best to honor that after this letter.*
>
> *I can't even begin to tell you how sorry I am. On Sunday, I sat down at my computer to organize my thoughts and try to explain why I did it. I could give you an excuse how I'd only intended to read the entry about our night, but then I was too fucking curious to stop, and was riveted by your words from start to finish.*
>
> *But there's no excuse. I did it because I wanted to know more about you, even the parts you chose not to share with me yet. I violated your trust and am ashamed I couldn't be patient enough to let you make that decision.*
>
> *I sat down at my computer and intended to write this letter, but something else came*

out. I went to the club looking for a story, and on Sunday night, I found it. It just wasn't the one I was expecting.

Enclosed you will find the first three chapters.

Shove it in a drawer. Set it on fire. Rewrite it. Or publish it. It's yours to do whatever you'd like. I haven't and won't share it with anyone else. It's not my story—it's yours.

If you'd like me to continue or have notes, I am here for whatever you need.

-Grant

P.S. I'm sorry for using one of Ruby's envelopes, but I wanted to make sure you read this.

I dropped the letter, letting it flutter to the table, and snatched up the book, flipping to the title page. It was written in simple, unassuming font.

THE BLINDFOLD CLUB

by Tara Vannett

- based on a true story –

Intrigued, I turned to the first page and began reading.

Usually when I arrived at the club, I went to the lounge, changed into my robe, and chatted with the other girls about how their week had gone, but tonight I went into Julius's office.

He was sitting at his desk, and the wall of monitors behind him was dark since the club wasn't open yet. When he saw me, he motioned for me to have a seat. "Shut the door."

Julius's door was always open. Was he firing me?

I pulled it closed but refused to sit. Just like everyone else, he'd been lying to me. I'd texted him a week ago from the back of my cab after leaving Regan's apartment, tears stinging my eyes. I'd asked if he knew who she really worked for, and he'd answered by telling me it was complicated.

Which meant yes.

"How did you find out?" he asked softly.

"Her boyfriend slipped."

He steepled his fingers together, his elbows on the desktop. "I'm sorry I couldn't tell you. Nobody knows, and I'm not supposed to talk about it." His expression was reassuring. "You're safe. They do their thing and we do ours, and everyone stays happy." He eyed the black book I had clutched in my hands. "What's that?"

I dropped it on his desk with a thud. "The first three chapters of the book I'm thinking about publishing."

He leaned forward, picked it up, and opened to the first page, only to pull back like the book had burned his fingers. His stunned gaze snapped to meet mine.

"Read it," I said. "Change what you need to, so you're covered."

"They won't let you publish it."

An evil smile curled on my lips. "Unless you tell them, I don't know how they can stop me."

I didn't give him a chance to respond. Instead, I turned, tugged open his door, and walked across the hall to the lounge.

A large part of me didn't want to be working tonight. It felt wrong and weirdly disrespectful, but I didn't know any other way to make my feelings go away. I just wanted one evening where my thoughts were quiet, my body numb. To escape thinking about the South African who'd broken my heart.

I scanned the board to see my room number for the evening, then checked again to confirm Regan wasn't working tonight. We hadn't talked since I'd left her place. She'd texted and called, and I'd left them all unanswered. Eventually, I would deal with it, but she'd kept me in the dark. It'd do her some good to see how it felt.

"Hey," Nina said in her husky voice. "I haven't seen you in a while. What have you been up to?"

She hadn't changed yet into her robe. She wore a black leather skirt that fit her so perfectly, it looked painted on, and a black tuxedo jacket. It was buttoned, but she wasn't wearing a bra, and it was miles of skin and cleavage.

"Nina," I gasped, "you look fucking hot tonight."

She gave me a genuine, flattered smile. "Aw, thanks, girl."

She scanned my outfit, maybe wanting to return the compliment, but it would be wasted. I'd put on heels, black cigarette pants, and a purple backless top. The bare minimum of effort.

"You should probably get changed," she said, her gaze drifting to the white silk robe hanging in cubby number five.

It finally clicked why she was dressed, when all the other girls were in their robes already. I grabbed the hem of my shirt and tugged it up over my head. "Are you my assistant again tonight?"

She nodded. Seeing me topless had no effect on her. At this point, we'd seen it all, and many times too. She leaned in, lowering her voice so the other girls wouldn't hear. "Rumor is your appointment tonight is with somebody special. Julius won't even put his name on the schedule."

My hands slowed. "Mr. Gold?"

"Fuck, no. Someone new."

There was relief it wouldn't be Katzenberg, but otherwise I didn't feel the excitement I would have a month ago. I moved like a robot, striping off my clothes and slipping into the robe. It used to feel luxurious, but tonight it was cheap and scratchy on my skin.

When I was ready, we went down the stairs and turned into room five. My complacency continued as I shed the robe and climbed on the table. The chandelier overhead didn't seem as bright. The crystals were dull and ordinary.

"You okay?" Nina asked as she handed me the blindfold. "You seem . . . unhappy."

I was unhappy. Last week I'd been ready to walk away from this place for Grant. And now, here I was one week later, already back up on the table. Like it had all meant nothing. I donned the blindfold and tugged it over my eyes, not wanting to see the concern in hers.

"I'm fine," I announced, telling myself more than her. I

just needed to get through tonight. Then I'd get my life back to the way things used to be, and in a few weeks, I'd head to New York for *Dance Dreams* selection week.

She Velcro-ed closed the ribbons around my wrists and radioed to Julius that room five was all set.

I'd hoped that putting on the blindfold and the restraints would have calmed me, but it had the opposite effect. There was nothing else to focus on, other than my thoughts, and nowhere to run.

Why had Grant signed my name on the book he was writing, and not his own? Or at least, both of ours? We'd collaborated so well on the audition piece, but maybe seeing our names together would have been too much.

Once Nina had walked to the wingback chair in the corner and sat, the room was quiet as a tomb. I wanted it to feel like that. To be dead inside when the man came through the door and offered his hard-earned money to use my body however he wanted.

This feels fucking wrong.

I was a breath away from telling Nina I'd changed my mind and didn't want to take the client, when the door creaked open and footsteps came in.

"Oh my God," she gasped.

We'd had plenty of celebrities come through the club, and we didn't get starstruck, so it was fucking weird to hear her start off negotiations this way. It'd been a few weeks since we'd been partnered together, though. Was this some new tactic she was using? She'd really sold it. Her pleased surprise had sounded real.

Her high heels tapped across the floor in a hurried

rhythm, like she was running at him. "It's so good to see you. Congrats on the wedding!" Her voice muffled. Was she . . . hugging him? "I saw the pictures online, and they looked amazing."

"Thank you," a very male, very familiar voice said.

"What are you doing here?"

"I need to talk to Tara. Would you excuse us?"

My heart suspended so I could hear better. That voice couldn't be who I thought it was. He didn't come here when the club was operating, and he certainly wouldn't come as a client.

"Of course." Her heels clicked away.

When the door opened, he spoke again. "Oh, and Nina? Tell Julius to cut the feed. No cameras in here tonight."

Had she nodded? There was no response from her, other than the door closing.

The room was silent, and I whispered it. "Joseph?"

"Hey, honey."

The straps were undone as he released my wrists, one then the other. I clawed at my blindfold, pushing it up and blinked as he came into view.

I hadn't seen him in months. He'd kept distance from the club he'd created for the sake of his wife, not wanting scandal that could damage her company. And physically, he looked exactly as he always did. Broad shouldered, dark hair, deep eyes.

His wedding ring glinted as he placed the robe over my body, and I marveled at the sight of it. I'd expected the silver ring to look out of place, but it didn't. He'd sworn for years he'd never marry, and told me repeatedly that nothing lasted forever.

Oh, how he'd changed.

She'd done that—taught this old dom some new tricks.

"What are you doing here?" I cried, holding the robe against me as I sat up.

His expression was an enigma. "I came for you."

I glanced around the room, confused. "Where's Noemi?"

They'd eloped on a beach in Hawaii a few months ago. I'd known about it for two weeks before the pictures leaked online, and Nina had been right. They'd looked amazing. Standing on a beach, her in a white dress, both of them gazing at each other with so much love.

"She wanted to come, believe me." Something clouded in his eyes, then vanished. "We haven't told anyone yet. It's too early to say anything, but she has horrible morning sickness."

My mouth dropped open with surprise, then widened into a huge grin. "Oh my God. Joseph, congrats. You guys sure didn't waste any time."

"Our situation is complicated. We've been trying for a while." He made a face. "I mean to say, thank you. We're excited, and I'll be much more excited when she's not miserable for ninety percent of the day." He grabbed the lapels of his black suit and tugged them, getting his jacket to hang properly on his shoulders. "We need to focus on you right now. I came tonight to make you an offer."

His eyes were intense, and I found it difficult to breathe. "What kind of offer?"

He didn't break my gaze as he reached into his suit pocket and pulled something out. He laid it beside me on the table, and it squeezed the air from my body. It was black leather with a steel clasp at the back.

A collar.

"One night," he said. "You give me total control. I can't promise you'll like everything I tell you to do, but I know you're struggling right now, and I think I can help. I can promise you'll feel better when we're done."

Before I could even consider it, my thoughts went to Noemi. "Your wife is okay with this?"

"Yeah." Heat warmed his expression. "If she gets to feeling better, she'll FaceTime. She wants to watch."

"Oh." My gaze drifted from him down to the band of leather. I'd only been Joseph's submissive for a month, and that had been years ago. He'd never collared me then, and he was married now. "Why?"

He followed my gaze. I'd forgotten how good he was at reading me. "The collar? So there's no mistaking who's in charge." He was so serious tonight, all business. "I'll step out for a minute and let you make your decision. If you accept, put it on, and we can begin."

I didn't know what to say as he moved toward the door and opened it.

He turned over his shoulder as he crossed the threshold. "Think carefully. If you wear that, you're agreeing to my rules. It only comes off when I say so, or with a safe word."

And then he disappeared, pulling the door shut behind him. I frowned and pulled my arms through the robe, cinching the sash tight around my waist. As far as I could tell, Joseph had never lied to me. He'd been the one to set me free, and my submissive side wanted to fling herself at his offer.

But he'd also told me I wouldn't like some of the things

he'd demand.

Joseph wasn't cruel, but he was . . . intense. He lived to push. I was fragile right now. What if his pushing made me break?

I stared at the collar. It was a simple piece of leather and metal, but it carried heavy meaning. Rules, and pleasure, and likely pain. I'd come to the club to be numb, and he was offering the opposite.

But if I didn't do this, I'd be filled with regret. Worse—I'd still be the same way I was now. He'd promised I'd feel better, and he'd always delivered on his promises.

I picked up the collar and slipped it around my neck, trembling as the cold steel kissed my skin.

chapter THIRTY-FOUR

TARA

Joseph had only been gone a minute, but I waited in tense anticipation for a century for his return. What would he do to me? Would I find release and be able to purge the sadness from my fractured heart?

My breath hitched as the door opened. He stood in the hallway, his hand still on the doorknob as he peered into the room, and his gaze found the dark collar ringing my neck.

His posture straightened, his shoulders pulled back. His expression filled with satisfaction, and power rolled through him. Shivers of pleasure shook my body. He could do that in a single look. Let me know how pleased he was with me. It flooded me with warmth.

His smile reached deep into his eyes. "You've made the right decision."

He stepped into the room, and people trailed behind him. Silas, Regan . . .

. . . and Grant.

I scrambled backward on the table, so close to the edge I nearly fell off. "No," I cried. "Stop. Red."

"Yes," Joseph's tone was plain. "Those are all safe words you can use once we get started. But first, we need to go over the ground rules."

He stood in front of me, and Silas and Regan were

together on my left, their hands linked. Grant lingered alone near the back of the room, his eyes fixed on me. I tore my gaze away, refusing to look at him. I focused back on Joseph, and anger clenched my stomach.

"No, Joseph—"

His expression went hard, and I'd swear I could feel his eyes tugging on my collar as a reminder. "It's 'Sir' tonight." He turned and spoke to the rest of the room. "And that goes for all of you."

Holy. Shit.

He'd given me the collar, he'd said, so I wouldn't mistake who was in charge. Because in this room, there were four dominants, and I'd submitted to each of them.

"At no point," he continued, his voice demanding attention, "will you speak, unless you are told to do so."

I swallowed hard. Silas looked unaffected, but Regan's gaze dropped to the floor. She'd maintained a position of power here at the club, and being told what to do by anyone, especially a man, would be a struggle.

"You all agreed to this. I give the orders, and I expect them to be fucking followed."

"No," I said. "Stop. Red."

Joseph came to me, and I expected disappointment. I was safe-ing out so early, but this was a different Dominant than the one I'd had before. His edges were sharper, but the rest was smoother. Softer. He gently grabbed my shoulders, making it so I couldn't look anywhere else. He was forty now, but time had only made him more handsome.

He spoke quietly, just for me. "I'll always respect those words, but you're safe. I'm not going to let anything bad happen. You're wearing my collar, Tara."

It meant my safety, both physically and emotionally, were his responsibility tonight. I had surrendered to him. I gazed up at the chandelier, trying to drain back the tears in my eyes. "I don't think I can do this."

"I know you can. Everyone came for you. We're all here for you."

I shouldn't have done it, but I couldn't help myself. I looked at Grant.

His attention had never left me. There could have been a million people standing between us. The room could have burst into flames, and he wouldn't have flinched. Right now, only I existed.

He wore a classic blue suit and a bright white dress shirt. No tie. He looked amazing, but also like a fucking liar. He'd told me he'd do his best to make sure I wouldn't hear from him again, unless I wanted that.

So, what the fuck was he doing here?

Then again, Joseph had said no one was allowed to talk. Grant's eyes were filled with a thousand words, but he'd left them unspoken. Technically, he was keeping his promise.

I shifted back to Joseph, whose expression was pure persuasion. "Trust me," he coaxed.

He'd never given me a reason not to. It was a ghost of a word. "Okay."

"Good." He kissed my forehead, right at my hairline, as he released me. It wasn't sexual or romantic. It was a reward and helped to define our roles. He turned his attention to Grant. "Bring in the chairs and shut the door."

I had my legs tucked beside me and my hands in my lap,

worrying a cuticle on my thumb, as he disappeared into the hall for a moment and returned with two black folding chairs, one in each arm. He set them up side-by-side on the wall opposite the white wingback chair, then returned to the door and pulled it closed.

Trembles crawled along my legs, but I couldn't tell if it was with trepidation or excitement. The closed door signified the start of the scene.

"Sit," Joseph ordered Silas and Regan, motioning to the pair of chairs.

They complied, but neither looked comfortable. Regan's back was straight, and she was literally on the edge of her seat. She wanted to be somewhere else. She hated this, and yet, she remained.

Everyone's here for you.

Joseph took my hand and helped me down off the table, then nodded toward the series of drawers beneath it. "Two sets of handcuffs, please."

Oh, God. I tightened with apprehension, making my hands clumsy as I opened the top drawer. I knew in my gut these restraints weren't for the people sitting, and they definitely were not for Joseph. That left me and Grant. Was he going to handcuff us together and force intimacy on us?

I pulled out the metal ones, but Joseph shook his head. "The soft ones with the longer chain. In the back."

He knew the contents of each drawer. It wasn't his club anymore, but he still carefully curated each item in the room, per Julius's request.

I found which ones Joseph wanted and placed them in his outstretched hand. I must have looked nervous, because amusement dashed through his eyes. "You think either of these are for you? You'd be wrong." His head swung toward Grant. "You'll sit there."

He meant the white upholstered chair.

Grant didn't hesitate. He strode to the chair that looked a throne in comparison to the others in the room, but I'd learned long ago, looks could be deceiving in Joseph's scenes. If his sub was comfortable, he wasn't pushing hard enough.

"This one," he said as he gestured to Grant, "struggles with self-control, so we're going to make it easier on him." He passed back one set of the handcuffs to me. "One on the wrist, and one on the back chair leg."

I was frozen in place while I watched it unfold. Grant didn't look at Joseph as he pulled back his suit coat sleeve and offered his wrist. It was powerfully sexy, made more so because his piercing stare was locked on me. It announced he would do anything for me.

Including submitting to another man.

The muscles low in my belly tightened, creating a dull ache.

Once Joseph had the wrist cuff done, he took a knee beside the chair and fastened the other end around the foot of the chair. His sharp tone was a threat. "Do I need to repeat myself?"

"No, Sir."

I went to the chair and bit down on the inside of my cheek. I didn't know if I could touch him and not break apart. My body clamored for him, while my head demanded I stay far away. My heart was a battleground, and neither side could claim victory yet.

I ripped open the Velcro and wrapped it quickly around his wrist, touching him as little as possible. Relief swept through me when it was done, and I bent to finish my task. Only I'd been so focused, I hadn't realized he'd dropped his arm over the side of the armrest, and he brushed his knuckle against my cheekbone.

I jerked away, falling backward on my bottom, and a panicked sob burst from my lips. It had been a featherlight caress, but it both lit me on fire and scared the hell out of me.

"I'm sorry," Grant whispered.

For the touch? For everything?

Joseph must have predicted Grant would try something, because he was ready, waiting with a riding crop he'd retrieved from the middle drawer. It swung through the air and slapped across the top of Grant's thigh.

His eyes went white with surprise, and he hissed in discomfort, flinching from the strike.

"Not another word," Joseph barked. He extended a hand and helped me to stand. His evaluating gaze took me in from head to toe. "You all right?"

With everything I'd done in the club, it was ridiculous that a single, innocuous touch had me unraveled. I refused to let it get to me. "Yes, Sir."

He led me to the front of the table and asked me to sit, and when I did so, he set his sights on the couple. Or more specifically, Regan.

"You. Come here."

He didn't use names often in scenes. They had to be earned. Until then, you had to work for his respect.

But it was clear who he was calling up, and she stood

reluctantly, smoothing her nervous palms down the sides of her black pencil skirt. Her face was a mask, but her eyes gave away her fear, especially when she risked a glance at the riding crop he held at his side.

"Face Tara," he ordered.

She did. Her makeup was muted, softer than the way she usually wore it when working at the club. Her hair was down. She looked more like the woman I knew outside of this place.

Joseph's tone was the same as a parent talking to a disobedient child. "Is honesty important between a dom and a sub?"

"Yes," she said quietly.

He lifted an eyebrow. "I can't hear you."

"Yes, Sir," she corrected, louder this time.

"You violated this trust, didn't you?"

Her blue eyes flooded with remorse. "Yes, Sir."

"So, what should we do about that?" His expression was dark, wicked excitement. "What happens if your sub lies to you?"

Her tremble was so subtle, I barely noticed it, but Joseph did. His eyes flared with power. Regan barely squeaked it out. "She gets punished."

He seized a fistful of her hair and jerked her head back. It was rough enough, it startled everyone, and most of all her. She gasped, but it didn't seem to be in pain—only shock. Silas was out of his chair, but she put up a hand, signaling for him to stop.

This was a test. If Silas couldn't handle this, he'd never make it through the next part.

"Tell him it's all right," Joseph commanded.

292 | NIKKI SLOANE

"It's all right," she said instantly, her voice tight. With her head held back, she struggled to get her gaze on him. "I've got this."

Joseph's attention drifted to Silas. "I don't have an issue with you." He turned back to the table then nodded toward Grant. "But these three? They're all guilty to some degree, and you need to let me work through it. Understood?"

Silas didn't look happy as he begrudgingly lowered back into his chair. His hand curled into a fist as it rested on his knee.

But Joseph looked pleased. "Yeah, we've got some shit to work out, don't we, *Andrea*?"

I blinked against my confusion. Why was he calling her—

Oh. Hurt seeped in. She was undercover, which meant I didn't even know her real name. Fresh betrayal stung my insides, prickling my eyes.

"Can I say something?" she begged.

When Joseph released her with a shove, it sent her flying into me, and her hands landed on my legs. Her palms were warm against my bare skin, and it tingled where we were connected, even though I didn't want it to.

"Speak," he ordered.

"It's Regan. The person I am when I'm here, when I'm with Silas . . ." She gazed at me with desperation. "When I'm with you—that's the real me. I hid my whole life until I became Regan." Her expression was pure and bare. "Andrea is the lie. You know the real me."

I didn't have a reason to trust her, but this, I believed.

It was silent for a long moment, until Joseph broke it with his cold command. "Pull up your skirt and bend over."

chapter THIRTY-FIVE

TARA

Was Regan really willing to do this? For me? She'd do what she hated for the chance to earn my forgiveness.

My heart leapt into my throat as she reached down, grabbed the sides of her skirt, and tugged the fabric up to her waist, her ballet pink panties exposed. Her skin was so pale and the fabric so thin, she was essentially naked.

I had to lie back as Regan leaned over me, preparing to receive Joseph's punishment.

"You're like me," Joseph said. "Good at reading people. You might even be better. Anyone else, and I would have caught them. But you," he lifted the crop, sending my pulse soaring, "slipped right past me. I let you into my club, and it created a mess for Julius."

The crop sliced through the air. Its violent stroke ended in a soft crack, and she jolted.

My mouth fell open. Not so much that she'd taken a hit, but that I was certain Joseph had pulled up at the last second and delivered a sweetheart blow. Barely more than a tap.

"That one was for me," he said. "This one is for her."

And on that strike, he did not hold back. The thin rod made a whooshing noise as it came down, and the sound of impact was very different. It was a sharp, biting crack, and it caught her by surprise. Pain colored her stunned eyes and her breath cut off.

Silas was on his feet again. I could see over Regan's shoulder, and his death glare was pointed at Joseph. He waited, ready to pounce like a predator. All she had to do was say the word. But she didn't.

Joseph gently laid the crop across my lips, and as I'd been trained to do, I bit down, holding it in place, at the ready for him.

"Tell her you're sorry," he demanded.

"I'm sorry," Regan said between two breaths, recovering.

"Tell her you had no choice. Tell her you wanted to say something but couldn't."

"It's true. I wanted to tell you so badly, but I wasn't allowed."

"Ask if she can forgive you, and in time, let you work to earn back her trust."

Regan softened into me. She ran her hands over the silk robe, seeking out a better connection, and pressed her face against my stomach. She turned to the side, her red hair spilling over me. "Forgive me."

I had no idea where he'd struck her. If it was across the prefect cheeks of her ass, it probably didn't hurt much anymore. It would be red and hot to the touch, but the pain would fade quickly. If he'd whipped her across the backs of her thighs, she'd still be experiencing the dull, painful ache. It seemed to linger in that spot.

I couldn't tell from her reaction. The only pain she seemed to be feeling was what she'd caused me. As her submissive, I lived to bring her pleasure, and watching her suffer was awful. It wasn't necessary any longer.

He grabbed the crop and lifted it away. "Speak."

"I forgive you," I whispered instantly.

She murmured it into the silk. "Thank you."

Her hands continued their slow slide, working their way beneath my robe. She pushed the silk out of her way, kissing along the top of my thigh. Joseph set the riding crop back on my lips, and once again, the taste of the cane filled my mouth.

Regan was content to explore and work her way toward my pussy, her hands at the knot of my robe, until she remembered she wasn't in charge. She looked up at him, begging permission with her eyes.

"After you put your skirt down, yes. She's earned a little reward." He stepped back, as if letting Regan have the stage with me. Silas sank down into his seat as she shimmied her skirt back into place and moved eagerly to undo my robe.

The air was cool against my skin as she pulled the fabric back, and my nipples perked instantly. Regan didn't waste time teasing. She was ravenous, and as soon as her head was between my legs, her tongue found me.

I clenched the crop so hard with my teeth, I wondered if it would be permanently bent when Joseph pulled it from my lips. Her mouth was hot and incessant. It had me writhing and whining as the men watched, and I couldn't imagine a more erotic image.

I clutched handfuls of the silk by my side. What did Grant think about this? Did he enjoy watching a woman go down on me? The one who had forbidden him from doing it? I wanted to know if he was turned on.

The whole time we'd been together, he'd known I worked here. He'd read my entire journal. And yet he hadn't run away—he'd come back for more. Didn't that mean something?

No. I refused to let it. I closed my eyes and enjoyed the stroke of her lush tongue. Goosebumps blossomed on my legs, and tingles raced along my spine.

Joseph snapped his fingers over my face, making my eyes fly open. "Look at him," he demanded, pointing to Grant. "Let him see how much you like her tongue in your pussy."

It was an order, so I had to obey. I lifted my head and turned to look at him.

It was a miracle the rod didn't snap in two in my mouth. The way he fucking looked at me, while restrained to that big, white chair, it nearly sent me over the edge. Desire was in his expression, but so was love.

You aren't allowed to love me, I wanted to yell. *You forfeited that right.* But I couldn't say anything because the riding crop was nestled in my teeth, and I wasn't sure if I believed it, anyway.

When I was panting and dangerously close to coming, Joseph put a hand on Regan's shoulder, easing her back. "That's enough for the moment. Go back to your seat."

Normally, she would have delighted in denying my orgasm, but she looked disappointed tonight. She ran her hand over her lips, wiping away my arousal, and shuffled back to her chair beside Silas.

The crop was pulled from my mouth. "Up," Joseph said.

As I stepped down from the table, the open robe slipped off a shoulder. He caught it, pulled it the rest of the way off, and left me standing naked in the center of the room as he went to hang it on the back of the door.

I held my head high. He'd taught us girls at the club to realize confidence was sexy, and better yet, powerful. I felt that way, until Joseph gave me my next set of instructions.

"Unbutton Grant's shirt."

My shoulders slumped. How the fuck was I going to do that? He was chained to the chair, and I was naked, and I'd have to lean over him to do it . . .

The riding crop slapped against my breast, right across a nipple, drawing a gasp from me.

"We're waiting."

Fuck Joseph and his authoritarian tone. He was so good at making me yo-yo between being angry to thrilled and back again in the same scene. I stormed over to Grant's chair. If I was going to do this, I'd do it in the most unsexy way possible. I grabbed his shirt and plucked at the buttons furiously, not making eye contact.

This time, Joseph's crop landed on the back of my thigh, and I yelped.

"Slower," he hissed.

It was pointless to fight. He always got his way. I slowed my movements, undoing one button at a time. It was unavoidable, since our faces were only inches away, that our gazes met, like a magnetic force pulled us together. And the second Grant realized I was looking at him, the words tumbled from his mouth.

"Tara, if this is all we—"

I jumped out of the way as the crop came down and smacked across his thigh. It wasn't cute or playful or even corrective. This was punishment, plain and simple. Joseph would not be disobeyed or lose control of a scene, and he needed Grant to understand.

"Motherfucker," Grant groaned under his breath.

"Since you can't control your mouth, I'll do it for you." Joseph's gaze swung to me. He didn't have to ask. I went to the top drawer, pushing aside the other items until I found the piece he wanted.

Grant's eyes nearly bulged out of his head as I approached with the black ball, a leather strap on each side. I wasn't a fan of wearing a ball gag. It made my jaw hurt and turned me into a drooling mess, but the idea of Grant in one? That wasn't so bad.

"Wait—" he started.

I didn't. I shoved the ball in his mouth, found the right notch for the correct fit, and did the buckle behind his head.

"If you want to stop," Joseph tapped the crop repeatedly over the palm of his own hand, "stomp your foot. I'll undo the handcuffs, and you'll leave immediately. There will be no discussion. Understood?"

Grant's eyes were loud and unhappy, but he nodded.

Joseph traced the tip of the crop over the last button on Grant's shirt I hadn't yet undone. "Finish. Then I want his pants and underwear down around his ankles."

The room became a vacuum. Both Grant and I inhaled sharply. Shouldn't I have been glad I'd no longer be the only naked one in the room? I couldn't feel anything but concern. The rules tonight were Joseph's. I'd never seen him play with other men, but I'd heard rumors back when he ran the club. He was omnisexual, and before Noemi, he'd fuck anyone with a pulse.

My hands shook as I undid the final button. I knelt on the ground, the hard floor unforgiving on my knees, and focused on Grant's belt. My blood roared in my ears, and I was only dimly aware Joseph was at the table, rummaging around in drawers. How deep would he go? And was he aware Grant was still new to all of this?

A grunt came from the man before me as I slid down his zipper. He wasn't hard, but the brush of my hand obviously felt good. I tried to ignore it and complete my task. He helped by lifting his hips as I worked his pants and underwear down. He was a fool for wanting to help. Joseph's punishment of Regan had only been a taste of what he could do, and to be the dominant in charge of four people? It was amazing Joseph hadn't already power tripped right into domspace.

I sat back on my heels and admired the view.

Grant's suit coat was still on, but his shirt was wide open, and his pants were bunched around his shoes. His bare, beautiful chest was working fast, like his heart was beating in overtime and he was struggling to keep up with it. His semi-hard cock lay across his leg.

He wasn't as dominant as Regan—at least, not yet. But being vulnerable like he was would be hard on anyone, and worse for someone who liked control. I wasn't supposed to feel bad for him. He'd broken my heart, and I wanted to be petty and vindictive.

Yet . . . I couldn't.

Just like with Regan, it was difficult for me to see him uncomfortable. I wanted to ease the strain.

Joseph had collected whatever he was looking for and moved to Silas and Regan. His instructions were given quickly and too quietly for me to hear. But as he turned away and crossed the room to return to me, I saw Regan's hand undoing Silas's zipper.

When I realized what Joseph was holding, my mouth went dry. Surely the vibrator was for me, but I hoped the plug and the bottle of lube were also, and not for Grant.

"Hey, there, big boy," Joseph teased, lifting an eyebrow as he stared unabashedly at the other man. Grant's head swung away, embarrassed, although he shouldn't have been. Joseph had meant it as a compliment.

He squatted beside me and set his items on the floor, the plug on its base so the tip pointed upward. His expression turned serious. "You lied to this man. Did you say you were sorry?"

"What he did was worse."

Displeasure flashed over him. "Answer me. Yes or no."

I was irritated. "No, Sir."

"That tone will get you in trouble." He studied me, as if unsure how to proceed. "Tell him you're sorry."

I turned my insincere eyes toward Grant and said it devoid of meaning. "I'm sorry."

"Keep digging that hole, Tara. Tell him your sorry again, and this time, you'll do it while he's in your mouth."

Oh, *fuck*. I split in two. I didn't want to, and oh, how did I. Going down on him had been against the rules. He was handcuffed to the chair and gagged and at my mercy. I could do this.

I placed one hand on his knee, and as I reached for him, Joseph clarified his instructions. "Just the tip."

It was evil, and I loved this kind of punishment, where it felt good, but just not good *enough*. It didn't satisfy, it only made you hungry for more. I gripped Grant's swelling cock by the base, steadying him, and slowly push my lips down on the head.

He groaned through his gag. The pleasure was enough to make him throb and harden against the tip of my tongue. I mumbled my apology, which sounded stupid, but seemed to appease Joseph.

"Get on all fours," he said. "I want to play with you as you finish your apology."

Now that Grant was fully hard, his dick stood at attention, its slight curve angling toward the ceiling, and I wouldn't need a hand on him. I placed my palms flat on the ground, putting my ass in the air, and lowered my mouth on him once more.

The head of the wand vibrator was set against my clit, but not turned on. "Fuck him with your mouth, but just the head, and look at him while you do it."

The vibrator buzzed to life, and the pleasure was instant. I did exactly as told, eager now. I sucked on Grant, hollowing my cheeks, and watched lust twist in his eyes. I flicked my tongue, I traced the ridge, and when Joseph told me to, I ran my tongue down the sensitive underside.

I kissed the hard column of flesh, smiling as he jerked from the simple press of my lips. His moans and grunts were muffled by the ball in his mouth, and shiny drool dripped down, landing on his chest. The Velcro on the cuffs creaked as he pushed against them. He wanted to use his hands. Probably to hold my head steady so he could push deeper into my mouth. He rocked his hips, trying to gain ground, but I met his actions with my own, never letting him get further past my lips

The vibrator felt so good, I was drunk off it. But as I

teased Grant, Joseph teased me, pulling back and reminding me I didn't have power over anyone else. I was just a tool for him, which he was currently using to dominate Grant.

The buzzing ceased, and my body wanted to riot, but I held my position. When I was good, good things happened to me.

Cold lube was dripped onto my body and ran down between my crack, and breath tightened in my lungs when I felt the tip of the plug prodding. Grant's breath came and went rapidly through his nose as his wild gaze bounced between my eyes and what the man behind me was doing.

"That's a good girl," Joseph said, his voice like velvet.

I shivered with the praise, but also the strange, yet not unpleasant, sensation of the plug as he slid it ever-so-slowly inside me, all the way to the base. As soon as it was done, the vibrator was switched on and set back at its place on my clit.

I whimpered with satisfaction.

"Feels good, doesn't it?" Joseph whispered. "With that plug in your ass?"

God, it did. I pulled off Grant just long enough to answer, and then returned to my task. "Yes, Sir. Thank you."

"All the way down now," he said.

Meaning he wanted me to open my lips and take Grant's cock as deep as I could. His eyes lidded. Was he lust-drunk like me? I flattened my tongue and inched down, all the way until his tip hit the back of my throat.

His moan was loud and desperate, and he tipped his head back for a moment, as if watching me go down on him was too much to endure. I moaned, not just from the vibrations rocketing through my body, but from the way he looked.

From how I was making him feel.

It was dangerous thinking, wanting to please him.

But I did it regardless. I pumped my mouth on him, from base to tip and back again, swirling and cartwheeling my tongue as he groaned and sighed. He throbbed when I ran the edge of my teeth over him. Not enough to hurt. Just enough to give a different sensation.

As I closed in on my orgasm, so did he.

But the vibrator's mechanical hum stopped once more, and it disappeared from my skin.

Joseph straightened. "You two, come here. Silas is going to fuck this pussy."

Oh. My. God.

chapter THIRTY-SIX

GRANT

My jaw hurt, as did the corners of my mouth, from the gag. The cuffs around my wrists were tight and uncomfortable. But none of it mattered because Tara was looking at me. Seeing me.

It also helped that her mouth was wrapped around my cock. Her tongue had my toes curling inside my shoes.

A gamut of emotions knifed through my chest as my gaze went across the room. Jealousy was strong, but so was my curiosity. Carnal fascination. I wanted to watch her fuck another man. The idea was arousing, but what about in reality?

Regan had been slumped over in her seat, her head bobbing up and down on Silas's dick while he had his hands clenched, holding her hair back, but she pulled off him at Joseph's order.

He stood deliberately from his seat, holding up the sides of his suit pants, and strode toward us, her following him. My gaze fell back down to the beautiful woman on her hands and knees, her blonde strands picking up highlights from the chandelier. The only thing she wore was that thick black collar.

Tara's mouth moved on me, generating more heat with each pass. I wasn't allowed to come. Joseph had scripted the evening, giving me a bare outline of how he expected things to happen. He'd left plenty of room for improvisation, though.

Like this gag, and I was pissed about it.

Although this wasn't one of them, I'd given him my limits. I'd told him I was comfortable with him touching me in a non-sexual way, but I was hetero, and this was one area I wasn't curious about. I wasn't into men. Tonight, he made me uneasy, like he wanted to test how far he could push that line.

When Silas knelt behind Tara and ran one hand along her spine, my mind went blank. My body filled with fire. Less jealousy now, more desire. His pants fell from his hips, and he undid the buttons of his shirt, his gaze on Regan who knelt beside him.

Off his suit coat and shirt came, and they were passed to Regan.

His tattoo covered the expanse of his chest, flowing down his arms, and like the artwork he'd put on her, it was intricate and stunning. I didn't look for long, though. Regan handed a condom to him, and as he tore the wrapper open, I focused back on Tara.

She studied me as much as I studied her, wondering how I was going to react. I'd tried to tell her I was into this, but now I'd have the chance to show her. To make her believe, since she didn't trust me.

When Silas was ready, he set a hand on her hip and wedged the other between their bodies. It was unmistakable when he brought them together. Her eyes melted. A moan gurgled out of me. I wanted to tell her it was so hot, but the gag prevented me from forming the words.

All I could do was sit there, strapped to the chair, while she sucked me and took another man inside her body. I

306 | NIKKI SLOANE

hadn't adequately prepared for it. I'd hoped I'd be all right. Possibly enjoy the experience.

But this was so far beyond that.

It was erotic. Pornographic. I nearly came from the sight.

Regan's face was flushed, and her hands slipped over Silas's arm, like she wanted the physical connection to him. She looked so full of sexual tension, she might rip apart at the seams. Joseph stood nearby, watching the scene. He was far more controlled than her and surveyed us like we were merely sufficient, instead of the hottest fucking thing in existence.

Silas established his tempo and latched a hand on her waist, his other going around Regan's waist to hold her close. His expression was full of bliss, like he was savoring both women, but then his gaze drifted up to find mine. The corner of his lips turned up in competitive smile. It was adversarial. He might as well have said, "*Mine.*"

Tara wasn't. The instinct to defend my territory was hard-wired, and the chains snapped taut as I tried to lunge at him.

"Boys," Joseph said, making a tsk-tsk sound. Which was fucking ridiculous. Silas was at least thirty, like me, and I'd stopped being a boy years ago. It was just a way for Joseph to keep us in our place. He took a few steps until he was right beside my chair. "This is your fantasy, isn't it? Him fucking her while you're in her mouth?"

Was he going to make me regret telling him that?

Tara retreated to catch her breath, and she peered up at me with surprise, her cheek resting against the inside of my thigh. Behind her, Silas was driving hard, and the slap of their bodies made her jolt with each thrust.

I moaned as she took me again, and this time, she

seemed to be enjoying it so much, I wondered if she loved it.

"You like it." Joseph said it like he was throwing it in my face. "You love the way she sucks cock when she's getting fucked, don't you?"

I didn't answer. It was getting hard to think, and not coming was taking all of my focus.

He ran his cold fingers down my chest, through the streams of drool I couldn't stop, and lifted his hand away to show me the glossy strands as they dripped from his finger-tips. "You messy fucking thing. You're going to answer me."

He grabbed my nipple between his thumb and the knuckle of his index finger and squeezed. It burned hot un-til he began to twist, and it graduated to full, sharp pain. I groaned into the gag, my teeth clenched down on the rubber.

His voice was loud in my ear. "You fucking love this, don't you?"

There was no other answer. I nodded vigorously, sling-ing more of the embarrassing drool around.

He laughed. "Shit, I love topping men. They're never as strong as women." He released his hold, and the pain shot away. "They give in so easy."

I had no idea how to feel about what he'd just said. The competitor in me wanted to prove him wrong, but bloody fucking hell, that hurt. It had temporarily distracted me from wanting to come, so at least there was that.

Joseph's attention shifted away like he was done with me for now and settled on Tara. "How about you? You like all that dick in you?"

She moaned approval.

"I bet you do, you slut. I bet you want one in your pussy,

and one in your ass."

Abruptly, she pushed back. "Sir."

"What is it?" He was displeased she'd spoken out of turn.

"My knees."

Realization washed down him, and he turned deadly serious. "Silas, stop."

Silas pulled back, and as Joseph helped her to stand, he did the same with Regan, then yanked his pants up to sit low and undone across his hips. There were angry red marks on her knees. The position had been hard to hold, and she was smart to protect her body. Irritation simmered in my chest. What if she had gotten injured? He could have put her dancing in jeopardy, when she was finally getting traction.

"Are you okay?" He sounded deeply concerned.

She stretched her legs out, one and then the other. "Yes, Sir. I'm fine."

Cautious relief glanced through him. "You're sure?" When she nodded, he placed a hand on her arm. "Thank you for telling me."

In a strange way, it felt good to see that beneath the overbearing dominant, he was fallible. Human.

He must have pushed the reset button, though, because his strict persona snapped back into place. He flung a hand at the table. "Silas. Everything off and on your back. Knees at the edge of the table."

The room waited with bated breath as this was done. Was everyone else wondering Joseph's next move, as I was? He picked up the vibrator and the bottle of lube off the floor, handing the lube to Regan, and the vibrator to Tara.

"Put that away and then you'll get on Silas. Face the door

when you do it."

Meaning he wanted her to ride him reverse cowgirl. I dry swallowed, since all my saliva was running the opposite direction and down my chin. I watched as his plan was carried out. And when it was done, the image of Tara sliding down on him, her tits bouncing with the impact, was seared in my mind.

Joseph didn't let them do this for more than a minute. He doled out more instruction, this time to Regan. He put her in charge of final preparations.

The plug was removed from Tara, and Regan disappeared from view behind the table to put it away. Lube was applied, and Silas grunted as his girlfriend stroked her fist down over the condom, coating him.

The end of the table looked to have drawers too, but they weren't. Joseph bent, grabbed a silver handle, and pulled it out, revealing it was a step. When Regan finished cleaning off her hand with a wipe she'd pulled from a dispenser, she climbed up.

With her heels on, it made her nearly level with Tara.

I was dizzy with desire as the women kissed, and it was vertigo as Regan helped ease Tara's ass down on Silas's thick cock. It looked like a lot to take, and she went slow, aided by Regan.

The table was a symphony of moans, and Joseph stood to the side, listening and admiring.

Blood surged through my veins. My heart ran at breakneck speed. It was a decadent, filthy display, and I was torn between wanting to watch and being desperate to join them. Regan was still fully dressed in her skirt, blouse, and heels, lording over the naked couple fucking in front of her on the table.

She threaded her hands through Tara's hair and nipped at her neck. Silas had his hands on Tara's ass, forcing her to rock her hips and ride him. She swayed and rolled with his thrusts, and her unfiltered gaze somehow found mine.

Was I projecting, or was she looking at me like she wanted me to join them too?

I wasn't imagining it, because Joseph picked up on it as well. He undid the buckle at the back of my head, and I spat the gag out, beyond grateful to have it gone. As I ran my tongue over my lips, he continued to release me. He tugged at the Velcro around my left wrist, and it tore open with its scratchy rip, setting my hand loose.

First thing I did was wipe off my chin with the back of my hand, as Joseph released the other.

Second, I fought every desire in me to leap out of the chair. I sat impatiently waiting. He'd undone the handcuffs, but he hadn't set me free. Not yet.

"I think she's ready," he said quietly. He pulled a condom from his pocket and threw it at me. "That's all you're wearing when you get up there." His eyes were hard and nearly black. "Don't fuck this up."

THIRTY-SEVEN

TARA

I allowed myself, just for a moment, to imagine what it would be like if Grant joined us. It was all in my head, a safe place away from my heart. I pictured his mouth on my tits while Regan's was on my neck. His fingers sliding inside me while Silas fucked my ass. Three people all focused on me at once.

I shivered.

Joseph's voice broke through the fog. "Regan. It's Grant's turn."

I tensed, and beneath me, Silas slowed to a stop. Everything else happened too fast. Regan stepped off the stair, and Grant climbed up. He was gloriously naked. The impressions from the gag were fading quickly from his face, and he looked very much like he usually did. Sexy. Beautiful. Like the man I'd fallen in and out of love with.

Wasn't I lying to myself about that last part? I hadn't been able to turn off my feelings for him, no matter what I did, which meant I was still just the teeny-tiniest bit in love with him.

He stood motionless, waiting for direction, but looked ready to take me as soon as Joseph snapped his fingers.

He didn't snap them, but he pointed to the edge of the table and looked at me. "I want your feet here."

I sucked in a breath, knowing what was coming next if I

followed his order, and what would happen if I didn't. I could plead my case that I didn't want my first time with Grant to be like this, but my mind roared back it didn't matter. Because the first time was also supposed to be the last.

I'd spent years separating emotion from sex. Why the fuck couldn't I do it now?

Joseph was annoyed at my delay. "Is what I'm asking you to do physically challenging?"

"No, Sir," I whispered.

"Then do what I fucking said."

That sounded more like the Joseph from three years ago. His dark tone spurred submissive me into compliance. I leaned back, placing my hands on Silas's hard chest, awkwardly unfolded my legs, and slid them forward. I brought my knee up and planted one foot, then the other, while keeping him uncomfortably lodged inside my body.

It opened me up. Made space for Grant to move in. For him to have and share me.

The tremble in my arms had nothing to do with muscle fatigue from supporting my weight, and everything to do with him. Why was his dick hard? Why did he look at me like he was dying to have this?

"Do it," Joseph said.

It was emotional warfare, and Joseph had weaponized Grant against me, and most of me didn't care. We'd been waiting for this moment for so long, how it happened wasn't relevant.

The question hung in Grant's eyes. *Are you sure?*

I pressed my lips together and nodded. He moved in, nudging his tip against me, and then inside.

"Fuck," all of us said as a single unit. Joseph allowed it without discipline.

Tight. That was the only word I possessed, the only thought I had. I was so full, stretched beyond comfort and verging dangerously close to pain. But like most pain I received in this room, it came with pleasure too.

I gasped for breath, swallowing air as Grant advanced, pushing deeper.

I'd had double penetration before, but never with two men. It had always been a toy or a finger subbed in. This was shockingly different. Not just in its physical feeling, but to know I was being shared. Two men taking their pleasure from me at the same time.

My pussy clenched, choking on Grant's dick, and he latched onto my waist, as if needing to hang on. His gaze was intense, and I couldn't look away. I wouldn't dream of it. There was nowhere else to look but him.

No directions came from Joseph. Silas began to move as Grant did, and the men fumbled along until they found a rhythm. It was like a dance, in a strange way. The trio of us working together, everyone's movement relying on the others.

Heat filled my core. I wasn't going to last long like this. It felt so different, so new, and way, way too good. The muscles of Silas's chest beneath my hands bunched. He groaned in succession, getting louder as we hit our stride.

Grant had one hand on my waist, and he scooped the other behind my neck, helping to hold me steady. We were only a breath from each other, and his gaze dropped down to trace my lips. He was thinking about kissing me. I was thinking about it too.

But then I began to cross over, where the need for release pushed everything else out of its way. I half-moaned, half-sobbed as I tried to convey what was coming, warning the men. Grant froze, but it was too late for Silas. He continued to pump and tipped us both over the edge.

My cry was panicked as it rang in the room, followed by his deep gasp and a bunch of curse words. I rode out my orgasm with both men inside me, and as I came, I hung onto the back of Grant's neck, mirroring his hold.

He watched me, his mouth hanging open. Could he feel every pulse of my body on him? Could he feel Silas's? The orgasm was sharp and intense, but so overwhelming, I was almost relieved when it began to let up.

Everything was hazy in the aftermath. I was lifted off Silas, and he slid back, out of my way, so I could sit on the edge of the table and wrap my legs around Grant's waist. Joseph was there, handing a handful of wipes to Silas as he climbed off the table.

As I continued to recover, Grant simply watched me, fascinated. The air in the room began to swirl and shift. Silas cleaned up and pulled on his clothes, but Joseph moved in, standing at the side of the table. I got the sense that whatever he'd planned for the evening, it had all been leading up to this moment, when I was at my weakest.

I yanked up my shields, preparing for the next round. Grant was still inside me, and I was sure now Joseph wanted him to get inside my mind too.

"Tell her you're sorry," Joseph said.

Grant's expression was heartbreaking as he whispered it. "I'm so sorry."

"No," I said.

But it was ignored. "Now tell her you know what you did was wrong, and you will never, ever do anything like that again."

Before Grant could repeat it, I snarled it out. "*No.*"

"Put your fingers in her mouth," Joseph commanded.

Grant reached up and pushed his first two fingers past my lips, all the way to the top knuckle, stopping my tongue from moving. His expression pleaded with me to listen. "I promise you, I'll never do anything like that again."

"Tell her it doesn't have to happen tonight, but you need her to forgive you. Not want, but *need.*"

My tremble was back and picked up steam. Shudders rolled down my legs.

Grant sounded desperate. Lost. "I need you to forgive me."

"And ask her where your needs fit in the hierarchy."

Fucking Joseph. Hot tears stung my eyes. The sub's needs were first, but the dom's needs were next, and Grant had put mine first at every step of the way. He'd helped with my audition. Learned a new piece of music. Given up his rugby game for me. Gone to the terrible dinner with my sister.

Not to mention, he'd followed every rule Silas and Regan had dished out. All for me.

He'd honored the hierarchy, and I had to do the same. Thankfully, his fingers retreated from my mouth, so I could answer.

"Speak," Joseph said.

Only he wasn't specific in who his order was for, and Grant seized the window of opportunity. It spilled from him like wine from an uncorked bottle. "If this is all we can be, I'll take it. If you only want me around to play cello, or watch, or be your fourth with Silas and Regan, yes. I'll do it." He took in a deep breath. "If all you have left for me is scraps, I want them." His voice was solid. Absolute. "Anything to be with you, Tara."

I couldn't stop the tears. I blinked, and they streamed hotly down my cheeks. "Why?"

"Because I love you."

I was done. Obliterated by his admission, and then by his kiss. He hadn't asked for permission, but I was glad. It would have slowed down the time it took before our lips met, and I needed the connection to him right that instant.

His mouth roved against mine, tasting like love.

"*Speak*," Joseph ordered, and it was very apparent who he was talking to.

I broke the kiss and wiped my tears from my cheeks with a shaky hand. "I love you too."

He pushed me down and onto my back, climbing on top of the table. "Forgive me."

"Yes," I whispered. And I said it again as he slid inside me. "*Yes.*"

Gone was Joseph's hard voice. This one was gentle, as if the moment had moved him. "Take off her collar."

Because I didn't belong to Joseph. Nor Regan, or Silas.

I was Grant's.

Every piece of me, even the ones I'd tried to hide. He wanted them all, and I would give them, because he was mine. He raced to get the collar undone, and when I was free, he dropped it over the side of the table. By the time it thudded to the ground, everyone else was moving toward the door.

They sensed we needed this time together alone. I wanted to thank them, but I got lost in Grant's urgent kiss. It was full of so much passion, it nearly restarted my tears. Then, his hips moved, reminding me of all the places we were connected.

I was fragile, but he pieced me gradually back together on the table.

His slow movements built until we were breathless, sticky with sweat, moans pouring from our lips. He laced our hands together, whispered he loved me, and showed it with every kiss.

And when I came, he followed right behind, collapsing on top of me with a gasp.

I loved the weight. The feel of him.

As he caught his breath, he drew a finger over my forehead, brushing the hair out of my face. We lay like that, together on the table, wrapped around each other until our bodies cooled.

Finally, I had to break the silence.

"How many more chapters have you written?" I asked.

A smile hinted on his lips. "A few."

"I have notes."

A soft laugh came from him. "I'd love to go over them with you, but can it wait until the morning? I have other things I'd like to do with you first." He kissed me deeply and slowly, making the promise there'd be many more to come.

chapter THIRTY-EIGHT

GRANT

TWO MONTHS LATER

Leave it to Tara to be late to her own party. By the time we arrived at Kyle and Ruby's place, everyone else was already there. We set our bottle of wine on the kitchen island, beside the other bottles the guests had brought, and the tray of macarons Ruby had no doubt stress-baked.

"There she is!" Payton said when she spied us sneaking in. She was McAsshole's younger sister, and the resemblance was apparent. "Cutting it close. It's almost eight."

The TV was on, a commercial playing in the background as people chatted over the sound. In a few minutes, *Dance Dreams* would come on. It would be the fifth episode of the season—New York selection week. After that, they went to the live shows.

Tara had signed an NDA about whether she'd made it as a contestant and was forbidden from telling anyone. So, tonight, our friends were finally going to find out if Tara was going back to New York, or if her journey had ended.

Of course, she'd already told me. We'd decided we were done with secrets after the blindfold club—at least, secrets from each other.

Joseph poured a glass of wine for himself and a glass of

ginger ale for Noemi. She was still struggling with morning sickness, and I felt bloody awful for them both. Seeing his wife sick was especially hard on him, because it wasn't something he could control.

She was here, though, so hopefully it was beginning to ease.

"Shh," Ruby announced to the group. "It's coming on." She squeezed onto the couch between Kyle and Julius, breaking up their bromance.

I'd spent months trying to track down the blindfold club and was seriously annoyed when I discovered McAsshole was best friends with Julius. All that work when I could have gone right to the source. At least now we were all friends. Maybe I could work on Julius's girlfriend Courtney to convince him to try out for rugby. He'd played football in college, she'd told me last week at our previous 'watch party.'

Tara and I sat on chairs gathered from the dining table. Silas and Regan weren't the guests of honor like us and must have gotten last pick, because they had been relegated to folding tailgate chairs. But once the show was on, everyone was quiet, and our gazes were glued to the large screen.

Every time there was a shot of Tara, no matter how brief, the group would cheer, and Elena was the loudest. The girls catcalled when she was shown at practice, her chest drenched with sweat and in a low-cut sports bra. My girl was so hot, I felt that way every time I looked at her.

When it cut to commercial, the group would break into discussions, and I wanted to laugh each time the show returned, and they fell silent. They were all so invested in her success. It was powerful and wonderful to watch.

320 | NIKKI SLOANE

"Where's Hot Cello Guy?" Kyle's brother-in-law Dominic said during the next break, reading Twitter aloud from his phone. "The people want to know."

I smiled and shook my head.

They'd edited it down to less than three minutes on-air, but *Dance Dreams* had shown Tara's audition during the Chicago episode, and they'd included the part where Rita called me hot cello guy. #HotCelloGuy had been a reality TV star for thirty seconds, and for one night, I was trending on Twitter. My parents probably died with embarrassment.

Finally, it came time for Tara's segment on the show. She'd been grouped together with nine other hopefuls. They'd spent a grueling week practicing a routine together, and then performed for the choreographers. If they liked what they saw, they'd pick dancers to fill out their team.

There were trades and steals among the choreographers too. Things to give the show more drama, but none of that mattered at this stage. If a dancer was selected tonight, they were in.

Our friends lost their collective minds when Tara was picked second from her group. The women screamed and leapt from their seats, and Silas clapped me on the back, as if I had anything to do with it. I grinned anyway.

"You're going back to New York!" Elena shouted in disbelief. She looked so fucking thrilled for her friend.

Tara was all smiles.

Yes, we were going back to New York. While she was at practice, I'd meet with our literary agent. We'd submitted the first half of the book five weeks ago and turned in the final when she'd come home from selection week.

There was a six-figure advance coming our way, plus offers for movie rights.

And we'd told no one.

Well, except for Joseph and Julius. It was to protect the club they'd built and run. We let them read it and change what they needed to, covering their clients' identities, starting with setting the book in New York instead of Chicago. I couldn't help but wonder . . . would Julius's business suffer when the book came out? Or would the subtle publicity help? He'd lose some clients, but people loved being part of something infamous.

We were able to get him alone in a quiet corner after the show ended and update him on the book's progress. He listened, not saying a word.

Tara bit her bottom lip. "I know you're not thrilled we're doing this, but—"

He lifted one of his hulking shoulders. "Would my life be easier if you weren't? Yeah. But it's not all bad. You're just pushing up my timetable." He gave half of a smile. "I've been planning a move and an expansion, and the Feds want to upgrade the systems."

"Oh, wow. That's good. But about the," she lowered her voice, "FBI. We kept them out of the book, but I have a condition. I need you to come clean about them with everyone at the club."

Julius's brown eyes filled with concern. "I'm not supposed to and you gotta understand—they offer all of us protection."

Her eyebrows tugged together. "I get that, but you can't keep them in the dark. They deserve to know, and you need to let people decide for themselves if they want to keep working for you."

His expression went firm but before he could say anything, she set her hand on his arm in a calming gesture.

"If the FBI gives you shit about it, tell them it was the deal you had to make to keep their cover."

He sighed and put his fists on his hips. He didn't like being challenged, but it was clear as he considered his options, he saw he had none. If we put the FBI's involvement in the book, it would doom his club.

"Fine. I'll tell them, but you're lucky I like you," he grumbled.

She rose up on her toes and planted a kiss on his cheek. "You like everyone, Julius, and they like you because you're a great guy."

The party went late, and afterward, Tara and I snuggled together in the back of a cab. She laced our hands together. "I made a decision."

"Yeah?"

"No pen name. Anonymous."

We'd gone back and forth on the author name. It was her story, and she'd slaved over every scene, helping me fill in details. I'd done the bulk of the writing, but she wanted us to share credit as equals.

We'd been pitching pen names to each other all day, but it quickly devolved into jokes. "You don't want to be Harry Balls?"

"Tempting, but no. I like being anonymous. I thought it was kind of fitting."

I pressed my lips against her hairline, breathing in the

scent of her fruity conditioner. "How's that?"

"We spent so much time trying to be seen, and now we're willing to walk away from it."

"Uh, people are going to be seeing you. Or did you forget you're on a television show now?"

Her knowing smile was lit by the neon lights of a store as we sped through the heart of downtown. "You know what I mean. This might sound stupid, but it's like, I just needed one person to see me. *Really* see me. And now that I've found that person, I'm good. I don't need anything else."

It made my chest tighten to hear her say that. As if my heart was suddenly a little too big to fit comfortably inside it. I gave her the biggest smile I had. "I feel the same. I don't need anything else." I squeezed her. "Just this."

OTHER BOOKS BY NIKKI SLOANE

THANK YOU

I wrote this one faster than any other book. 84,000 words in forty-five days. In early November 2018, I committed to the publish date when I had only written the first chapter, determined to put the novel out before the end of the year. It was ambitious because I'm not a fast writer, but I needed to do it. I was coming off a book that took more than a year to write and I still didn't feel confident in it at the end. I needed to find my groove again.

Writing the first half of this book went well. The words were flowing, and I felt confident I was going to make the deadline.

The week before Thanksgiving, we received a devastating call. My husband's younger brother passed away very unexpectedly, and everything stopped. It was some of the hardest days of our lives. The title took on more meaning for me, because when I finally returned to the keyboard and escaped my grief by writing, I had tremendous guilt about not being there more for my husband.

But he supported me regardless. He understood and encouraged, and with his strength and help, I was able to finish. So, more than any other book I've ever written and probably will write, I need to say thank you.

Thank you to my gorgeous and perfect husband, who I love more than I think anyone has ever loved another person.

To my beta-readers, copy editors, and dearest friends—Nikki Terrill and Andrea Lefkowitz—thank you! You save my ass, make me laugh, and are absolutely amazing.

To my editor Lori Whitwam—thank you so much for fixing my words and bringing a smile to my face.

Thank you to my readers. You make it all possible, and I am so, so grateful.

ABOUT THE AUTHOR

Nikki Sloane fell into graphic design after her careers as a waitress, a screenwriter, and a ballroom dance instructor fell through. For eight years she worked for a design firm in that extremely tall, black, and tiered building in Chicago that went through an unfortunate name change during her time there.

Now she lives in Kentucky, is married and has two sons. She is a three-time Romance Writers of America RITA© Finalist, also writes romantic suspense under the name Karyn Lawrence, and couldn›t be any happier that people enjoy reading her sexy words.

Website: NikkiSloane.com

Goodreads: Nikki Sloane Author Page

Twitter: @AuthorNSloane

Facebook: Nikki Sloane

Instagram: nikkisloane

Printed in Great Britain
by Amazon

86604745R00192